WHat YOU LeFT BehiND

jessica verdi

sourcebooks
fire

Published by Sourcebooks Fire, an imprint of Sourcebooks, Inc.
P.O. Box 4410, Naperville, Illinois 60567-4410
(630) 961-3900
Fax: (630) 961-2168
www.sourcebooks.com

Verdi, Jessica.
  What you left behind / Jessica Verdi.
      pages cm
  Summary: Seventeen-year-old Ryden's life was changed forever when his girlfriend discovered she was pregnant and stopped chemotherapy, and now, raising Hope with his mother's help and longing for the father he never knew, he meets smart and sexy Joni and gains a new perspective.
  (alk. paper)
  [1. Babies--Fiction 2. Teenage fathers--Fiction. 3. Single-parent families--Fiction. 4. Fathers and daughters--Fiction. 5. Dating (Social customs)--Fiction.] I. Title.
  PZ7.V584Wh 2015
  [Fic]--dc23

                              2014049306

        Printed and bound in the United States of America.
              VP 10 9 8 7 6 5 4 3 2 1

For my mom.

Chapter 1

I f there's a more brain-piercing sound than a teething baby crying, I can't tell you what it is.

I fall back on my bed, drop Meg's journal, and rake my hands through my hair. It's kinda funny—in an ironic way, *not* an LOL way—that even with the endless wailing filling my room and ringing in my head, I notice how greasy my hair is. It's gross. When was the last time I washed it? Three days ago? Four? I haven't had time for anything more than a quick soap and rinse in days.

And to think I used to *purposely* go a day or two without washing it. Girls have always liked the chin-length hair that falls in my face when I'm hunched over a test in school and that I have to pull back with a rubber band during soccer practice. But now it's gone past sexy-straggly and straight into flat-out dirty.

God, I would kill for a long, hot, *silent* shower. I would lather, rinse, repeat like it was my fucking *job*.

Ever since Hope was born six months ago, I've been learning on the fly, getting used to the diapers and formula and sleeping when she sleeps. I spend all my time reading mommy blogs, figuring out which supermarkets carry the right kind of wipes, and shopping at the secondhand store for baby clothes, because they're basically as good as new and Hope grows out of everything so fast anyway.

The learning curve has been pretty damn steep.

I sit up. Tears squeeze between Hope's closed eyelids and her little chubby feet kick every which way. Her pink, gummy mouth is open wide, and you can just begin to see specks of white where her teeth are coming in.

Her crib is littered with evidence of my attempts to get her to *please* stop crying—a discarded teething ring, a mostly full bottle, and this freakish, neon green, stuffed monster with huge eyes that my mom swore Hope liked when she first gave it to her, though I have no idea how she could tell that.

I pick up Hope and try massaging her gums with a damp washcloth again like they say to do on all the baby websites. It doesn't do much. I bounce her on my hip and walk her around my room, trying to murmur soothing, *shhhh*-ing sounds. I rub her head, as gently as my clunky, goal-blocking hands can manage. Her hair is soft, dark, and unruly, like Meg's was. But nothing works. The screams work their way inside me, rattling my blood cells.

Yes, I changed her diaper. I even brought her to the doctor last week to make sure nothing's actually wrong with her, some leftover sickness from Meg or something. There's not.

She always cries more when I hold her than when my mom does—but it's never been this bad. This teething stuff is no joke. According to the Internet anyway. It's not like Hope's giving me a dissertation on what she's actually feeling. Whenever I get anywhere *near* her, she shrieks her head off. Which means no matter how hard I try or how many books I read or websites I scour, I'm still doing something wrong. But what else is new?

Lately I've had this idea that I can't shake.

What if I'm missing some crucial dad gene because I never had a dad of my own? What if I'm literally incapable of being a father to this baby because I have zero concept of what a father really *is*? Like beyond a dictionary definition or what you see of your friends' families and on TV.

I have no idea what that relationship's supposed to be like. I've never lived it.

And inevitably that thought leads to this one:

Maybe finding my dad, Michael, is the key to all of this making some sense. Maybe if I tracked him down, I'd finally figure out what I've been missing. The real stuff. How you're supposed to talk to each other. What the, I don't know, *energy* is like between a father and a kid. Not that I'm into cosmic energy bullshit or anything.

If I could be the child in that interaction, even once, for a single conversation, that could jump-start my being the father in *this* one. Right? At least I'd have some frame of reference, some experience.

But that would require getting more info about him from Mom. And I've already thrown enough curveballs her way to last a lifetime.

The music blasting from Mom's home office shuts off. Five

o'clock exactly, like always nowadays. She loves her job making custom, handmade wedding invitations for rich people, and before Hope, Mom would work all hours of the day and night. But it turns out babies cost a shitload of money, and despite how well Mom's business is doing, it's not enough. So the new arrangement is that during the day, Mom gets to turn her music on and her grandma duties off while I take care of Hope, then Mom takes over when I go to work at five thirty.

In a few days, that schedule's going to change, and I don't know what the hell we're going to do. That's another topic I haven't brought up with Mom. She keeps saying we need to talk about our plan for "when school starts up again," like she's forgotten that soccer practice starts sooner than that. Like it doesn't matter anymore or something.

But I can't *not* play. Soccer is the one thing I kick ass at. It's the whole reason I'm going back to school this fall instead of sticking with homeschooling, which I did for the last few months of last year after Hope was born. Fall is soccer season. I need to go to school in order to play on the team. And I need to play on the team because I'm going to UCLA on an athletic scholarship next year. It's pretty much a done deal. I've spoken to their head coach a few times this summer. He called me July 1, the first day he was allowed to according to NCAA rules. He's seen my game film, tracked my stats, and is sending a recruiter to watch one of my games in person. He wants me on his team. This is what I've been working toward my whole life. So Mom's delusional if she thinks I'm giving it up.

I wipe the tears from Hope's face and the drool from around her mouth even though she's still crying, then set her down in her crib. She grasps onto my finger, holding on extra tight, like she's saying, "Do something, man. This shit's painful!"

"I'm trying," I tell her.

I meet Mom in her office, where she's sitting on the floor, attempting to organize her materials. Stacks of paper and calligraphy pens are scattered among plastic bags filled with real leaves from the trees in our yard. Three hot glue guns are plugged into the wall, and photos of the Happy Couple glide across Mom's laptop screen.

"Hippie wedding in California?" I guess, nodding at the leaves. The people who hire Mom to make their invitations always want something unique to who they are as a couple. Mom and I started this game years ago—she tells me what materials she's using, and I try to guess what kind of people the Happy Couple are. I'm usually pretty good.

Mom shakes her head. "Hikers in Boulder."

Or I *was* pretty good. Now everything is so turned around that I can barely think.

"That was my next guess," I say.

Mom smiles. She's been so great about everything. She's not even pissed about me making her a thirty-five-year-old grandmother. She says she, better than anyone, gets how these things happen. But this is not your typical "oops, got pregnant in high school, what do we do now?" scenario, like what happened to her. This is the much more rare "oops,

I killed the love of my life by getting her pregnant in high school and ruined my life and the lives of all her family and friends in the process" situation.

And I know that deep down, Mom knows our situations are not the same at all. Her eyes are green, like mine, and they used to sparkle. They don't anymore. It's not because of the baby—she loves Hope to an almost ridiculous level. It's because of me. She's sad for me. Even though the name "Meg" is strictly off-limits in our house, I can almost see the M and E and G floating around in my mom's eyes like alphabet soup, like she's been bottling up everything she's wanted to say for the past six months and is about to overflow. I need to get out of here.

"So, I'm out," I say quickly, clipping my Whole Foods name tag to my hoodie. "Be home at ten fifteen."

Mom sighs. "Okay, Ry. Have fun. Love you."

"Love you too," I call back as I head to the front door.

She always says that when I leave to go somewhere. *Have fun.* She's been saying it for years. Doesn't matter if I'm going to school or work or soccer practice or a freaking pediatrician's appointment with Hope. *Have fun.* Like having fun is the most important thing you can do. Like you can possibly have fun when you're such a fucking mess.

• • •

I'm restocking the organic taco shells in the Mexican and Asian foods aisle, trying to block out the Celine Dion song that's playing over the PA system, when I notice a kid climbing the shelves at the opposite end of the aisle. His feet are two levels off the ground, and he's gripping onto a shelf above him, trying to raise himself up another level.

"Hey," I call. "Don't do that."

"It's okay. I do it all the time," he says, successfully pulling himself up another foot. He lets go with one hand and stretches toward something on the top shelf.

"Wait." I start to move toward him. "I'll get whatever you need. Just get down."

But there's a determined set to his jaw, and he keeps reaching higher, the tips of his fingers brushing a bag of tortilla chips. I keep walking his way, but I slow down a little. He really wants to do this on his own, you can tell. I'm a few feet away, and he's almost got a grab on the bag, when his grip on the edge of the shelf above him slips and his Crocs lose their foothold. Suddenly he's falling backward, nothing but air between the back of his head and the hard tile floor. I move faster than I would have thought possible, given how tired I am. I shoot my arms under his armpits and catch the boy just before he hits the ground.

The kid rights himself, plants his feet safely on the floor, and looks at me. My heart is beating way too fast, but I tell it to chill the fuck out. The kid is fine. Crisis averted.

"Thanks," he mumbles.

"No problem."

He ducks his head and starts to walk away.

"Hey," I call after him.

He stops.

I grab a bag of chips off the top shelf—funny how easy it is for me to reach; sometimes I still feel like that little kid who the world is too big for—and hand it to him.

He takes it, no *thank you* this time, and disappears around the corner.

I'm dragging my feet back to the taco shells, back to the monotony, when there's a voice behind me.

"Why, Ryden Brooks, as I live and breathe."

My spine stiffens. Apparently today is Weird Shit Happening at Whole Foods Day. I haven't heard that voice since before I left school in February. I turn and find myself face-to-face with Shoshanna Harvey. Her soft, southern belle accent comes complete with a delicate hand to the chest and a batting of long, thick lashes. I fell for that whole act once. Before I found out about a little thing called real life.

I saw Shoshanna in the store about a month ago but ducked down a different aisle before she saw me. This time, I'm not so lucky. "You do know we live in New Hampshire, not Mississippi, right?"

Shoshanna purses her lips and studies me. Her ponytail swings softly behind her, like a metronome on a really slow setting. "How are things, Ryden?"

"Things are great, Shoshanna. Really, just super."

"Really?" Her eyes are bright. Clearly, she's never heard of sarcasm. "That's *so* great to hear. We've been worried about you, you know."

"We? Who's *we*?" You never know with Shoshanna—she could be talking about her family or she could be talking about the whole damn school.

Just then, another familiar voice carries down the aisle. "Hey, Sho, how do you know when a cantaloupe is ripe?" It's Dave. His hands are placed dramatically on his hips and he's got three melons under his shirt—two representing boobs and one that I'm pretty sure is supposed to be a pregnant woman's belly. A flash of rage burns through me, but I smother it deep inside me to the place where all my unwelcome emotions reside. It's getting pretty crowded in there.

"*Dave*," Shoshanna loud-whispers, her eyes doing that as-wide-as-possible thing that people do when they're trying to get some message across to someone without saying the actual words.

He follows Shoshanna's nod toward me and drops the doofy grin. "Oh. Hey, Ryden." He relaxes his stance, and the cantaloupes fall to the floor, busting open. Orangey-pink cantaloupe juice oozes from the cracks. Great. Now I'm gonna have to clean that up.

I look back and forth between Shoshanna and Dave, and it all clicks. They're the *we*. My ex-girlfriend and my former best friend are *together*. That kind of thing used to require at least a "Hey, man. Cool with you if I ask out Shoshanna?" text, but I guess we left the bro code behind right around the time my girlfriend up and died and I became a seventeen-year-old single father. Yeah, Dave and I don't exactly have much in common anymore.

"You work here?" Dave asks.

"Nah, I just like helping restock supermarket shelves in my free time."

"Oh. I thought…" Dave looks at my Whole Foods name tag, confused.

"He was kidding, Dave," Shoshanna says.

Ah, look at that. Sarcasm isn't completely lost on her after all.

"Oh. Right. We're, uh, getting some food for the senior picnic tomorrow down at the lake. You coming?"

I stare in Dave's general direction, unthinking, unseeing. I forgot all about the picnic, even though it's been a Downey High School tradition for pretty much ever.

Dave keeps talking. "Coach said you're coming back to school in September. You are, right? We really need you on the te—"

"Hey, Ryden, can you help me with a cleanup in dairy?" a female voice asks, cutting him off. "Some asshole kids decided to play hacky sack with a carton of eggs."

I blink a few times and push the picnic out of my mind.

The source of the voice is a girl with short, brown hair that is juuust long enough to fall in her eyes, skin a shade or two lighter than her hair, earrings stuck in weird places in her ears, and tie-dyed overalls over a black tank top. She *looks* like she works in a Whole Foods.

"Uh, yeah. Sure," I say. I turn back to Shoshanna and Dave, glad to have an excuse to bail on this happy little reunion. The cantaloupe juice can wait. "Gotta go."

"Bye, Ryden!" Shoshanna's voice travels down the aisle after me.

"Yeah, see ya tomorrow, Ry."

I shake my head to myself as I follow tie-dye girl to dairy. Good thing that wasn't awkward or anything.

Once we're out of sight of the Mexican and Asian aisle, tie-dye girl stops walking and spins on her heel. "Right, so…" she says as I screech to a halt behind her. "There's no cleanup in dairy."

"Huh?" That's all I got. I'm so tired.

"Sorry, it just looked like you were having a moment there. Thought you might need a little help with your getaway."

I lean back against a shelf of recycled paper towels. They're soft. I could totally curl up right here on the floor and use one of the rolls as a pillow.

"Thanks," I say. "How did you know my name?"

She points to my name tag.

"Right," I say. "Where's yours? Or do you not even work here?"

She pulls the top of her overalls to the side to reveal a name tag pinned to her tank top. *Joni*. "I'm new. Started the day before yesterday and already blew my first week's paycheck on ungodly amounts of pomegranate-flavored soda. That stuff is like crack."

I smile for the first time in centuries. "Nice to meet you, Joni," I say.

"I saw you catch that kid," she says.

"Oh."

"That was cool."

I shrug. "I guess." There's an awkward pause, like she's waiting for me to say something else. "Well, see ya," I say and book it out of there as fast as I can.

"Nice to meet you too, Ryden," Joni calls after me.

Chapter 2

In the break room, I pull Meg's journal out of my bag. It's the only thing I have left of her—the old her, the person she was *before* I destroyed her life by getting her pregnant. She was constantly writing in these things. The first time we met, she was scrawling away in this very notebook, though I didn't know it was a journal until I got to know her better. Turned out she had hundreds of these books—single subject, college ruled, all different colors—filled with her thoughts and experiences and observations of the world. She wrote about almost every single thing that happened to her, every single conversation she had.

She once told me she started keeping the journals because they helped her cope with everything that was going on.

"I remembered what Mom was like after she got the call that Granddad had died," she said. "Instead of breaking down and crying, she went straight into practical mode—making funeral arrangements, calling relatives, packing up his house. When I was diagnosed, I realized that was what I needed to do too— keep myself busy. Make lists, keep a journal, dive into schoolwork. It turns out it's a lot easier to deal with stuff when you have a plan."

I didn't say her mom probably did that because she wasn't exactly the "breaking down and crying" type. That didn't matter. What mattered was that writing everything down helped Meg make sense of what was happening to her.

But I think she wrote for the joy of it too. Her entries are more like little stories than memories. Perfect moments preserved forever.

Not that things with us were always perfect. There was a big chunk of time in the middle that was pretty rough, actually. When she found out she was pregnant, and I realized what that meant not only for us, but for *her*, we, shall we say, disagreed on what course of action to take. But things happened the way they happened, and there's nothing I can do about it now. Apparently there was nothing I could do about it then either.

Last August, we sat in her massive living room with her parents, her sister, and my mother. Everyone was well aware of the pregnancy. Meg had been scheduled to go back for her second round of chemo at the end of June, but that obviously hadn't happened. Meg's parents were disappointed, outraged, embarrassed—all the things a couple of uptight robots are programmed to feel when their perfect daughter doesn't follow their perfect plans. My mom was just sad.

But it wasn't a done deal yet. Meg could've still gotten an abortion. She could've still gone back on chemo. If we acted fast, her treatment plan would've barely been interrupted at all. To me, it was a no-brainer. Her parents agreed. It was probably the only thing we ever agreed on.

Meg saw things differently. And as I had come to learn over the last several weeks of shouting and crying and pleading and futile attempts at reasoning, her opinion was the only one that mattered. "I'm having the baby," she declared.

My mom didn't say anything. Neither did her sister Mabel. Neither did I. I was still so, so mad.

"I feel good," she said. "Better than I have in a long time. All I have to do is hold out another seven or so months, and then I'll go right back on treatment. I promise."

"But, Megan," her mother said, "you know how quickly things can change. Seven months is a very long time when it comes to cancer."

"I don't care."

Her mother shook her head and glared at me. Me, the asshole who knocked up her sick daughter. Believe me, anything she was thinking, I was thinking ten times worse.

"Everything is going to be fine," Meg said. "You just have to trust me."

Well, it wasn't fine. Not even close.

But there was so much good stuff in our relationship too. So much. I loved her. I miss her. And her journal helps me remember. Everything is so out of control lately. I'm so tired, and it's really hard to just *think*. Sometimes I worry I'm going to forget her. Forget the time we had together, as if it was some strange, wonderful/horrible dream. I can't do that. I need to tell Hope all about Meg when she gets old enough. I can't control the fact that Hope's going to grow up without a mom, like I grew up without a dad, which really fucking sucks, but I *can* give her what I never had—as many details as possible.

When I read the journal, Meg's words latch onto my tired brain, and the memories from those specific moments come flooding back. Not the big things, the mistakes. Believe me, I don't need a journal to remind me of that. The journal helps with the small things—the things I'd forget without Meg's notes, the things I need to tell Hope someday.

I wish I had more journals, more reminders.

Meg left this journal at my house sometime at the end of sophomore year, after she told me about the cancer but before we found out she was pregnant. I kept it without telling her. There's writing in it up to the very last page, which is probably why she never missed it—she was ready to start a fresh one anyway. I couldn't have known at the time that it would become my most valued possession in the entire freaking world.

I open it up.

May 20.

Ryden Brooks spoke to me in Honors English today.

I can't do this again. The crush is absolutely, positively <u>not</u> coming back. I am going to carry out the rest of my high school days the same way I have for the past few months—in a rational, sane, Ryden-free mental state. Yup.

Reasons why I love this part:

1) I never knew Meg had a crush on me before we started going out. She never told me that, even after everything. So I know something I never would have known.

2) I love the "yup" at the end. Like she's agreeing with herself. It's really cute.

3) She wrote this entry the day we met. She goes on to document exactly what we said to each other. Which means our crazy conversation in Mr. Wheeler's class meant something to her too.

I keep reading, and it's like a play button has been pressed in my mind.

"There's gum on that chair." Those were the first words she ever said to me.

I froze, my ass hovering above the seat, and looked over to find myself staring into the darkest pair of eyes I'd ever seen.

I zoomed out from the eyes a little and found they were attached to a girl. Her hair was just as dark as her eyes, but her skin was pale. Really pale. Like, Styrofoam-marshmallow-Casper-the-Friendly-Ghost pale.

She was gorgeous.

And she was smiling at me.

Wait, scratch that. She was *laughing* at me.

"What?" I asked, starting to feel kind of angry. I wasn't used to getting this kind of reaction from anyone—especially not girls.

"Nothing." She grinned. "You just look kind of…confused."

"Huh?"

She nodded in the direction of my still-frozen-in-midair butt.
Oh. Right.

I guess I did look a little mental, squatting over the chair and ogling this girl like she was a topless supermodel, when all she'd been trying to do was save me from sitting in a wad of Bubble Yum.

I straightened up. "Sorry. And, uh, thanks."

"No problem."

I switched my chair with the chair from an empty desk nearby and tore a page out of my notebook to alert any future unsuspecting asses who wouldn't be lucky enough to have a pair of mysterious, dark eyes looking out for them.

Don't sit. I wrote. *Gum.* I was about to tear it out of the book and put it on the chair when a little giggle stopped me. She was laughing at me again. What was with this girl?

I sighed. "What now?"

"What are you, a caveman?" she asked. "Don't sit. Sit bad. Gum bad."

She was putting on a kind of gruff voice, her eyebrows pulled together, her shoulders hunched. She was totally making fun of me. I should've been pissed. Normally I *would* have been pissed. But it was funny. *She* was funny.

"What's your name?" I blurted out like an idiot.

All traces of humor vanished from her face and she raised an unamused eyebrow. "Really?"

"What?"

"I've gone to school with you for four years. And we've been in *this* class together since January."

I was a complete and total asshole. "Oh. I knew that. Sorry, um…"

"Meg," she prompted. "Meg Reynolds?"

No way. That wasn't Meg Reynolds. Meg Reynolds was the girl from my eighth-grade gym class who couldn't hit a ball or jump a hurdle to save her life. The girl who'd completely destroyed our chances of beating Coach Bell's class in Downey Middle School's End-of-Year Olympics.

When did Meg Reynolds get *hot*? And where the hell was I when it happened?

"Right. Of course. Meg! I'm—"

"Ryden Brooks," she said. "Star goalie of the state champion Pumas, future prom king and homecoming king, and recipient of the Most Likely to Conquer the World award." She rolled her eyes. "I know who you are. Because we've been going to school together *since seventh grade*."

I nodded and focused on the front of the classroom, desperate, for the first time in my life, for class to start early. Where the hell was Mr. Wheeler?

Since my *Don't sit. Gum.* sign had been deemed unacceptable, I flipped to a new page and started over. *Please don't sit here.* I wrote neatly. *There is gum on this chair.* Meg wouldn't be able to object to this one. I used full sentences and everything.

I tore it out and held it up, but she wasn't looking my way.

Her head was down, and she was writing something in a note-book. Her hair was all over the place, tumbling over the desk and obstructing her face, but she kept writing. Her handwriting was really small, like she was afraid of running out of room and was trying to squeeze as much information onto the page as possible.

I watched as her pen moved confidently across her paper. Whatever she was writing, she was really into it.

I couldn't imagine writing *anything* like that, all intense and continuous. The only time I ever write anything is when we have to do essay questions in those blue books or type up term papers, and even then I feel like I have to stop every three words to figure out what the hell I'm supposed to say.

"Hey, Meg," I said.

Her pen kept going. Didn't she hear me? Or was she still pissed that I hadn't known her name?

"*Meg*," I said again, louder.

The pen stopped. She looked up. "What do you want?"

Yeah, she was still pissed.

"Is this okay?"

She read my sign, and her dark eyes changed from coal to velvet as she laughed.

I felt an inexplicable rush of relief. Fifteen minutes ago, I'd completely forgotten this girl existed. And now I cared whether she was mad at me or not? What the hell was wrong with me?

"It's better," she said. "But kinda stilted, don't you think?"

"Stilted?"

"Yeah, you know, too formal. Not enough personality."

"I know what it means," I said. "But it's just a sign about gum. Why does it need personality?"

She tapped her pen at the corner of her mouth, right where her top lip and bottom lip met. The skin there looked really soft. I had the sudden urge to run my thumb over it. "How about doing a play on one of those no trespassing signs? Something like, *No Sitting. Violators Will Be Prosecuted.*"

I laughed. "Or, *Private Gum Residence. Trespass At Your Own Risk.*"

"Yes! Amazing. Or… *Beware of Gum.*"

"*Private Chair. Gum Only. No Butts Allowed.*"

Meg cracked up. "Yes! Do that one."

I was putting the finishing touches on the sign when Meg's laughter cut off. I looked up, and she pointed to the chair, her eyes wide.

Someone was sitting in it. We'd been so busy trying to come up with something funny for the sign that we'd forgotten the whole *point* of the sign. Oops.

The guy sitting in the chair was Gary Fleming, this dude who always pushed around the underclassmen and wrote things like "homo" and "slut" on people's lockers.

I felt bad for about a second, and then I was kind of glad Gary sat in the chair. If anyone deserved it, he did.

I turned to Meg. She actually looked *scared*, like Gary was going to think *she* was the one who'd made him sit in the gum and make her life a living hell because of it. *Huh.* Was that what people like him did to people like her? I'd never really thought about what school was like for other people.

I shook my head. "That guy's a douche bag," I whispered. "Don't worry about it."

She stared at me, her eyes latched on mine as if she was trying to figure me out. I smiled. She smiled back hesitantly.

It felt good, holding her gaze like that. Safe. Comfortable.

But then Mr. Wheeler came into the classroom muttering something about a broken Xerox machine in the teachers' lounge, and Meg turned away.

There were a million thoughts going through my head—and, let's be honest, a million feelings in the, um, lower half of me—but one thing was certain: I'd never forget Meg Reynolds again.

Chapter 3

There's so much noise. I pace around my room, bouncing Hope on my hip, rubbing her back, trying to soothe her. The vibrations from her little crying body seep into me. The music pumping through my earphones is like Febreze—it covers the sounds of Hope's crying and Mom's office music, but it doesn't erase it. It's an illusion. I still know the noise is there—outside me, inside me—and all this trying to fool my brain into thinking otherwise is a giant waste of time. And probably causing cancer.

Fuck. Why'd I have to go and think that?

I put Hope in her swing, pull off my earphones, wipe the baby drool from my cheek, and run my finger over my laptop trackpad. The *Futurama* screen saver vanishes, and I pull up Google. But I don't know what to type. "Guy named Michael with a son named Ryden Brooks" doesn't bring up much.

Mom doesn't like to talk about my father. She wouldn't admit that, and she's actually told me many, many times since I was a little kid that if I have any questions about him, I should ask her. But I get the feeling that talking about him makes her sad, so I've tried not to ask many questions. Sparing her that pain is one small way I'm able to take care of her.

Here's what I do know about him:

His first name is Michael.

He was twenty years old when Mom got pregnant with me; she was eighteen, still in high school.

They met at a concert in Boston, which was where he lived. They were together for four months, and he drove back and forth the two hours between her town in Vermont and the city to see her.

He left her when she told him she was keeping the baby.

Mom graduated from high school with a giant belly (I've seen the pictures). She didn't get to go to college.

I don't know what he does for a living.

I don't know his last name.

I don't know what he looks like.

I don't know if he has other kids or not.

I don't know anything.

I've thought about him a lot over the years. I've sort of come up with this vague, faceless image of him in my mind—a guy who wears his hair longish, like me, who's a little bit taller than I am, who plays a musical instrument (maybe the piano), runs marathons, and travels the world doing something really important.

I know it's stupid.

At different points in my life, I've found myself hoping he would come looking for me—not to replace my mom or anything, but to, I don't know…complete the picture? Tell me how to, like, *exist* in the world. Things Mom couldn't know. Guy things. But I never seriously considered looking for him.

Meg thought I should. She was always trying to convince me to track Michael down and fill in that blank in my mind. I think it had something to do with her own parents being so cold and distant—both to each other and to their kids. I think she imagined that somewhere in my unknown, I might find the happiness she'd never been afforded. But meeting him was always something I knew I would do *someday*. I never felt any sort of urgency.

Until now. Hope changed everything.

Because now it's not about me being curious. It's about me being *deficient*. A clueless, shitty excuse for a father with a baby who won't stop crying.

I really need to talk to Mom.

The computer monitor flashes the time: 12:14 p.m.

I could go knock on her office door, but I don't want to drop the Michael bomb in the middle of her workday. I'll talk to her tonight.

I look at the clock again, and it hits me. There's somewhere else I could be right now.

Before I can really think about what I'm doing, I run around the house collecting things to pack in Hope's diaper bag—diapers, wipes, baby sunscreen, ointment, bottles, burp cloths, a change of clothes (please, God, no explosive diarrhea today), three pacifiers and five teething rings (enough to replace the ones she'll inevitably throw on the ground), her baby sun hat, and the freakish green monster—and throw on my bathing suit and a T-shirt.

Hope whines as I transfer her from her swing to her car seat, but the motion has calmed her some and she's not all out crying, so hey, win. With her in one hand, her diaper bag in the other, and a beach towel tossed over my shoulder, I peek my head into Mom's office.

"We're going out!" I shout over the P!nk song Mom's singing along to. "Be back by five."

She looks surprised. "Okay, well, have—" But before she can finish, I've pulled the door closed and am on my way.

I drive toward the lake.

Press down on gas.

Check mirror.

Flip blinker.

Merge.

Press gas harder.

Just keep moving forward, Ryden.

Before too long, I'm pulling my beat-up 2002 Mercury Sable into the makeshift parking lot at the southeastern side of the lake and lugging Hope (who drifted off to sleep during the drive—double win) and all her crap down to the beach. It's not until I crest the hill that I stop. There's a ton of people here. Probably the entire entering senior class plus their friends/girlfriends/boyfriends from other years. Oh yeah. This is what summer is like.

There's a beach volleyball game going, the girls are lounging in bikinis on their towels, and there's a keg set up right in the middle of it all. Almost everyone has a red Solo cup in their hands. There's no one here over the age of twenty, and no one under fifteen or so. Except Hope.

The exhaustion haze clears, and I come back to myself. *What the hell am I doing?* We can't be here. I may not be the world's most qualified parent, but even *I* know you probably shouldn't bring a baby to a keg party.

I take one last look at the scene below, then turn to go back to the car. Instead I collide with Shoshanna and Dave. Perfect.

No one says anything for a long second. Shoshanna looks from me to Hope and back to me, clearly trying to find something to say, and Dave just unabashedly stares, literally open-mouthed, at the baby.

I sigh. "Yeah, so, this is Hope." I lift her car seat to give them a better view, as Hope brushes her little clenched fists against her face in her sleep.

They still don't say anything. It's like they've never seen a baby before.

"Anyway, we're gonna go."

I move to duck around the statues that used to be Shoshanna and Dave, but suddenly Shoshanna animates. "Oh. My. God. Ryden. She. Is. *Adorable!*" "Adorable" comes out in a high-pitched squeal, and my poor, battered eardrums cringe.

"Um. Thanks." It feels weird taking credit for something like that. All I did was have sex with Meg. Genetics did the rest.

"Look at her, sleeping there like a little angel!" Shoshanna says. "Look at those tiny fingernails! And those chubby cheeks! Come on. We *have* to introduce her to everyone." She pulls me by the wrist, and before I know it, we're skidding down the hill to the beach. My flip-flops sink into the soft, hot sand, and I have the sudden urge to roll around in it and cover my entire body in its warmth.

"Hey, everybody!" Shoshanna yells, waving her hands to get people's attention. "Ryden Brooks is here!"

And then I'm being swarmed by people I used to know— the soccer guys, the varsity cheerleaders, the student government officers—and it takes everything I have to smile and act like everything's great, and yes, I'm *so* glad to see them too, and yes, this is my kid, and *please* don't wake her up.

Matt Boyd, the new captain of the varsity soccer team (that should have been me, but the vote was held at soccer camp this summer, and you can't win a contest when you're not there), tries to give me a fist bump, but it doesn't really work so well since my hands are kinda full. "Training starts Monday, Brooks," he says. His nose is covered in not-blended-in sunscreen, and he's wearing a puka shell necklace. *Douche.* "You ready?"

As if I didn't know that training starts Monday. As if I haven't been trying to figure out how to make the schedule work all damn summer. Our soccer team is one of the top-ranked teams in the country, so practices are pretty intense. I may have gotten a pass on camp this year—for obvious reasons—but there's no way in hell Coach O'Toole is going to give me any leeway on the regular practice schedule. Practices are from nine to four, five days a week for the two weeks before school starts, and then from two fifteen to four thirty after school every day. Those are

Mom's work hours. How's she supposed to keep a steady hand for her calligraphy with a baby in her arms?

"Yeah, man," I tell Matt. "I'm ready."

And then they're dispersing again, going back to their beer and their games, laughing and making out and grilling hamburgers. They're doing fine without me. A few groups of people whisper to each other as they glance my way. I'm nothing more than a novelty.

I don't know what I was thinking coming here. I guess I thought I could, for a moment, go back to being "Ryden Brooks," instead of "Hope's dad." But that's who I'll be for the rest of my life. Even if I don't have the first clue how to do it.

Shoshanna runs off, strips down to her bikini, and jumps in the water. Dave claps me on the back and says, "You want some food?"

I shake my head. "Nah, man. I think I'm just gonna go."

Dave nods. "Cool. See ya, Ryden."

I'm working my way back up the hill, my feet sliding around in my sand-covered flip-flops, the back of my neck sweating from the sun and all the heavy stuff I'm carrying, when footsteps close in behind me and the diaper bag is suddenly snatched out of my hand.

"Hey, what the—" I stop short. "Alan."

Alan Kang. Meg's best friend.

Shit.

• • •

I met Alan the day after I met Meg. Or re-met her, I guess. That part's in the journal too.

May 21.

Today was one of the most embarrassing days of my life. And you know I've had a lot of those. I started feeling sick in English (the one class I have with Ryden, of course) and had to run out before the bell. I refused to give myself permission to throw up until after I got to the bathroom, and luckily I made it to a toilet just in time… But what had Ryden thought about me running away with my hand over my mouth like that? I was mortified. And I really, <u>really</u> didn't want to have to explain about the chemo.

So then, ten minutes later, I left the bathroom…and Ryden was waiting for me! I think I may have actually gasped when I saw him there. <u>So</u> embarrassing, on every level.

That part's sorta funny to me, because what did *she* have to be embarrassed about? She threw up. It happens. *I* was the one feeling like a total tool, standing outside the bathroom, listening to the muffled sounds of her puking, clueless about what to do. I didn't know if I should go in or not. I mean, it was only a bathroom, right? Nothing I'd never seen before. But what if they were doing, like, *girl* stuff in there? Passing around tampons and stuff.

A few minutes went by, and the crowd in the hall started to thin out. I felt so useless. What if she needed someone to call the nurse? There had to have been other girls in there, but I wasn't sure if Meg would ask them for help or not. She kinda kept to herself.

The door swung open. It was Meg. And yup, she gasped. It made me smile.

"Are you okay?" I asked.

She nodded. I noticed she was chewing a piece of gum. "Were you waiting for me?"

"Yeah." I held up her backpack. "What happened? Do you have the flu or something?"

"No. I'm fine."

"Do you want to go to the nurse?"

"No!" she said, a little panicked. "It passed. Seriously, I'm fine. You should go to lunch. Thanks for your help." She held out her hand for her bag.

A few minutes ago, she was spewing her guts, and I should've been grossed out, but she was still really pretty, with that crazy hair and soft-looking mouth.

"Can I walk you to lunch?" I asked.

She hesitated and narrowed her eyes. "Did you really friend Alan Kang on Facebook?"

"What?" How was that a response to my question?

She spoke slower. "Did...you...friend...Alan...on...Facebook?"

I held her gaze. "Yes."

"Why?" It was like she was accusing me of something, like friending Alan Kang on Facebook was all part of some master scheme to take over the world.

"Because *you're* not on Facebook. I checked. And I saw you sitting at lunch with him yesterday and figured one degree of separation was better than nothing."

Her eyes widened.

My Alan Kang Facebook recon mission had been surprisingly useful—his relationship status was "single." Which meant Meg wasn't his girlfriend.

"So," I repeated, "can I walk you to lunch?"

"One more question," she said.

I waited.

"What about Shoshanna?"

Huh? "What about her?"

"Shouldn't you be walking *her* to lunch instead?"

"Um, why?"

Meg's face got all flushed, and she looked down at her shoes. "Aren't you two…?"

I shook my head. "We broke up a couple of months ago."

If I hadn't been looking so hard, I would've probably missed it. But there it was. Meg's features relaxed with the smallest hint of relief.

"So?" I asked. "Lunch?"

She met my gaze. "I have to go to my locker first."

We started to walk. "Why?"

"Alan will be waiting for me there. And I need to get my lunch."

"You bring your lunch?" I asked. Yeah, it was small talk, and yeah, it was awkward, but it was better than saying *nothing*.

"I don't really like the cafeteria food."

"Why not?" Cafeteria food was awesome. Nachos and burgers and fries and pretzels and those deep-fried pizza roll things.

She shrugged. "I try to eat healthy."

I nodded, as if I understood. "So you bring a sandwich or something?"

She full on smiled at that. "No. Steamed veggies and tofu, kale chips, organic fruit, stuff like that."

"Right. Cool." *What the hell is a kale chip?*

We got to her locker, and sure enough, there was Alan. He blinked at the sight of the two of us together.

"Hey," Meg said, giving him a look that I probably wasn't supposed to notice but that obviously meant, *Stay cool.*

"Hey," he said. "Hey, Ryden Brooks."

"Hey."

More uncomfortable silence. "Hey" couldn't be the only thing we had to say to each other, could it?

"Sorry I'm late," she said.

"No problemo."

Meg fumbled with her lock as I racked my brain, trying to come up with something to talk about. What had I seen on Alan's Facebook page again? Hip-hop and Korean movies. I guessed I could bring up one of those topics. But which one? I knew nothing about hip-hop, and I didn't want to sound dumb. I could ask him about the movies, but would it sound like I was only asking him about Korean stuff because he was Korean? Coming off as an insensitive racist was the last thing I needed.

God, why was I so nervous?

Come on, Meg. Get the damn locker open already.

"So, Alan," I said, hating the desperation that came through in my voice. "On Facebook I saw that you like Korean cinema." *I'm such a loser.*

Alan's eyes lit up. "Yeah! Have you ever seen *Shiri*?"

"Uh, no."

"Oh, man, it's so badass. What about *Joint Security Area*?"

I shook my head.

"Dude, you gotta Netflix it. It's about these two soldiers who are killed in the DMZ. It's really good."

I glanced at Meg as she clicked her lock open. About time. Her wild hair was blocking most of her face, but I could just make out a smile through the tangled web. She was happy. Whether it was because she finally showed that lock who was boss or because of something I'd said, I had no idea. But I wasn't about to stop.

"What's the DMZ?" I asked Alan.

"The demilitarized zone between North Korea and South Korea. Dude, don't you watch the news?"

I shrugged. "Not really." *Why didn't I keep my mouth shut? They're going to think I'm a moron.*

Meg turned to us and held up an insulated lunch bag. I hadn't had one of those since second grade. "Got it," she said. "Let's go."

"Do you like Korean movies too?" I asked her, trying to keep this train wreck going for some reason.

"I've seen a lot of them. But I'm not really into them like

Alan is. I don't understand how he can watch the same ones over and over." She rolled her eyes.

"You're know you're just jealous of my mad cultural pride," Alan said.

She patted him patronizingly on the back. "That must be it."

"Hey, you liked *Il Mare*!"

"Yeah," she conceded. "That one was actually pretty good."

"*Il mare*?" I asked, my ears perking up at the familiar words. "Like, *the sea*?"

Alan and Meg stared at me.

"What? I take Italian. I'm not a complete idiot, you know." *Shut up. You're making it worse.*

Meg smiled. "I know. You're in Honors English."

"Yeah, my guidance counselor has been trying to get me into honors classes for a while. I finally agreed this semester because I figure it'll help seal the deal on my scholarship with UCLA."

Meg was quiet for a moment, then said, "UCLA, huh?"

"Yeah. My mom and I went on a road trip to see a bunch of soccer schools over Christmas break. As soon as I got to the UCLA campus, I knew that's where I wanted to go. They have a kickass team, and the weather's nice, like, all the time. Plus, it's California, so the people are generally cool. I talked to the coaches and did the whole unofficial visit thing, and they're really interested in me."

Meg nodded and got this far-off, dreamy look in her eyes.

Alan saw it too and obviously understood it better than I

did, because he immediately changed the subject. "Anyway, the Korean title of *Il Mare* is *Siworae*. It's about these two people who are in love but living two years apart. The only way for them to communicate is through this magic mailbox."

"There was an American remake with Sandra Bullock and Keanu Reeves," Meg said, clearly trying to get her mind off whatever it was that had upset her.

"*The Lake House*," I said.

Again, Meg and Alan stared at me.

I shrugged. "My mom loves that movie."

We arrived at the cafeteria and went our separate ways. But it was clear that things had changed. I was one step closer to being a part of Meg's world.

• • •

"You looked like you could use some help," Alan says, dragging me back to the here and now. Of *course* he'd be at a party meant for the whole incoming senior class. Of *course* I'd run into him here.

The look in his eyes is pretty damn close to the one in my mom's—M, E, and G bobbing up and down in a pool of sadness—but there's a difference. Alan isn't sad for *me*. He's just plain old sad. Because he lost Meg too.

Something starts to bubble up inside me, but I shove it down before it can show itself.

"Yeah," I say, clearing my throat. "Thanks." I sit down, right there, halfway up the hill, with Hope's car seat. She's kind of on an incline, but it's sturdy enough. And hey, when she wakes up, she'll have a great view of the lake.

Alan sits too. He rests his forearms on his knees. He's got his red WWSOD bracelet on. *What would Sandra Oh do?* The corner of my mouth turns up in a pathetic attempt at a smile. The guy is freaking obsessed with famous Koreans.

"I called you," he says.

"Yeah."

"A lot."

"Yeah."

"I came by your house too, but your mom said you weren't up for having visitors."

"Yeah. Sorry about that. I…uh…" I try to come up with a reasonable excuse for not returning his calls or wanting to see him, but I've got nothing. The truth is, I couldn't face him, knowing he was thinking what Meg's parents and everyone who was ever close to her were thinking—that she's dead because of me.

Eventually I give up trying to come up with a response. Alan doesn't seem to be expecting a real answer anyway.

We're quiet for a long time. I stare out at Lake Winnipesaukee. You can see across to the other side easily, but its size is deceiving because it's not round. It's all warped, with hidden bends and nooks. You could spend your whole life out here and it would keep surprising you.

I haven't been here in a long time.

After a while, Alan says, "She looks like her."

I blink out of my daze. "What?"

"The baby. She looks like Meg."

The name hits me hard, right in the gut. Even though it's always with me, I haven't heard it spoken aloud in months. I dig my heels into the grass and run soccer drills in my head. When all the bad feelings are safely restrained, I turn to Alan and find him staring at Hope. I look back at the lake. "You think?" I ask. My voice is flat.

I already know she looks like Meg. It's all I see whenever I look at her. Shoshanna was right—Hope is cute. Beautiful even. Like her mother. Especially lately, now that she's growing out of that smooshed-face, all-newborns-look-alike thing. Other than her eyes, which are a dark blueish (though my mom says that will probably change), everything else about Hope is pure Meg, right down to her fair skin, the shape of her lips, and her jet-black hair, which sticks out in every direction and is growing fuller every day. And she's only half a year old—as she grows up and becomes more of a person, it's gonna get worse. Her eyes are going to turn dark brown, almost black. I know it.

"It's uncanny." Alan's voice is full of awe. I don't think I've ever heard anyone use the word "uncanny" in actual conversation before. "What's her name?" he asks after another minute.

I startle. "You don't know her name?"

"How would I? You won't talk to me, Meg's parents won't talk about the baby, and no one else I've asked has known any more than I do."

Well, shit. Now I feel even worse.

"Her name is Hope," I say.

"Hope?"

"Hope."

He raises an eyebrow. "That's ironic."

This time, both corners of my mouth pull up. "Tell me about it."

A few people pass us on their way down to the picnic, but they don't stop. They just wave and hurry down the hill.

"So," I say after a few minutes. "I'll see ya."

I stand and start to gather Hope and all her crap.

"Wait, Ryden." Alan stands and brushes the grass off his butt. He nods toward Hope. "It's like...at least Meg didn't die for nothing, you know?"

He's totally serious, waiting for me to say, "Yup, I understand completely. Right-o." But that's not going to happen. Because if I could go back in time and do it all differently, I would.

It's not that I blame Hope or want her to go away or anything like that.

I just wish I'd realized that Meg's birth control pills weren't going to work because of all the chemo. I wish I'd used a condom. I wish Meg had listened to me and gotten the abortion—I wish I'd fought even harder for that. Because if any of those things had happened, Meg might still be here.

But Hope is here now, and Meg's not. That's the way it is, and I'm trying to do my best with it.

I don't respond to Alan's question. Instead, I sling the diaper bag over my shoulder and say, "Later, man."

Then I walk to the parking lot and don't look back.

Chapter 4

That afternoon at work, Joni comes up to me as I'm squee-geeing the refrigerator doors. She's wearing jeans and a sweater that looks like it was made in a beginners' knitting class. The holes between the stitches are really big.

"Aren't you cold?" she asks, nodding at my bare arms.

"Nope."

"If you say so."

"Where's your name tag?" I ask.

Joni reaches under her loose collar and pulls out the top of the tank she's wearing underneath. The name tag is pinned to the thin white cotton.

"You know you're supposed to wear it where people can actually see it, right?"

She shrugs. "All they said was that we had to wear it. They didn't say where."

"Have you always had such a problem with authority?"

She sticks her tongue out at me. It's tinted blue.

"What the hell have you been eating?" I shift my squee-gee and bucket down to the next frost- and fingerprint-covered door.

She holds up her left hand. There's a blue Ring Pop on her middle finger.

I put on an appalled face and point a finger accusingly. "How dare you taint this hallowed ground with corn syrup and artificial dyes! Sacrilege!"

She laughs. "What can I say, I'm a rebel. You wanna take a break?"

I laugh too, a little. "I only get a fifteen, and I haven't even been here an hour yet. I try to go as long as possible before going on break, 'cause then the second part of my shift goes by quicker."

"Crafty."

I tap my temple. "Yep."

"Well, I get a fifteen and a forty-five, so come find me when you want to go on break."

"Um. Okay."

"Um. Okay," she mimics and skips off down the aisle with all the random stuff that doesn't have a logical home—the paper plates, the dog food, the colanders.

I straighten a few bags of frozen veggies before moving on to the next door. I probably should have said no. I don't know why I didn't. My break at work is the one tiny sliver of my day where I don't have to do anything.

But Joni's cool. She's easy to talk to. I get the sense that she's not into guys, so there's no chance of being anything more than friends.

And the best part is, she doesn't know anything about me.

• • •

A couple of hours later, I go in search of Joni and find her working register fourteen. I wave from my safe space, off to the side, away from the never-ending checkout line, and she turns off her light.

"Follow me," she says as she makes her way over to me.

I trail her through the store. When we get to the deli, she punches a code into a door I've never been through before and holds it open. I walk through to find that we're in the employees-only section behind the deli counter. There's a little corridor with a few turnoffs—the one closest to the door is where the deli guys stand to talk to the customers over the counter.

"Hey, Julio," Joni says to the guy at the meat slicer. "¿Cómo estás?"

"Hola, Joni." He says her name like ho-ni. "My daughter drew you a picture. I left it in the back for you."

"Awesome! ¡Gracias!"

We keep walking down the hall, past doors marked "Refrigeration. Keep closed at all times," and wind up in a little break room. It's empty and spotless. The main break room on the other side of the store is rarely empty, and it's never this clean. There are about a million employees at this place, and I've never seen anyone wipe down the tables or clean out the microwave. There's a child's drawing on the table: a beige piece of construction paper with what I'm pretty sure are fish swimming around under the ocean. To Joney, it reads in wobbly black crayon. From Annalisa.

Joni picks it up and smiles. "Aww. Sweet kid." She gestures to the empty chairs. "Have a seat." She pulls two long, oval-shaped things wrapped in white paper out of the fridge and tosses me one.

"What is this?"

"It's a sandwich, dummy."

"Where did it come from?"

"The deli. Those guys love me."

Okay, I'm really confused. "Haven't you only been working here for a few days?"

"You can make friends in way less than a few days, Mr. Ryden Whatever-Your-Name-Is."

Joni bites into her hero. A glob of mustard squirts out onto her chin. Rather than using a napkin to wipe it away, she tries to lick it off. I laugh as she squints and strains her tongue to try to reach the spot. It doesn't work, obviously, so eventually she uses her sandwich to wipe it off and then licks the glob off the bread.

"That is disgusting," I say.

She just grins and takes another bite.

I dig into my sandwich too. It's Swiss cheese, lettuce, tomato, pickles, and olives. Not what I would have chosen, but I only have a few minutes left of my break and I'm suddenly starving.

"Tell me something about yourself," Joni says.

I swallow the bite of hero in an attempt to force down the lump that's risen in my throat. "What do you want to know?"

She shrugs. "I dunno, basic stuff."

Basic stuff I can do. "All right, shoot."

"How did you get this?" She points to the thin scar that cuts through my left eyebrow.

My stomach twists, and I shake my head. I've never told anyone that story—not even Meg. At the time, it was *her* scars that were more important. In particular the one on the back of her thigh, where they extracted a big chunk of skin and tissue around her cancerous mole. "More basic."

"More basic than that?"

"Yup."

She sighs. "Okay. What's your last name?"

"Brooks. What's yours?"

"Ríos. How old are you?"

"Seventeen. You?"

"Seventeen."

That surprises me. I thought she was older for some reason. "When's your birthday?" I ask.

"March 6. You?"

"March 6!"

Joni's eyes get huge and she sits up straighter in her seat. "Are you serious?!"

I burst out laughing. "No. It's actually January 13. That would have been crazy though, right?"

She throws a tomato from her sandwich at me. "You jerk."

I peel the tomato off my shoulder and eat it. It feels good to joke around like this. "Moving on. Where do you go to school?"

"Clinton Central." That explains why I've never seen her before—Clinton's a few towns away from Whole Foods in the opposite direction of Downey. "And you go to…let me guess… Haverford Prep."

I almost choke on my last bite of sandwich. "Why the hell would you think *that*?"

She studies me. "You strike me as one of those angsty, life-is-so-*hard*, privileged types whose daddy is making him work a part-time job to learn the value of a dollar. Why else would you be so miserable all the time?"

My good mood burns a fiery death. "You really don't know what you're talking about." I push back my chair and toss the hero wrapper in the garbage. "My break's over. Thanks for the sandwich, but please just leave me alone from now on, okay?"

I don't know what I was thinking when I thought I could be friends with this girl. I'd wanted it to be different, to have someone fun to talk to and hang out with who wouldn't look at me with pity. But she's just as judgmental as everyone else.

Finding someone you can *really* connect with is like winning the fucking lottery—it happens basically never, but if it does, you really shouldn't blow it.

• • •

May 23.

"How are you feeling?" Ryden asked me the moment I hopped off the school bus this morning.

The first thought I had was that he'd found out about the cancer. _Panic._ "What do you mean?"

"What do you mean, what do I mean? You were out sick yesterday, right? And there was that whole running-out-of-English incident the day before?"

Relief. "I'm better now. Thanks."

"Good."

I know I'm not supposed to think about him. No more crush. Focus on school. That's what's important.

I started to walk again, but he caught my arm. "Meg."

I know this would probably sound crazy if I ever said it out loud to anyone, except maybe Mabel, but I think that was the best moment of my life so far. Because I've never felt anything as good as when our skin first touched. It was like time stopped Heat passed between us like fire when his hand clasped my wrist. Okay, maybe not fire, but something really, really hot.

"Go to the dance with me tomorrow?"

Every possible answer went through my mind: Yes. No. I can't.

I broke eye contact and looked down at my feet. Someone's old Math II quiz was being pushed along the ground by a mild gust of wind. It was crinkly, like it had been wet and then dried in the sun. There were footprints all over it. It had been through so much, but it was still here.

"Ryden…"

"Don't say no. Just come with me tomorrow, and if you don't have fun, I promise I'll never bother you again."

There was a little tremor in his voice when he said the word "bother." I really wanted to say yes.

The wind picked up, and the math quiz was carried away.

The parking lot was emptying out—first period was going to start soon. But I knew I had to give him an answer.

Finally, I said, "Dances aren't really my thing." Obviously it was the truth, since I'm not supposed to do anything overly physical lately, but it sounded stupid even to me.

He let go of my arm, looking incredibly dejected. But here's what I still don't get: <u>why</u>? He can have anyone he wants. Why me?

"That's cool, I get it. See you later, Meg."

"Wait!" I called out as he walked away.

He turned back.

"Do you want to do something else tomorrow night? Something more…low key?"

A huge, gorgeous grin crept over his face. "Yeah, absolutely. School dances are lame anyway. What did you have in mind?"

Honestly, we could sit on the side of the road counting cars for all I care. I just can't wait to be alone with him. But I do have an idea: the secret beach. "You'll see," I said, and I still can't believe how cool I was able to play it.

Holy crap. I'm going on a date with Ryden Brooks. Mabel's going to flip. ☺

Chapter 5

There's Daddy!" my mom says to Hope as I slam the front door. She holds the baby out to me as I pass by the living room on my way to my room. "How was work?"

"It sucked." I keep walking.

Mom follows me. "Aren't you going to say hi to Hope?"

I stop at the door to my room and slump against the doorjamb. My fingers grip Meg's journal. Hope's happy and babbling in my mom's arms, trying to grab her necklace.

"Can't you keep her in your room tonight? I've had a really shitty day. I need sleep."

"No, Ryden. I can't."

"But look at her—she obviously likes you better than me."

Mom sighs. "No, she doesn't. You're her father. She loves you. I just have more experience handling babies—that's what she's responding to. You'll get it. You just need to keep practicing."

"I don't want to." The words are out before I can stop them. I don't even think I really mean them. Or maybe I do. I don't know.

I did everything wrong with Meg, and I really don't want to do everything wrong with Hope too. But there's a part of me that thinks I might as well stop busting my ass trying. Stop trying to get her to respond to me the way she does with my mom, stop trying to get her to stop screaming and crying and fussing whenever she's alone with me, stop trying to get her to sleep through the whole night *one fucking time*.

Until I find that missing piece of me, it's hopeless.

Mom frowns. A lot of women her age haven't even had kids yet, and here she is, a single, working grandmother. I know none of this has been easy on her either, but she's so much better at managing it all than I am.

Mom passes me and walks into my room. She puts Hope down in her crib, turns on her mobile with the different colored dragonflies, and then sits on my unmade bed, patting the spot beside her. "Come here."

I drag my feet across the floor and collapse face-first onto the bed. The mobile serenades us with a tinny, four-note tune.

"Ryden," Mom says. Her voice has that serious tone that I heard for the first time about a year ago. "We need to talk."

"Can we talk tomorrow?" I ask into the sheets.

"No. Now."

The lake, Alan, Joni…and now this, whatever this is. It is so not my day. I sit up and lean my head back against the wall. "What?"

"We need to figure out what we're going to do when school starts up again in September. You're not dropping out," she says firmly.

"*What?* Why the hell would you think I want to drop out?"

"Don't look at me like that. Do you know how incredibly

common it is for teen parents to drop out of high school? It's a hard balance, being there for your child, going to school, keeping up with your homework, and providing financially for your family."

"Mom, it was *my* idea to go back to school this fall, remember?"

She continues as if I hadn't said anything. "So, you're not dropping out, and you're going to have to keep your job. But we need my job too, which means I won't be able to watch Hope while you're at school *and* while you're at work."

Don't forget about soccer practice.

"So we need to work something out."

"What about day care?" I ask.

Mom raises an eyebrow. "Day care is expensive."

As if I don't know that. We looked into a few places in our neighborhood back when Hope was first born before we decided I'd do homeschooling for a while. The cheapest one we could find was $425 a week.

"Maybe Grandma and Grandpa could help."

"You can't drive back and forth to Vermont every day, Ryden. Besides, they're too old to take care of a baby."

"No, I mean I could ask them for some money. To pay for day care." After all these weeks of trying to figure out what to do with the baby when soccer starts up again, that's the best option I've managed to come up with.

Mom's expression doesn't change. "You really think that will work."

I shrug. "It's worth a shot."

Mom holds up her hands. "Well then, by all means, don't let me stand in your way. Can't wait for the checks to start rolling in."

I may not know my dad, but there's no question of who I got my sarcastic gene from.

I ignore her. "I'll call them tomorrow."

Mom gets up. "Great. Then tomorrow night, we'll talk about plan B." She's about to leave, but Hope starts doing her baby talk thing again, and it sounds a lot like, "Da-da-da-da-da."

Mom stops in her tracks and blasts me with the most massive, out-of-control grin I've ever seen. "Did you hear that? She's trying to say Daddy! That's right, Hope, daaaa-deeee. Daaaa-deee."

It suddenly feels like there's some sort of Panic Creature with lots of legs and super sharp claws crawling around my stomach, through my chest, and up to my throat.

There's no way Hope is trying to say "Daddy." She's too young for that. Right? My fingers twitch with the impulse to grab my computer and look up "average age of baby's first word," but suddenly there's something even more pressing, something I need to do *right now*, just in case she really *is* trying to say what Mom thinks she's trying to say.

I can't be Daddy. Not yet. Not before I know what it even *means*.

"Hey, Mom?"

"Daaaa-deeee. Daaa—"

"Mom!"

She snaps out of it. "Yeah, bud?"

"I need to ask you something, and I really hope you won't get upset."

She lowers herself back onto the bed, and the joy in her eyes melts into worry—the same worry that was in her eyes the day Meg and I told her about the pregnancy. To her credit, she didn't freak out then. I hope she won't now.

"What's going on?"

I wish I didn't have to do this. But I'm desperate.

"I…um…was wondering if you could tell me a little more about my father. Michael."

I watch Mom carefully. The changes are small, but they're there. A line of confusion between her eyes. A swallow of surprise. The downturn of her mouth as she deliberates. A rise and fall of her shoulders as she understands what I'm asking.

"Do you want to find him?" she asks finally.

I look away, and my gaze lands on the corner of Hope's light green baby blanket sticking out through the slats of the crib. "Da-da-da-da-daaaa," she sings.

I nod.

"Why now?"

I open my mouth to tell her the truth, but for some reason I can't say it. "I don't know." It's lame and obviously a lie, but Mom doesn't push it.

"Okay," she says after watching me for a second or two.

Her voice sounds surprisingly steady. "I'll tell you everything I know."

I look back at her. "You don't mind?"

She sighs. "I knew it was going to happen sooner or later. You know I was never keeping secrets from you, right?"

"I know."

"But, Ry…" I wait as she seems to work something out in her thoughts. "I really don't have a lot of information. The last time I tried to track him down, I hit a dead end."

The last time she…*huh?* "You've tried to find him?"

"A couple of times. So I could have the information for you when…well, when this conversation happened. And…I guess I wanted to see what he's been up to all this time. I wouldn't mind some answers too, you know." She fiddles with the frayed edge of her cutoff shorts, and for the first time, I see it: she was in love with my father. That's why she doesn't talk about him all that much. He broke her heart when he left her.

Suddenly I'm thinking about all the fights with Meg, her insistence on not terminating the pregnancy, her absolute refusal to even *listen* to my side of it. Even though she didn't think she was going to die, and even though it was my fault she was in the position where she had to make that choice… in a way, when she decided not to have the abortion, she was choosing to leave me too.

Mom's not the only one with a broken heart.

I put my arm around her, and she rests her head on my shoulder. "I'm sorry, Mom."

She pats my knee. "I'd do it all again. It got me you."

And I guess that's where our similarities end. I wouldn't do it all again. Not even close.

Hope is quiet now, asleep. The mobile continues its song.

After a minute, Mom straightens up. "His name is Michael Taylor."

Michael Taylor. My father. The picture is becoming clearer already.

"He'd be about thirty-seven or thirty-eight now. When I checked a couple of years ago, he was no longer living in Boston. Or if he is, his information isn't listed anywhere. I actually called every Michael Taylor in Boston—came up with nothing."

"Mom," I whisper, "I can't believe you did that."

She just shrugs. "There are a *lot* of Michael Taylors in the United States. And all I have to go on is his name, his incredibly common name." She shakes her head to herself.

"You don't know his parents' names? Or what he does for work? Or anything that will help narrow it down?"

"I'm sorry, Ry. I wish I did. He was a concert promoter at the time—the kind of job you do in college, working off the books for cash. He could be doing anything now."

"Yeah, I guess."

She gives me a kiss on my forehead. After she leaves the room, I start Googling.

Michael Taylor. Approximately 531 million results.

Michael Taylor concert promoter. 126,000 results, most

having to do with lawsuits against Michael Jackson's concert promoter or second-market tickets to Taylor Swift concerts.

Four hours later, I fall onto my bed, smother my face into my pillow, and scream as loud as I can.

Why does *everything* have to be so impossible?

• • •

"Hello?"

"Hi, Grandpa," I say into the phone. "It's Ryden."

"Hello?" he says again.

"*It's Ryden*," I say, louder.

"Ryden! How are you?"

"I'm fine, Grandpa. How are you?"

There's a clicking on the line. "Hello?" my grandmother says from another phone somewhere else in their house.

"It's Ryden, Sylvia," Grandpa says.

"Ryden!" Grandma says. "How are you?"

I quietly bang my head on my desk. This is never going to work. My grandparents are older than they should be. They had four kids in a row in their twenties and then got pregnant with my mom when they were forty. Unplanned babies: a Brooks family tradition.

"I'm fine, Grandma, how are you?"

"Oh, we're doing fine. How's our great-granddaughter? Is that her crying I hear?"

Clearly Grandma's hearing isn't as bad as Grandpa's. "Yeah,

she's teething. Actually, that's what I'm calling about. I'm going back to school for my senior year in a few weeks, and I'm going to have to put Hope in day care. I was wondering if you guys would be willing to help pay for it. I have a part-time job, but it's not enough."

I cross all my fingers. *Please.*

There's a pause.

"Well," Grandpa says. "How much are we talking here?"

"It's over four hundred dollars a week," I admit. "I know it's a lot, but—"

"Ryden, I'm sorry," Grandpa says right away. *Can't he even take some time to think about it first?* "We would help you if we could, but we just don't have that kind of money."

"I understand," I mumble.

"How about this—we'll send you a check for a hundred dollars. I know it's not much, but it will help."

"Yeah. It will." Not enough though. Not nearly enough. "Thanks."

"And please bring that little cutie around to visit us soon," Grandma chimes in.

"I will. I promise." I pause, debating whether to ask them my next question. Oh, fuck it. "Do you guys remember my father?"

"Your father?" Grandpa repeats.

"Yeah."

"If I ever meet that bastard, I'm going to wring his neck with my bare hands until he's pleading for mercy." *Jesus, Grandpa.* He's shouting now; his bald head is probably beet red and shiny with sweat, his veiny, wrinkled hand surely gripping the phone way too tightly.

"Never mind, it's okay," I say, not wanting Grandpa to rage himself into a heart attack. One death on my hands is more than enough, thank you very much. But then his words sink in. "*If* you ever meet him? You mean see him *again*, right?"

"Never met him, never want to." The disgust in Grandpa's voice is heavy.

I let all the air out of my lungs. Michael must have been even more elusive than I thought. "So you don't have any information about him?"

"Information? Not a chance. He never even saw fit to grant us the courtesy of an introduction, Ryden. We could see him every day—he could be our *mailman*, for crying out loud—and we wouldn't know it."

Another dead end.

"Okay, well, thanks anyway. And thanks for the money."

I hang up the phone. A hundred dollars. I mean, it's a hundred dollars I didn't have yesterday. But that money will only pay for one day of day care.

What the fuck am I going to do?

Humans should be more like deer: a few minutes after they're born, they start to walk; a week later, they start going to look for food with their mothers; and a year after that, they're on their own. Simple.

I don't want to go to Mom—not yet. If I let her take over the plans, soccer will be the first thing to go.

A thought creeps into the back of my brain: if it's this hard to figure out what to do with Hope now, what's it going to be like when I'm at UCLA? I highly doubt Mom will move to California with me, and I can't leave Hope here with her. That's just…not an option. Even if Mom were willing. And even though it would be easier. It's the same reason I wouldn't consider giving Hope up for adoption—Hope is Meg's baby. There's no way in hell I'm giving away anything—or anyone— that's part of her. No matter that the alternative is pretty sucky. Plus, my mom didn't give *me* up for adoption or leave me with her parents while she went off and did stuff. And I'm really glad about that, even though I know having me made her life really difficult.

Hope's lying in her crib, babbling to herself, swatting at her mobile. At some point while I was on the phone, the crying stopped. I lean over the top of her crib and place my hand on her chubby belly. Her heartbeat pulses under my fingertips.

One of the all-time craziest moments of my unusually crazy life was when Meg and I heard that heartbeat for the first time. The doctor had a machine at the office. Before Hope had arms and legs and everything, she had that heartbeat. It was loud and it was strong. It was the first tangible proof I had that she was real and that she was here to stay.

I pull my hand away and sigh. If I'm going to keep soccer, which I *am*, I need to come up with a solution—for this summer, for the school year, for college, for all of it—and fast.

I stare at the photo of me and Meg on my computer desktop.

It was taken at one of my games last season. She looks so happy. And healthy. And alive.

There *is* one other thing I could try…

It's not going to work. But I'm kind of out of options.

I put Hope in her car seat—she starts crying immediately—and bring her into the bathroom with me. I shave, brush my teeth and rinse with Listerine, and pluck the two rogue hairs between my eyebrows. Then I get in the shower. The sound of the water slightly drowns out the sound of her crying, and I stand under the stream and try to focus on each individual drop pounding down on my head.

Today, I wash my hair.

Fifteen minutes later, I'm standing on Meg's front porch. Being back here after all this time makes me want to throw up.

Her house is big, way nicer than mine, and has a fancy brass doorknocker in the shape of a horse's head—but it's all shiny and I don't want to mess it up with my sweaty fingerprints, so I just knock on the door old-school style.

The two brand-new Lexuses (Lexi?) in the driveway stare me down. When did they get those? Meg's parents already had nice cars, and they weren't even that old. I bet they bought them for each other and put big red bows on the roofs like those rich people in the commercials. Meanwhile, I was getting a job and trying to figure out how the hell to take care of their granddaughter.

I knock on the door again and then try the doorbell, which is less like a bell and more like a freaking classical orchestra.

There's no answer.

But I know someone's home because the curtains behind the large foyer window move slightly. I glance down at Hope in her car seat on the porch beside me. She's clearly visible from the window, the bright red of her sun hat standing out like a giant "you are here" arrow. Meg's parents know Hope and I are here, and they don't care. Not like I should be surprised—they haven't contacted me once since Meg died, not even to check up on the baby.

I've never understood them. For two people who don't seem to like each other that much, they sure are perfect for each other. Both are workaholic control freaks, attached to their kids in all the wrong ways—making sure Meg and Mabel were on the Ivy League path, behaved like perfect little clones at their work functions, and kept company with the right people. (I, of course, wasn't the right people.)

But the cancer made them more psycho. They couldn't control Meg's disease. Or her choice to continue the pregnancy. And now I guess her death amped the crazy up that much more.

I knock one last time. Nothing.

"Well, I never liked you very much either," I say. If they're on the other side of the door, they probably heard me. I hope they did.

As I make my way back to the car, I have an impulse to call someone and freaking *vent*. And for some reason, Joni is the first person who pops to mind. But then I remember that (A) I don't have her number, and (B) she and I are not friends. I don't know her, she sure as hell knows nothing about my life, and we're gonna keep it that way.

I'm about to pull out of the driveway when some movement catches my eye and Meg's younger sister, Mabel, steps out from around the side of the house. She looks directly at me and makes the international extended-pinkie-and-thumb phone gesture. Then she disappears the way she came.

I grab my phone out of my jeans pocket and discover I have one new text. Meet at the four-way stop sign at the end of our street in five min.

What the hell?

I coast down to the end of the block, and a few minutes later, I see Mabel approach in the rearview mirror. I get out of the car.

"Hi," she says. She's gonna be a sophomore this year. Meg and I hung out with her sometimes, especially when Meg was mostly confined to their house. She's very different from Meg. Lots of sparkly nail polish and pushup bras (not that I was looking) and considers "shopping" a legitimate hanging-out activity. Honestly, if I'd never met Meg, I probably would have ended up hooking up with her sister. Mabel's exactly the kind of girl I used to go for.

"Hi, Mabel."

She opens the back door of my car and goes to unbuckle Hope out of her car seat.

"Wait, no—" Hope is asleep and I'd like to keep it that way. I'm beginning to think I should just drive around all day. It's the only thing that actually mellows her out. But I'd probably have to sell a kidney in order to pay for the gas.

Mabel lifts her up as if I didn't say anything, grunting a little with the weight of her (six-month-old babies who have been fattened on formula and pureed sweet potatoes are way heavier than you'd think—sixteen pounds at her last doctor visit), and cradles her against her chest. Hope squinches her face up and makes little fists. I brace myself for the inevitable wailing, but she settles in and falls right back into her slumber.

Why does Hope seem perfectly happy with everyone except me? I'm about to reach out to take the baby from Mabel—out of nothing more than spite and jealousy—when I notice the tears running down Mabel's face.

"Hey, you okay?"

She just sniffles and nods and breathes in Hope's baby smell. That smell is pretty amazing, I have to admit.

Remembering my conversation with Alan, I say, "Her name is Hope."

She smiles. "Good. I know that's what my sister wanted." She's holding on to the baby like she's the most precious thing in the entire world, and something gurgles up from that place deep inside me. Hope is Mabel's niece. Her family. She's known her for all of two minutes and is already head over heels in love.

I wonder if this is what Meg would have looked like, holding the baby like this, gazing at her with adoration...

No. Stop.

I clear my throat. "Mabel, listen." She looks up at me. "I'm sorry."

She blinks. "For what?"

For forcing my way into your sister's life during those early days even though she was clearly trying to hold me at arm's length. For not doing everything in my power to make sure she didn't get pregnant. For not finding some way to convince her to get an abortion.

"For not bringing Hope to see you sooner," is all I say.

She shakes her head. "Don't say that. I know my parents are being complete jackasses. Do you know they actually *blame* you for Meg dying?"

I stare at her. I did know that, yeah, but no one's ever said it directly to my face before. It's strangely satisfying—so much so that it almost trumps the stab I feel at the sound of her name. Almost. "They're right."

Mabel rolls her eyes. "Oh yeah, because you're the one who gave Meg cancer, right?"

"No, but the chemo was working. The tumors were shrinking. If she didn't have to stop going, she would have gotten better. And guess what? I'm the reason she had to stop going. So, A plus B equals…" Thinking about this, everything hurts. My arms, my legs, my heart, my brain. The pain is physical, debilitating. I want to keel over in the middle of the road and wait for a speeding car to run me over. Too bad there're never any speeding cars around here. Goddamn four-way stop sign.

I sit on the curb.

Mabel sits next to me, stroking Hope's head. "You're wrong," she says. "And Meg thought so too."

I lift my head slowly. "How do you know? Did she tell you that?"

"No. But..." She reaches into her purse—one of those giant leather ones with the brass buckles that all the girls carry around—and pulls out a notebook. It has a red cover.

Holy shit. Is that—

She hands it to me.

It's probably just a regular notebook. Don't get your hopes up.

I open it and am immediately overcome with a feeling I'd forgotten even existed. When exactly what you want to happen, the thing you're wishing for, actually comes true.

This is one of Meg's journals. I flip through quickly. It's full.

It doesn't matter what's written in it. Just the fact that it's here, in my hands, means I get more of her.

I hold it tight against my chest. Sort of the same way Mabel's holding Hope. Like it's the most precious thing in the whole world.

"I started reading this after she died," Mabel says. "It made everything feel a little better, you know? Like she wasn't all the way dead. She was still here, a little."

"I know."

"She wrote this one when she was about seven months pregnant, I think. It was in my room when my parents boxed up all her stuff. That's why they missed it. Everything else went into storage."

I swallow. "Everything?"

"Her room is a guest room now." Mabel lowers her eyes. "Like we don't have enough of those already. They painted it this disgusting pea soup color and bought all new furniture. My parents are fucking crazy."

Have to agree on that one.

"Anyway," she says. "I think you should have it."

I should probably say something like, *Oh, no, you don't have to do that. She was your sister. You should keep it.*

Yeah, that's not going to happen.

"Are you sure?" I ask.

"Yep. But, Ryden…" She looks at me, her eyebrows quirked warily.

"What?"

"There's some pretty intense stuff in there. What she was going through… Anyway, I thought I should warn you."

Guess what? We were all *going through some pretty intense stuff then.*

"I'm sure I'll be fine." I make the split-second decision not to read the journal all in one sitting. If I read it slowly, piece by piece, my time with her will last longer. "Thanks, Mabel."

She kisses Hope on the forehead and passes her to me. "Can I see her more often?"

"Of course. Come over whenever you want."

She smiles.

Chapter 6

Back at home, I hand Hope off to Mom. "I'm gonna go to my room for a while, 'kay?"

"What's that?" Mom asks, nodding to the notebook tucked under my arm.

"Nothing, don't worry about it."

"We have to talk about—"

I close the door on her and slide onto my bed, backing up so I'm wedged in the corner. I open the book.

January 11.

She wrote this more than seven months after the green journal, five weeks before she died. It's a short entry.

I know Ryden blames himself for me getting pregnant. I wish he wouldn't. It's not his fault. It's not anyone's fault. "Fault" is the wrong word. "Fault" implies something bad, regretful, unfortunate. If he could only see what I see, he would know this baby isn't something to be sorry about at all. It's a happy thing. It's amazing. Maybe someday he'll understand that. I hope so anyway.

I shake my head. Even that late in the game, she was still so sure she was going to make it through. But I know that if she'd opened her eyes and seen what the rest of us saw—that she was deteriorating, fast—she would have felt differently about blaming me.

Just one more, and then I'll stop reading...

January 16.

I told Ryden what I want to name the baby today. Hope Rosa Brooks. I like the sound of that. Pretty. Strong. The name of someone who has her two feet solidly on the ground and knows which direction to walk.

I remember that conversation. We were in my room, under the covers, sharing a pillow, staring at each other. (My mom didn't care. Meg was already pregnant, so what difference did it make if we were in bed together? Anyway, we were fully clothed.) Even seven months pregnant and close to death's door, Meg was so beautiful.

Things were good between us again. The only thing we'd ever really fought about was the abortion, and yeah, that was an enormous fight, and it lasted a long time, right up until it was too late for her to have one and the fighting became pointless. But even through her blatant disregard for my opinion, for my concern for her well-being, I'd never considered breaking up with her. We were in the shittiest of shitty situations, but we were in it together.

I brushed her hair out of her eyes. God, I loved that crazy hair.

But then I felt sick for thinking that, because the fact that Meg still had her hair meant she'd stopped chemo, which meant she wasn't getting any better.

"Hope Rosa Brooks," I repeated, testing the feel of the name on my tongue, trying to distract myself from Meg's hair and all its implications.

"What do you think?" she asked.

"What does it mean?"

"What do you mean, what does it mean?"

"I know you, Meg. You're the most organized person I've ever met. I know you have a reason for everything. Usually a long, thought-out reason."

She smiled. "Okay, fine. So, Rosa because of Rosa Parks."

"That bus lady? Why?"

She rolled her eyes. "I want our daughter to grow up knowing she can do anything she puts her mind to."

I nodded. "Okay, what about the Brooks part? Shouldn't it be Reynolds?"

"It's traditional for a child to take the father's last name," she said.

"I have my mom's last name."

"Yeah, but that's because you don't have a dad." She gave me a look that gave extra meaning to her words: I didn't have a dad, but maybe I could if I wanted. If I decided to track down Michael.

I shook my head at her. I wasn't ready for the Michael stuff yet. "But this baby will have a mom *and* a dad," I said. "So that's not a good argument. And since you won't marry me…"

"Ryden, come on, we've talked about this."

We had. A couple of times, actually. And she kept shooting me down. Don't get me wrong, it's not like I *wanted* to get married. Jesus, getting married at seventeen is nuts. But so is having a kid. And since we were doing that, I wasn't going to leave her when she needed me the most. I wanted to show her how much I loved her. But she kept saying no. She said it "wasn't something she felt she needed to do."

"I'm just saying, all things being equal, I don't get why the baby automatically has to have my last name. *You're* the one doing all the heavy lifting." I put my hand on her huge, round stomach. The baby didn't kick, which was fine by me—that shit freaked me out.

"Yeah, I am," she agreed. "So I get to decide. And I want her to have her father's name. The end."

I sighed. Whatever. Fine. I wasn't going to fight with her about something as stupid as a last name. "And what about the first name? Hope?"

"Hope."

"Why Hope?"

She just stared at me, like I was slow.

"What?" I asked.

"Because it's *hopeful*, you dumbass. She's stuck inside here"—she rubbed her hand over her belly, linking her fingers with mine—"in this sick, all-wrong body, not getting the best start, you know? And…" She took a deep breath. "And I really don't know if she'll be okay, Ryden." Her lower lip started to wobble. "But I really hope she will."

I gently reached out and brushed my thumb over her quivering mouth, feeling like breaking down in sobs too but really, really trying to stay strong. What Meg said about the baby was exactly how I felt about *her*. I didn't know if she would be okay, but I really hoped she would. She wasn't looking so good lately. Her face was drawn, her skin had lost its luster, and her eyes looked so, so tired.

"Hope is a really good name," I whispered. And I kissed her.

I close the book when I reach the end of the entry, but something's nagging at me that I can't put my finger on. Meg recounted that conversation pretty much exactly the way I remember it, but though the memory is the same, it feels weird now. Off, like there's something between the lines, something I'm missing. Huh.

It takes every ounce of energy I have—which, let's be honest, isn't much lately—to close the book after the second entry. I'll read more tomorrow.

I bring the book to my face. It smells like her house, like Glade PlugIns and chocolate-cake-scented candles and carpet shampoo. That scent used to work its way into her hair. Whenever I had my arm around her—walking with her in the halls or around the neighborhood in the snow after she got too weak to go to school—I would lean down, kiss her head, and breathe it in. When that delicious, familiar smell hit me, I would have to stop, wherever we were, and kiss her. And every single time, she snuggled closer into me.

I lie down, place the book right next to me on my pillow, and let its lingering scent waft over me.

• • •

I jolt upright.

Shit. It's Sunday night. 7:36 p.m. Soccer starts tomorrow morning, and I haven't figured out what to do about Hope. I'm screwed.

Still half asleep, I reach out for my phone, and before I really know what I'm doing, I call Alan.

He picks up on the second ring. "Yo."

"Hey. It's Ryden."

"I know. It was your ringtone."

Okay, I have to ask. "What's my ringtone?"

"'99 Problems' by Jay-Z."

I think about that for a second. Weird, but whatever. *Alan's* weird. Plus, he's off by about a thousand problems. "What was hers?"

"Meg's?"

Punch to the gut. "Yeah."

"'Stronger' by Kanye West."

"Oh."

"What's up? Everything okay?"

No. "Yeah. Listen, I have a question. Soccer practice starts back up tomorrow, and I haven't exactly figured out what to do with Hope during that time. Any chance you want to watch her?" I clear my throat and spit out the rest before he can say anything. "It's kind of all day, Monday through Friday, up until school starts. I know it's a lot, and I know this is really random, but—"

"Yeah, okay."

"Wait, really?"

"Yeah. It's not like I have anything else going on. And I'd really like to get to know Hope. Just let me know what I need to do. I've never really babysat before."

Well, that was easy. Wonder why I didn't think to ask him earlier.

I hang up with Alan and fall back onto my pillow. But it's not as soft as it should be. The journal. Guess I turned around a lot in my sleep, because the book is now half on my pillow, half off, and it's fallen open.

I go to flip it closed but stop. There's something written on the inside back cover. The writing is small, but the letters are clear. It's a checklist of some sort.

☑ Mabel
☐ Alan
☐ Ryden

My heartbeat picks up slightly. Mabel, Alan, Ryden. What does that mean?

I grab the other journal off my desk, the green one from the first day we met, and flip to the back cover. Nothing. I turn to the front cover. Also blank.

I pull my phone out of my pocket and dial a number I've never called before. Mabel picks up immediately.

"Are there any more?" I ask.

"Any more what?"

"Journals. Meg's journals."

"No, that's all I have. I told you, my parents put all her stuff in storage."

"Yeah, but you had time to take this one from her room before that happened. Did you take any others?"

"I didn't *take* that one from her room," Mabel says. "It was *in* my room. I found it stuck in a stack of books on my night-stand a couple of days after she died. By that time, all her stuff was already in boxes and being loaded onto a truck."

I think about that for a minute. "You didn't take it," I repeat.

"No."

"It was already in your room."

"Yes."

"And you had never seen it before?"

"Nope. Or at least not long enough to distinguish it from any of the other books Meg was always writing in."

"So Meg must have put it there. She *wanted* you to find it," I murmur, almost to myself.

"I guess so, yeah." There's a short pause and then Mabel says, "But why?"

"I have no idea." But my mind is revolving with possibilities.

What if this checklist, this journal, *means* something? What if she left one for each of us, and there are two other journals out there, for me and Alan?

What if there's something Meg wanted us to know?

Chapter 7

In the morning, I'm actually feeling all right—which is crazy, considering how dead tired I am.

I spent a long time last night searching for a journal with a ☑ *Ryden* in the back. It was a fail, obviously. If Meg had left another journal here, I would have noticed it before now. Then I left Alan a voice mail asking if he's found any journals at his place and fell asleep reading more of Meg's red journal, the ☑ *Mabel* one, looking for a clue.

I was woken up by Hope an hour or two later. Same old story. But then something sort of miraculous happened. She was crying and crying, her sore little gums bared, two small white teeth only just starting to fight their way to the surface, her hands pulled into fists, making way more noise than a thing the size of a shoe box should be able to, and somehow I knew it was hunger crying, not teething crying, even though she had eaten right before I put her down. I *knew* it. So I made her some formula, pulled her into my lap, and she latched onto the bottle right away, her sobs subsiding almost instantaneously. It was like when my mom feeds her. Easy. Peaceful. Kind of awesome.

She went right back to sleep when her bottle was finished. It was the first time I've ever gotten her to do that on my own.

Since I was all amped up after that, I used the time to continue the Michael search.

Michael Taylor Boston 1998 Ryden Brooks: 160,000 results and clear from the first page that they were all scraps of completely unrelated nothingness. Sometimes the Internet can be ostentatiously useless.

So I switched missions and Googled *UCLA day care*. Way more productive. Turns out they have a campus day care that gives highly discounted rates to children of UCLA students if they meet the financial aid requirements. And hello, I'm poor as fuck.

It's all going to work out. Today is the day that my life finally starts to get back on track.

I meet Mom in the kitchen. She looks up from her coffee and her book in surprise. (Mom reads a *lot* of paranormal trilogies. You'd think she was one of the girls at my school or something.) Then she takes in my practice gear and Hope all ready to go in her car seat, and her eyes narrow. "What are you doing?"

"Going to soccer practice."

She blinks a few times, slowly, and then says, "You're bringing the baby?"

"No. Alan's gonna watch her."

"You paying him?"

"No."

"Ryden."

"Mom."

She sighs and puts down her coffee. "We need to talk, bud." She pulls out the chair next to her.

I glance at the clock. "I can't right now. I have to be at practice in an hour, and I still have to show Alan how to heat up bottles and shit."

"I really don't care. Sit down."

I don't have time for this. But I sit, because I know that tone of voice, and I know she's not going to let me go until I listen to what she has to say. "Fine. Let's get this over with."

"Enough with the attitude, okay?" she says. "I'm on your side."

"I know," I mumble.

"Good. Now, explain this whole soccer thing to me. How on earth is that going to work?"

"The same way it always does."

Mom gives me a look. "What did I say about the attitude?"

"I'm not trying to give you an attitude. I'm serious—soccer works the way it always does. I go to practice; I go to games; I come home. What's to understand?"

"What's to *understand* is that you have a daughter now, and a job. And school. We talked about this. You have obligations, Ryden. Important ones. Soccer's going to have to go."

I shake my head. "Soccer's important. I can't play in college if I don't play this season."

Mom stares at me, her eyes bugging out of her head, as if I told her I've decided to become a woman or something.

"What?" I ask.

"Buddy," she says softer, putting her hand on mine, "you can't go to UCLA. I thought you understood that."

I yank my hand back. "The hell I can't. That's been the plan for almost two years! The coach wants me. When he called a couple of weeks ago, he said that they just need to see me play live, and then they're going to make their official offer."

"Things are different now."

I push my chair back and get to my feet. "Do you honestly think I don't know that?"

"I don't know what you think, Ryden! You don't talk to me like you used to. And you *clearly* haven't been working to figure out the day care situation—"

"Not true! I told you, Alan is going to watch her."

"Yeah, during *soccer practice*. I'm not talking about soccer practice. I'm talking about when you go back to school. Unless Alan graduated early, he'll be going back to school in two weeks too. Which puts us no closer to a solution. This isn't going to magically work itself out. This is real life, Ryden. You need to start acting like it."

Now it's my turn to stare at her. "I can't *believe* you just said that. I've done *everything* I'm supposed to do. I'm trying everything I can think of to do right by Hope. I got a job. I haven't seen any of my friends all summer, and when I have, it's like they're freaked out they'll catch the fucked-up-life disease from me. Meg is *gone*. She's gone, Mom, and she's never coming back, and it's all my fault."

With no warning, all the bullshit inside me forces its way out in violent, hyperventilating gasps, and I'm suddenly reaching for my mom as she gets up from her chair, rubbing my back like she did when I was a little kid.

Goddammit. Today was supposed to be a good day.

"It's okay, buddy," Mom whispers. "Let it out."

I don't know how long we stand there like that, but eventually the shaking subsides and my lungs start working again. I pull away, slowly.

"Sit," Mom says.

I do.

"Talk to me," she says. "*Please.*"

And I do.

It's not like any of it is really news to her—she obviously knows all the major plot points of the story. But I've never told her the little things about Meg, the things I loved most about her, like how she used to concentrate really hard on what the teacher was saying in class, as if she was eager to soak up as much knowledge as she possibly could. Or how she used to talk me into letting her braid my hair when we were alone and how she used to laugh at how ridiculous I looked when she was done. Or how she was the only person I'd ever seen eat ice cream (okay, sugar-free, organic frozen yogurt—Meg wouldn't have eaten real ice cream) out of an ice-cream cone with a spoon.

I've never told her how Meg was always pushing me to track down Michael, how she thought there was some big question mark in my head where my dad's face should be.

I've never told her that sometimes when I look at Hope's face, really look at her, I feel sick to my stomach because she looks so much like Meg that it's like being haunted by a ghost.

I've never told my mom how much I hate myself for how everything turned out, how much I regret having sex with Meg without a condom, knowing she had cancer and that things would be bad if she got pregnant, and how I should have pushed harder for her to have an abortion. Even if it meant Meg hated me forever, I should have done whatever it took to make her think of *herself* for once, to stop her from sacrificing herself like this.

But I tell her now.

"It wasn't supposed to happen this way, Mom. Everything was supposed to be fine. Meg promised me! She was so *sure* she was going to make it."

Before she got pregnant and after, during chemo and post-chemo, right up until the end, Meg never once believed she was going to die. And if I'm being honest, despite all our fighting about her decision to stop her treatment, deep down she had me convinced of it too. I really did believe she would make it through…right up until that horrible day late in the sixth month of her pregnancy when I looked at her face and realized pieces of her were already gone.

All Mom says is, "It's okay, Ryden. It's all going to be okay." Even though I know she's wrong—it won't all be okay—it's the best thing she can say to me. Because she's not trying to contradict me or tell me it isn't my fault or any of that crap. She's letting my feelings stay my feelings. And I love her for it.

Mom deserves to know I'm not completely in denial and that I actually do think about our situation. "I called Grandma and Grandpa."

She nods. "They told me."

"They said they would send a hundred dollars."

"That's nice."

There are a few moments of quiet. Oh, fuck it. Might as well tell her everything.

"And I went to Meg's house to ask her parents to help pay for day care," I say in a rush.

Mom's eyebrows shoot up. "You did? When?"

"Yesterday."

She stares at me, clearly waiting for me to elaborate.

"They didn't come to the door. They were home though. They saw me. I know that for sure."

Mom lets out her breath all at once. "I'm sorry."

"I don't understand it. I know they hate me and blame me and all that, and I know they probably blame Hope too, and that's why they're acting like this, but those people have more money than God. Why wouldn't they throw us a few grand to make sure their own flesh and blood is being properly cared for?"

"They're complicated people, Ryden," Mom says.

"Yeah. No joke."

Complicated, yes. Crazy, yes. But if they truly loved Meg—and

I believe they did; they were always doing whatever they could to help her get better—why wouldn't they want to see Hope? I don't care if she reminds them so much of her that it hurts. I don't care that it's easier not to deal with any of it.

I could have put Hope up for adoption and moved the fuck on. But I didn't. I couldn't just erase Hope and Meg from my life. I made the hard choice, because it was the right one. They should have to too. Isn't that what parents are *supposed* to do?

Or is that just another thing I'm wrong about?

Mom walks over to the sink and rinses out her coffee cup. I glance at the clock. It's already nine. Practice is starting. I have to be there.

But Mom's not ready to let me go yet.

"Ryden?" she says.

"Yeah?"

"What changed?"

Could you be a little more vague, Mom? "What do you mean?"

"You said Meg wanted you to try to find Michael, right? We both know you would have done anything for that girl. But you didn't ask me about him then, not even when Meg asked you to. So why now? What's changed?"

I really don't want to talk about this. Plus, I don't know how to explain it. "I don't know." I pick up Hope's car seat. "I'm sorry. I have to go."

"Please, Ry. I want to know." Her eyes are almost begging. *Fuck.*

I put the car seat back down and pull the rubber band out of my hair and redo my ponytail just to have something to do with my hands. "Honestly, Mom, I'm totally sucking at this whole parenthood thing. I have no clue what I'm doing. Hope even seems to know that. So I thought…maybe…if I met my own father, things would start to click into place. Like, I don't know, on some basic level. What fathers act like when they're in the same room as someone they gave their DNA to. Or what it feels like to look at your father's face. Stuff like that. I thought if I had those experiences, things might start to make more sense for me and Hope."

Mom stares at me as if I'm speaking Korean. Finally she unclamps her jaw. "First of all, you're not sucking at *all*. You're doing amazingly well, actually."

Ha. Whatever. I'm not sure if I actually say that out loud.

"Second…you really think *Michael* has something to teach you about being a parent that I don't?"

Shit. Suddenly I'm realizing how that reasoning must sound to her. Like I think she wasn't enough of a parent. Like everything she's done for me was so lacking that a five-minute visit with my deadbeat, glorified sperm donor would be more meaningful than a lifetime with her. Goddammit. That's not what I meant at all.

"Mom…that's not…not *teach* me anything…more like what it *feels* like…I mean, you're the best—"

She holds up a hand to stop me. "It's okay, Ry." She takes a breath and then asks, "Have you started looking for him?"

I nod.

"Anything?"

I shake my head. "I think it might be a lost cause." But her question reminds me of all my other Googling, which provides me with the perfect opportunity to get far, far away from the subject of Michael. The news that the day care dilemma won't be an issue next year should cheer up Mom at least a little.

"I almost forgot—I did some research last night," I say. "UCLA has a day care for students' kids. And they give you financial aid. So I can take Hope to California with me. I know it's not gonna be easy, but I really think I can do it."

She crosses back over to me, places her hands on my shoulders, and really *looks* at me. Then she smiles a sad, weary smile. "You know what, bud? I think you can do anything, if you want it badly enough."

"So"—I pause—"I'm gonna go to practice."

Mom nods. "Have fun."

• • •

"I got your message last night," Alan says as I run him through the basics of child care.

"And?"

He shakes his head. "I haven't seen any of Meg's journals in months. Since she was still…here."

"Damn."

"What exactly are you looking for?"

I quickly explain my theory about the checklist and he goes, "That's so Meg."

"So you think I'm right? About her leaving us some sort of message?"

"I guess it's possible. Or at the very least maybe she left us each a journal. As a…" He looks like he's searching for the word.

"Souvenir?"

"Or like a gift? But I don't know where she would have left them if they're not at your house and they're not at my house. It's not like she was going out all that much."

"I know. That's the problem." But with every moment that passes, my desperation to find Meg's journals grows. Because if I'm not going to get answers about how to be a dad from my father, then maybe I'll get them from Hope's mother. What if Meg left pages and pages of motherly wisdom behind? What if, even though she's gone, she didn't actually leave me alone in this?

At this point, I don't care where the answers come from—Michael or Meg or somewhere else entirely. Soon I'll be "Daddy," and all too soon after that, Hope will be old enough to start remembering stuff, and I really need to figure out what the hell I'm doing by then, because I don't want to permanently screw her up. So you can be damn sure I'm going to follow any lead that comes my way.

I hand over Hope and all her stuff and book it across town to school. I get to practice at 9:55.

"Brooks," Coach O'Toole barks, not looking happy. "You're late."

"I know, Coach. I'm sorry. It won't happen again."

He nods toward the field. "Take your place with your team. We're doing windows."

I jump right into the passing and receiving drill, and after a few minutes, it's as if the last year didn't even happen. I'm back in time, the Ryden of old, the one who spent the summer before sophomore year hooking up with Shoshanna Harvey, swimming at the lake, drinking a lot of beer. The Ryden who knew absolutely nothing about baby feeding schedules or diaper rash or what the word *metastasis* means.

My foot connects with the ball over and over again, and each impact is like a jolt of electricity from a defibrillator. Out here on the field, I'm coming back to life.

Dave approaches me at lunch. "Dude." He gives me a fist bump.

"Hey, Dave."

"I didn't know if you were coming today. You seemed kinda freaked out at the lake. And you've been totally MIA all summer."

I take a bite of my sandwich and chew slowly, trying to figure out how to respond. I really don't want to get into a whole discussion right now. Eventually, I go with, "Yeah, well, here I am. So what's going on with you and Shoshanna?"

Dave's eyes glaze over a little, and I know exactly what he's thinking about. There are certain things Shoshanna Harvey is very, very good at. "Man, she's amazing. I think I'm in love."

I smile. He's not wrong. Sho *is* amazing, in lots of ways.

"That's cool with you, right?" he asks way too belatedly. "I mean, you're totally over her, yeah?"

"Yes, David. I'm over her. I'm happy for you, man."

He pops a straw into a Capri Sun and downs the whole thing in one sip. I watch as the pouch gets flatter and flatter, powerless as its insides get sucked out. "Whatever happened with you two, anyway? You never told me why you broke up."

I shrug. "Dunno. Just wasn't right, I guess." The truth is, Sho and I had fun, but the same kind of fun over and over again gets old after a while   at least, when there's nothing underneath. I was ready for something else. Looking back, I was ready to find Meg. Not that Shoshanna's stupid or anything. She's actually really smart. And she's cool too. And fun. But we weren't right together. And I told her so. She was really pissed off at first, but she got over it. Shoshanna always bounces back. Maybe that's why she wears so much makeup—it's a barrier against assholes like me, so nothing we say or do can cut through her mask enough to hurt.

After the break, we play a full game to get back into the rhythm. I block every single shot.

At the end of practice, Coach O'Toole has us all gather around. "Nice work out there, gentlemen. Welcome back." We all applaud. "Seniors, listen up. Some of you who will be playing D-One have unofficial offers already, and that's great. Keep talking to the coaches. Now that you're in your senior year, they're free to call you once per week. Let's turn those unofficial offers into official ones. For the rest of you, if you're planning to play in college, *now* is the time to start looking at schools and sending out your letters of interest. Don't dally. Recruiters' schedules fill up quickly, and you want to make sure they have time to come see you play."

"Hey, Ryden," Dave says after Coach lets us go. "A bunch of us are going to Chili's. You comin'?"

I shake my head. "Can't do it, man."

He nods, like he expected me to say that. "Cool. See you tomorrow then."

I shower quickly and hop in the car. I have thirty minutes to get to Alan's, pick up Hope, drop her off with Mom, and get to work.

But really, all I'm thinking about is writing the UCLA head coach. I know Coach said those letters were for guys who don't have any interest from recruiters yet, but I also know the UCLA recruiter needs to see me play one more time—in person—before offering me my scholarship. As far as I know, that visit hasn't been scheduled. So it couldn't hurt to remind them that I'm the guy for their team.

Chapter 8

Here ow'd it go?" I ask Alan as I bundle Hope into her car seat. She's holding on to her spider stuffed animal, staring up at me, a little like *Hey, I remember you.*

She starts to get cranky the second that recognition kicks in. *Of course.*

"Great!" he says. "She's amazing."

I walk out to the car, and Alan follows. "Thanks, man," I say. "I really appreciate it. So you're cool for tomorrow?"

"Yeah, no prob. My mom's in love with her too. She wants to make her Korean baby food. Is that okay?"

"Sounds good." I get in the car. "See ya, Alan."

"Ryden, wait."

I roll down the window. "Yeah?"

"You didn't call to check on her today." He's looking at me like he's trying to figure something out.

Huh. Calling to check on Hope didn't even cross my mind. I never do that when my mom has her while I'm at work. God, I'm so bad at this. Even when I try really freaking hard, I still screw up. "Oh, yeah, sorry. I, uh…practice was really busy. We didn't really have any downtime."

"Okay." I can't tell if he means it or if he's saying it sarcastically, like "yeah, right."

I make a show of looking at the clock on the dashboard. "Gotta get to work, man. See you tomorrow. Thanks again."

And I speed off.

• • •

I'm making a mental list of all the stats and info I should include in my letter to UCLA while taking all the expired containers of precut fruit off the refrigerated shelves in produce when someone taps me on the shoulder. I don't have to look to know who it is. But I turn around anyway.

"Before you say anything," Joni says, holding up a hand, "let me say my thing first." Her other hand's behind her back, like she's hiding something from me.

I wait. She's got a nose ring today. It's a really tiny green stone. I wonder if she just got it pierced or if she just wasn't wearing anything in the hole the last few times I've seen her.

"I wanted to say I'm sorry for being a total douche on Saturday. Sometimes I say things without thinking about how it will sound to the other person. It's a fault. I'm working on it." She blows her hair out of her eyes. "I don't think you're spoiled or angsty or anything else that I said. I actually think you're pretty cool. So will you be my friend again, please?" She bats her eyelashes at me.

Maybe it's the high I'm riding from conquering the hungry

baby dilemma last night and having such a good day at soccer, but I can't help but smile. "Yeah, okay."

"Rad." Joni brings her hand from around her back and hands me a package wrapped in aluminum foil.

"What is this?" I ask, taking it. It's warm and about the size of my fist.

"It's a vegetarian empanada."

I stare at her. "Why are you giving me a vegetarian empanada?"

"It's a peace offering. Duh. My dad made them this morning. He loves to cook, so even though there are about a thousand people in my house, we always have a ton of extra food around. I gave one to my bus driver this morning—he liked it so much, he gave me a pass for a free ride home."

"You take the bus to work?"

She shrugs. "Don't have a car yet."

I open up the foil. A mouthwatering smell hits me. "This better be recycled aluminum foil," I tease.

Joni holds up three fingers, in the shape of a W, and holds them over her heart. "Whole Foods honor."

I take a bite of the empanada. "Holy shit."

Joni grins. "Good, right?"

"Fucking amazing." I devour the rest of it in two more bites. I guess with all the running around after practice, I didn't realize how hungry I was.

"There's more where that came from, friend." She skips off just as some guy who looks like he came straight from the gym pulls an avocado from the middle of the display and about fifty avocados from the top of the pile, the ones that apparently weren't good enough for him, fall to the floor. Joni stops to help him pick them up, and I watch from across the produce section as she checks him out as he bends over. I don't mean checking him out in the "ringing up his groceries" kind of way. Her eyes are seriously *glued* to his ass.

Well, that was unexpected.

A couple of hours later, I take my break and open Meg's journal. I stare at the checklist, waiting for some meaning to float up off the pages. But I got nothin'.

I flip back toward the beginning of the book. That entry I read yesterday about the baby-naming conversation is still bothering me.

I read it again.

Yeah, still feels off. There's something about it that gives me an uneasy feeling—like I'm on my way to the beach and am about to realize I forgot to pack a bathing suit. But I still can't figure out *why* it feels that way. Maybe it's because I'm reliving that conversation about Hope's name with the power of hindsight behind me, and knowing how the whole situation pans out taints the moment with bitterness. That could be it.

But then, wouldn't *all* Meg's journal entries make me feel this way? Why is this one in particular driving me nuts?

I'm about to skip ahead to where I left off when Joni comes into the break room.

"There you are," she says. She pulls out the chair next to me and sits down. "I saw on the schedule that you're off on Friday."

"Yeah, why?"

"I'm off too. I thought we could do something."

"Do something?"

"You know, hang out. Chill. Socialize in a nonprofessional capacity."

Hmm. Does she mean as friends? Or something else? Because I'm beginning to think she's not quite as gay as I thought she was.

"I have soccer practice during the day," I say.

"After that."

"Uh, okay." Okay? *Okay?* What the hell are you doing, Ryden?

Oh, who am I kidding? I know exactly what I'm doing. Joni's the only person I know who doesn't know about Meg or Hope or any of it. Being back at soccer today proved that I can be the old me again, the Ryden Brooks who everyone loved, who could do whatever he wanted with zero consequences. And it felt really, really good. I think if I play this right, I can have two lives—the shitty one *and* the good one. And they don't have to mix.

"Awesome," Joni says. "What do you want to do?"

I shrug. "Whatever."

"Do you want to go with me to get a tattoo?"

I stare at her. She's looking back at me, all "what?" like she just said the most boring thing in the world. "Uh…I don't really want a tattoo," I say.

Joni rolls her eyes. "I wasn't talking about you. I was talking about me. It hurts like a bitch, and I could use a hand-holding buddy."

I consciously ignore the hand-holding part of that statement. "How do you know it hurts so bad? Do you already have a tattoo?"

She rocks back on her heels, her hands in her pockets. "Yup."

"Where?"

"Wouldn't you like to know." She grins mischievously and then says, "Okay, cool, so we'll figure out the details later. See ya." And then she's gone, the break room door swinging behind her.

• • •

That night, I write my letter to UCLA. If Meg were here, she'd watch over my shoulder for a few minutes as I struggled to get the words out on the screen. I used to read a lot, before I stopped having time, but writing has always been hard for me. How am I supposed to know what to say? Eventually Meg would gently put her hands on my shoulders and lean down and whisper in my ear, "Want some help?" She wouldn't say it condescendingly—she'd just want to know if I needed her help. I'd say yes, and she would sit on my lap and start typing, and in twenty seconds flat, she'd have the perfect letter written, no typos or misspelled words, and she wouldn't even have to use spell check. She never told me what she wanted to do after college, but I bet she'd have been an author. Or maybe a journalist. She did tell me she'd always dreamed of going to Dartmouth but that her plans changed after she got her diagnosis. That was why she'd gotten all sad that day outside the cafeteria when I told her about UCLA for the first time.

I read over the letter about a hundred times to make sure all the commas are in the right place and I don't sound like a complete dolt.

Stats, athletic background, academic background, game film, YouTube link, Coach's contact info, game schedule. *Long-ass paragraph of desperate pleading.*

I go outside to put it in the mailbox. It's a really quiet night. There are no cars going by, and the people across the street are on vacation, so for once, their dog isn't barking his head off. Even my own house is quiet. Mom's hanging out on the couch with Hope, the two of them watching *The Bachelor*.

I sink down to the curb and sit next to the mailbox, leaning back on my hands, staring up at the stars. I still don't quite get how each one of those stars is actually a sun, burning up its own part of the universe. It seems incomprehensible that something that big, that complex, that infinite, is out there, while we're here on this stupid planet watching reality shows and waiting in line for the new iPhone and buying all the chia seeds in Whole Foods because some article told us it was trendy, thinking we're tough shit, like any of it means anything. But we're miniscule. We mean nothing. And even in our own world, we don't stick around that long. Not long enough to matter. You're born—more likely than not an unintended by-product of your parents wanting to get laid—you do some stuff, and then you die. You get sick, you get hit by a train, you get old and fall apart. It all ends the same way. And that's it. Then your kids get horny, have a kid, and the cycle starts again.

What the hell is the *point* of any of it?

I brought Meg's journal with me. The light from the streetlamp casts the book in a muted golden color. I read a few entries. Meg writes about her family dinners, how her father has been drinking a lot more wine lately, shopping online with Mabel since she's not strong enough to go to the mall, watching the clock and counting the minutes until school gets out and I can visit her.

Her words break my heart into as many fragments as there are stars in the sky. But none of the entries have the same stomach-twisting effect as that baby-naming one.

I lie back on the narrow strip of grass between the street and the sidewalk and focus on one particularly bright star.

My voice is a whisper in the darkness. "I miss you."

Chapter 9

Over the next couple of days, I get a kind of routine going. Drop off Hope with Alan, spend all day at soccer, pick up Hope and drop her off with my mom, go to work, go home, get as much sleep between the crying fits as I can. I haven't managed to repeat the mellow nighttime feeding of the other night, but I have remembered to call Alan at lunch to check up on Hope. Plus, I've successfully avoided being in the same room as my mother for longer than two minutes at a time, so she hasn't been able to bring up the whole day care conversation again. I think she's been cutting me some slack because of our intense as all hell discussion at the kitchen table on Monday, but I see that look in her eyes—the reprieve isn't going to last forever.

"Where do you live?" Joni asks me Thursday at work.

"Why?"

"So I can pick you up for our tattoo extravaganza tomorrow."

Nope. No way she's coming to my house. "I thought you didn't have a car."

"I don't. But I borrow my stepbrother's car sometimes."

Well, that won't do at all. "Where's the tattoo place?"

"Laconia."

Perfect. "And you live in Clinton, right?"

"Yeah."

"It doesn't make sense for you to come all the way out to Downey to pick me up. It's way out of the way for you. I'll pick *you* up."

She shrugs. "Have it your way, Brooks. I was *trying* to be a gentleman."

I laugh. "You don't look much like a gentleman to me, lady."

We swap phones and enter our contact information. I feel a strange relief at knowing that I have a way to get in touch with Joni now. If I ever wanted to.

"Who's this?" she asks, holding up the home screen.

It's a photo of me and Meg at our spot at the lake, my arms around her as I give her a kiss on the cheek, her arm extended out in front of her as she takes the picture of us, her face all red and laughing. I look at that photo every time I use my phone. There's no reason for me to act weird about it now. Except for the fact that I can't tell Joni the truth.

"Oh," I say, taking the phone back and pushing the button that makes the screen go dark. "That's my ex." I keep my voice as nonchalant as I can.

"An ex and yet you still have her picture as the background on your phone." Joni looks at me all knowingly. "Methinks somebody's not quite over it."

I shake my head. "No, it's very over. Trust me on that."

"Then why the photo?"

A woman with long, gray hair stops her cart next to us and saves me from having to explain. "Excuse me," she murmurs and steps between us to study the various brands of sprouted quinoa. She has a bag of kale chips in her cart. Funny how when I first met Meg, I had no idea what a kale chip was, and now I work in a store where they fly off the shelves. One more thing to remind me of her.

We step back to give the woman some space, and I shove the phone in my back pocket. While we wait for her to go away, I straighten a few sacks of whole wheat flour.

"Can I help you find anything?" Joni asks her.

"No, no, just looking," she says. Finally she plucks a bag of quinoa off the shelf and leaves.

"So," I say to Joni right away, "what time should I pick you up tomorrow?"

"My appointment's at five thirty. Maybe, like, five? Does that work?"

That actually works out perfectly. Just enough time to leave Hope with my mom and get the hell out of there again.

• • •

"I'm going out, Mom." I stop at her office door on my way to get Joni. "Hope's in her swing."

Mom's office is covered in pink feathers. She's even got a couple sticking out of her hair. "Hold on." She looks up, glue gun in hand.

"What is this, a flamingo-themed wedding?" I ask, joking.

She smiles. "Actually, yeah."

"Really?" I haven't guessed one of these right in a while.

"Hey, as long as it pays the bills, I don't ask questions," Mom says.

"You do realize that exact sentence has been uttered by every person who was ever involved in anything illegal?"

Mom laughs. "So where are you going?"

"Out."

"Out where? You don't have work today."

"I'm aware of that. I'm going out with a friend."

"What friend?"

"You don't know her."

Mom's eyes pop a bit. "Her?"

I shake my head. "Don't do that. It's just someone from work."

"Listen, I'm glad you're making new friends, Ryden, but you've barely seen Hope all week."

"I'll see her tomorrow. Your hot glue is dripping." I point. "Gotta go. Love you."

She sighs, like she knows it's not worth a fight. "All right then. Have fun."

Joni's house is exactly the kind of place I would have pictured her living. It's big but not too fancy, there are a few kids' toys scattered in the driveway, and brightly colored flowers are planted along the front pathway. It's welcoming, like Joni herself.

There's a dude in the garage working on some sort of project.

I give him a quick wave on my way to the front door, but he stops me. "Hey, can I get your opinion?"

I look around. "Me?"

"Yeah. Come here a sec."

I go over. The guy is, like, twenty, and has dark skin but bright blond dreadlocks. He looks like he hasn't shaved in a few days. His hands are gray.

He gestures to the thing in front of him. It's some sort of sculpture done with clay and metal. It's almost as tall as I am and kind of like a tree—the trunk is all organic-looking, with intricately carved bark, but the branches and leaves are harder, more geometric, made from welded pieces of pipe and scrap metal. It's actually really cool.

"What do you think?" the dude asks. "I need another set of eyes on this."

"It looks like a tree."

"Yeah, but what do you *think* about it?"

"I don't really know anything about art."

"You don't have to *know* anything to *feel* something. Just tell me your first impression."

"Well…" I look at it some more. "I think it's…sad."

"Sad how?"

"I don't know, it's like it was natural and something happened, something came along right around here"—I point to the junction between the clay and the metal—"and corrupted it, changed it into something else. Something *less*."

He stares at it a minute. "Yes. That's exactly right. It's *sad*." I don't know if that's good or bad, but he holds out his hand to me and says, "Thank you. That's exactly what I needed."

I shake his hand, getting gray clay all over mine. "So…is Joni here?"

"Yeah, she's inside. You can go right in."

I feel weird walking into someone's house—especially someone I barely know—but after two rings of the bell, there's still no answer, so I open the screen door and go inside. "Hello?" I call out.

"Ryden?" Joni calls from somewhere upstairs.

"Yeah." I start up the steps as she comes bouncing down the hallway. She's wearing these baggy linen pants that sit low on her hips and a red tube top. She's actually got a hell of a body. I clear my throat.

She grins down at me from the top of the steps. "So you just waltz into people's houses willy-nilly?"

"I rang the bell. Twice."

"Mhmm, sure you did." She crosses her arms.

"The guy outside said I should let myself in. I'm sorry, I—"

She drops her arms and rolls her eyes. "I'm messing with you. Lighten up."

The door off the kitchen opens, and two little kids—a boy and a girl, both with a skin tone about halfway between Joni's and the dude outside's—come running in, shrieking at the top of their lungs and firing at each other with Super Soakers. A girl who looks like she's not that much younger than Joni and me follows them inside, towel-drying her hair and shouting at the kids that the house is a water-gun-free zone. They share a glance and turn fire on her.

"Stevie!" Joni says to the girl. *"¡Es tu trabajo para mantener a los niños lejos de los problemas de hoy!"*

"I *know*," Stevie says. "But it's hard, okay? There's *two* of them."

Joni sighs and motions for me to follow her.

"Willy-nilly?" I repeat as we walk down a hall with framed paintings covering the walls. The house smells like fresh-baked bread. "Who talks like that?"

She laughs. "I do, apparently." She pushes open the door at the end of the hall. "Welcome to *Chez Joni.*"

Holy. Shit.

Joni's room is *insane*. The rest of the house was pretty normal. Colors everywhere and lots of art, but nothing crazy. This is hands down the trippiest room I've ever been in. You step inside and it's like you're stepping outside. Or through a magical wardrobe or some shit. The ceiling is one large, angled skylight, with a few strategically placed crossbeams supporting the glass. Above us, the sun is still fairly high in the sky, and the leaves of an old elm tree rustle together like they're trying to keep warm.

The walls, closet door, and light switches are covered in the most intricate mural I've ever seen. It's a 360-degree panoramic view of a city park. The details, the depths, the lighting...it's like a photograph. I don't feel as if I'm looking at a wall; I feel as if I'm looking out a window.

All the furniture is white—the bed, the lamp, the desk, the dresser.

There's some sort of soundtrack being pumped out of hidden speakers somewhere. Street traffic, the constant slosh of water from a fountain, and someone playing the violin far off in the distance.

And the floor…

"Is this *AstroTurf*?"

"Yeah, my parents wouldn't let me plant real grass in here, so this was the best I could do."

"Where *are* we?"

"Washington Square Park," she says. "It's in New York. It's my favorite place in the world."

"I've never been there. What's so great about it?"

"I have this picture of me there with my mom when I was a baby. It's one of the only photos I have of just the two of us." She opens her computer and pulls up a picture of a young woman who looks a little like Joni, wearing a winter coat and hat and holding a fat baby about Hope's age. They're in front of a big arch. "I don't really have any memories of her, but this picture feels like a memory, if that makes sense."

I nod. It's like the journals. A poor substitute for the real thing, but better than nothing.

"So when my stepmom and my sister Stevie and my best friend Karen and I went on a trip to New York a few years ago, we all went there." She shows me another picture of the four of them under that same arch. A tall, darker-skinned woman who I guess is Joni's stepmother; the girl from the hallway, only younger; and a white girl with a huge smile. Joni's hair was longer then—and pink. "It's this perfect little square of music and art and history and intellect and nature and harmony, right in the middle of a bunch of screaming streets." She looks me in the eye and smiles. "It was incredible. Because those are all things we have inside us too. You know, the things that make us human? Even though pressure, rules, drama push in on us from the outside and try to take over. I like being reminded that if this little, unassuming park in the middle of Manhattan can fight back against the bullshit, so can I."

I gape at her for a long moment, slowly coming to realize that Joni is *my* Washington Square Park. My way to connect with who I was—am—in the middle of all the bullshit.

She gets it. I wonder how she knew that was the exact right thing to say to me.

"What bullshit are you pushing back against?" I ask. She always seems so perfectly happy.

She shrugs. "Family being all up in my business all the time. Friend drama. Karen and I…I don't know, lots of stuff."

I want to know more, but then she'll feel like she can ask me more about my life, and we're not going there. So I nod. "How did you even do this?"

"You'd be surprised what you can do with a little elbow grease and imagination." She grins. "Elijah did most of it."

"Elijah?"

"The guy in the garage? He's my stepbrother. Anyway, you ready to go?" She jumps up and down. "It's tattoo time!"

We wave to Elijah on our way out, but I don't think he sees

us, he's so immersed in his work. The kids are out of sight, but I can still hear them screaming and laughing.

"So what are you getting?" I ask as we drive. The evening is warm, and we have the windows rolled down.

"An outline of an elephant on my shoulder," Joni says as her short hair blows around in the wind.

"An elephant? Why?"

"Because they're beautiful."

Fair enough. "Your parents don't care?"

"Nah. My dad let me get my first one last year. I'd been telling him I wanted a tattoo for as long as I could remember—since I was six or seven. I've always loved the concept of decorating your body. Anyway, he kept saying, 'Sure, Joni, when you're sixteen, you can get a tattoo.' I think he thought I'd forget about it by then. But I turned sixteen and still wanted one, and my dad never goes back on his word."

Joni's dad's follow-through seems to mean a lot to her. I file that bit of information away for future negotiations with Hope.

"What did you get?" I ask, taking the Laconia exit.

Joni gives me a closed-lipped smile. "Tell me how you got your eyebrow scar and I'll tell you about my tattoo."

I shake my head. "No deal."

"Is it a soccer injury?"

I just look at her, expressionless. "Yup. Soccer injury."

She rolls her eyes. "I'll get it out of you one of these days."

"You can *try*."

We get to the tattoo place, and Joni fills out a bunch of

paperwork, chatting with the girl at the front desk about *Sherlock* like they're best friends. I'm beginning to think Joni is best friends with everyone she meets.

Then we're ushered to the back, and Joni's sitting in the chair. The tattoo artist is snapping on rubber gloves and placing the elephant stencil on her shoulder, saying, "Ready?"

Joni nods and grabs my hand and closes her eyes tight as the needle makes contact with her skin.

She squeezes my hand tighter and tighter the longer the needle presses down. "Jesus fuck, that hurts," she says.

"Are you okay?" I ask, unable to take my eyes away from the elephant slowly forming on her shoulder and the tiny droplets of blood the artist keeps wiping away.

"Yeah, I'm okay. It's a good pain. Addictive."

I shake my head. "There's no such thing as good pain. You're crazy." But I keep her hand tight in mine.

She squeezes so hard that my hand starts to go numb, and it's easy to imagine I'm holding Meg's hand instead, talking her through a contraction, wiping her sweaty hair away from her face as she pushes her way through labor. "I'm here," I tell her. "I know it hurts but it'll be over soon. You're doing great."

She smiles at me and squeezes my fingers as she follows the doctor's order to push again.

Is it possible to have a flashback to a moment that never happened?

The alternate universe only lasts a second, and then I'm back with Joni, and the tattoo guy is wiping off the last of the excess ink and showing her what it looks like in the mirror. Joni claps with glee, then he covers her shoulder in ointment and a bandage, she pays her bill, and we're back in the car.

"Thanks for coming with me," she says.

"No problem. It was fun…in a sadistic kind of way."

"You want to go get some food? I could use a sugar boost after all the bloodletting back there."

"Works for me." Really, she could suggest crashing a wedding or shoplifting a mouse from the pet store or going to buy nipple clamps, and I'd probably agree. Tonight, I'm free.

We get grilled cheeses and milk shakes and a giant tub of waffle fries to share and sit along the lakeshore. It's strange, hanging out with a girl who eats junk food. If I'd ever seen Meg eat a waffle fry, I would have collapsed in shock.

Joni tells me more about her family. Her dad and stepmom got married when she was four, and she has one full sister (Stevie, the girl I saw at her house), two stepbrothers (Elijah's the only one who still lives at home), and two half-siblings— the Super Soaker twins. Her real mother died in a boating accident when Joni was two, so she never knew her.

"What's it like having such a big family?" I ask.

"*Loud.*" She shakes her head. "I love my little brother and sister, but they're *intense*, man. Always running around and screaming and demanding attention. I got the job at Whole Foods 'cause I was sick of being stuck in the house with them all the time. I guess I'm not a kid person."

Not a kid person. Good to know. I make a point of taking a huge sip of milk shake so I don't have to respond.

"What about you?" Joni asks.

I wait a minute for the brain freeze to subside, and then say, "Not really a kid person either."

"No, I mean what about your family? Your life?"

I figure the best way to approach this conversation is to pretend the last year and a half never happened. Anything post-Meg is off limits. Anything pre-Meg is fair game. It's still being honest—just with some restrictions. I tell Joni about my mom and my nonexistent dad and soccer and UCLA.

"Have you ever thought about trying to find your father?" she asks.

Gee, what a timely inquiry.

I don't know if this information lies in pre-Meg green light or post-Meg red. It's a little of both. I decide to be as honest as I can, without fully *going there*.

"Yeah. I've thought about it."

"What would you say to him if you found him?"

What's with all the questions? In all our years of friendship, Dave never once asked me about my dad.

I don't know how to respond. We're getting too close to the danger zone. I shrug. "What would you say to your mother if you could see her again?"

"Well, that's different. My mother didn't *choose* to leave me," Joni says.

I suck in a breath.

"Oh shit, Ryden. I'm sorry. That's not what I meant." She puts a hand on my shoulder.

I stare at the setting sun. "I know, I know, you say things you don't mean. It's a fault. You're working on it."

Joni sighs. "What I meant was what I would say to my mother is different because—"

"Believe me, I know all the different ways someone can leave you," I bite out.

There's silence as the last of the sun disappears over the horizon.

"Can we go back to having fun now?" Joni asks, her voice more unsure than I've ever heard it.

I glance at her. She's looking at me with a hopeful grin, holding out a handful of Pixy Stix. I can't help it. I laugh. Joni's really freaking good at knowing exactly how to make me feel better—even when she was the one to make me feel shitty in the first place. "Another peace offering?"

"You could say that."

I take a blue one. "Where did you get these?"

"From my bag."

"What else you got in there?"

She holds it out to me. "See for yourself. I have no secrets."

"Except for the tattoo," I remind her.

"You know how to make that secret go away, friend." She points to my eyebrow.

I rifle through her bag. I've never looked through a girl's bag before. Meg didn't carry a purse, just a backpack filled with journals. And Shoshanna and the girls I used to be friends with acted as if their bags contained the secrets of the universe.

Joni's got all sorts of shit in hers. The expected stuff: keys, wallet, phone, lip balm. But she's also carrying a bottle of water, a large Ziploc filled with more candy than most kids score on Halloween, a book (*Tempted by Lust: Book 4 of the Bahamas Bikers Series*, which I hold up, eyebrows raised, causing her to just smile and shrug), an extra pair of flip-flops, an old-fashioned compass, and a tiny plastic pinwheel.

I hand the bag back to her and hold my hand out to help her to her feet. "So what's the *Bahamas Bikers* series about?" I ask as we walk back to the car. "I assume you've read the first three already?"

"It's a romance novel series, Ryden. What do you think it's about?"

I laugh and shake my head. So she reads books about hot guys. Major check in the not-gay column.

A little while later, I pull up in front of Joni's house but don't get out of the car this time. "Say hi to your magic room for me," I say.

Joni smiles. "Magic room. I like that." She leans toward me. "I'll see you at work tomorrow?"

She's really close. She smells like fresh air and Pixy Stix and the goopy ointment from her tattoo. She licks her lips, and her mouth is so close to mine I'm surprised her tongue doesn't graze my own lips along the way.

Holy shit. Not gay. *Definitely* not gay. My heartbeat speeds up, but I don't know if it's from anticipation or panic. This was *not supposed to happen.* Joni was supposed to be safe, a friend. "Yeah. Tomorrow."

And then she does it. The thing I knew she was going to do but wouldn't let myself believe. She kisses me. Her lips brush across mine. My body reacts before my brain can catch up. I pull her to me and drink her in. The kiss is frantic and hungry and wild. I'm acting on autopilot, doing exactly what I've done every other time a girl has kissed me.

And then Joni is in my lap. I don't know how she got there. I wasn't paying attention. But she's straddling me, her back pressed up against the steering wheel. She takes my hand out of her hair and guides it down her body. Suddenly, it's like the plug has been pulled on my adrenaline supply, and I'm more awake than I've been all night.

I break away from her, open the car door, and scramble out into the street, leaning forward, my hands on my thighs, supporting my own weight, desperate to catch my breath, desperate to go back in time and erase the last few minutes.

"I can't do this," I manage to get out. "I can't do this to her."

"Who?" Joni whispers, still on her knees in the driver's seat. "The girl in the picture?"

I nod, because with all the guilt and regret and pain and goddamn *anger* inside me, that's all I can do.

"I get it," she says and steps out of the car, righting her clothes and grabbing her bag. "See ya, Ryden."

I manage to collect myself enough to call after her when she's halfway up her front walk. "Joni." She pauses for a minute, then turns. Her face is less expressive than I've ever seen it. Does she really not care? "I'm…" But that's all I've got.

She raises a hand in a weak *don't worry about it* gesture and disappears into her house.

Chapter 10

I'm sorry," I say over and over again to the empty car on the drive home. "I'm sorry, I'm so sorry." I don't know if she's listening, but I hope she is. I really need her to know. "For now, for then, for all of it." I take a deep, agonizing breath and wipe my eyes. "Meg," I say, the name feeling so familiar yet so foreign on my lips. "I'm sorry. I love you."

It hurts so much, but I have to say her name. Because if she is listening, I need her to know I'm talking to her. I need her to know how perfect she was, and how I destroyed everything the moment I almost sat in that wad of gum, and how I will never forgive myself as long as I live.

Chapter 11

The next morning, Joni's waiting for me when I pull my car into the Whole Foods employee lot. Great.

"I wanted to say," she says as I get out of the car and clip my name tag to my shirt, "that I like you."

I groan. "I know, Joni, but—"

"No, wait. I mean, I like you as a person, above anything else. I like you the way I like *Last Week Tonight with John Oliver* and anything made from colored sugar and watching the roller bladers in Washington Square Park. And okay, yes, I thought I liked you the way the Bahamas Bikers 'like' their biker babes, and maybe you liked me that way too. But you're still not over the girl in the picture. And that's fine. Really. But I don't want to not be your friend, okay?" She holds out a Tupperware.

"What's this?" I ask, taking it.

"Chocolate pudding. One of Dad's specialties."

I sigh. I don't know if I can be friends with Joni after what happened last night. But I don't have the energy to actively avoid her either. "Thanks," I say.

"So we're good?" she asks, hopeful.

"You mean it? *Just* friends? Nothing else? You're okay with that?"

She nods.

"Then we're good."

"Woohoo!" She does a cartwheel, right there in the parking lot.

• • •

During my break, I eat chocolate pudding and open to the next entry in Meg's journal. I didn't read any yesterday because I was pretty sure I couldn't handle it after everything.

January 19.

I have a feeling Hope will be born soon. I know I'm not due for a couple more months, but I don't think she's going to wait that long. Theoretically, the longer she stays inside me, the healthier she'll be. But does that count for a pregnancy like this one too? Where the baby is trapped inside a rotting body? What if I'm poisoning her? I know I'm going to die, but what if I die before she can get out safely? What if she dies too and all of this will have been for nothing?

My heart is in my throat.

Meg knew she was going to die? She never once told me that. The only thing she ever said was that she hoped *Hope* would be okay—when it came to herself, her confidence never wavered.

Everything is going to be fine. That was her go-to line. She was *so sure*.

But now it seems she wasn't. She wasn't sure at all. And I never would have known that if Mabel hadn't given me this journal.

What changed for Meg between that day in August when she sat us all down and said she was keeping the baby and January 19, the day she wrote this entry? *When* did it change?

And what the hell else was she lying to me about?

Chapter 12

Fuck the read-the-journal-slowly plan. I need to find out what else is in here. I sit on my bedroom floor and read as quickly as I can while still paying attention to what the words actually say. Jesus. There's a *lot* more about how Meg hadn't been feeling well and how she didn't think she had much time left. She even went to her doctor by herself one day without her parents or me or anyone knowing to get checked out. She took a fucking *cab*—a weak, sick, pregnant, seventeen-year-old girl taking a *cab* to a secret doctor's appointment so she could find out how long she had to live. Goddammit, Meg. Why didn't you tell me?

The doctor told her there was no real way to know for sure, but it looked to him like she didn't have much time left. Weeks. The cancer was everywhere. Her organs were going to fail. He wanted to do an emergency C-section, get the baby out of her, give her body a final chance to bounce back. A Hail Mary pass, he called it.

She said no. It was too soon for the baby to be born. She'd accepted her fate; she just needed to hold out as long as she could—for the baby.

I throw the book against the wall and pace the room.

Why the hell would she do this? Why wouldn't she give herself every possible chance?

It wasn't a pro-life thing—Meg was always going on about women's rights and equal pay and gender inequalities and "the old, white jackasses in Washington who think having a penis gives them the right to govern vaginas." She was pro-choice. And she certainly made her choice, didn't she?

I pick the book off the floor and flip to the next entry, searching through her scribble for some kind of meaning, some hint, some answer.

By the time I reach the end of the journal, one word has jumped out at me more than any of the thousands of others, the very last word on the very last line: legacy.

Hope's been kicking a lot lately. It hurts when it happens, like I'm being beaten up from the inside out. But it's okay. Actually, it's the only thing that's okay lately. I can't look at my parents or Mabel, because all I see is anguish. They know I'm dying. They know it and they hate me for it. And Ryden…Ryden's still in denial. It's even harder to be around him. With him, I have to pretend. He still has hope, and I'm not going to take that away from him. It hurts to smile, but I will not stop. I will not take away his hope. I love him too much. And it makes me want to cry.

But then Hope kicks and I feel better, because she's okay, she's healthy. My little legacy.

That's it. There's nothing else in the book. Except the checklist.

Legacy.

Is that why Meg insisted on keeping the baby? Because she wanted something to *leave behind*? She could have written a book or donated her college fund to a charity or planted a god-damn tree. No, she had to do the one thing that guaranteed she would even *need* to leave something behind in the first place, the one thing that would ensure her thirty percent chance of survival plummeted down to a big fat zero.

I sink to my floor, the journal clutched in my hands.

Somewhere deep in my brain, sirens are going off, warning signals. Of what, I have no clue. But I go back to the beginning and start to reread.

When I get to the conversation about naming Hope, the one that sat funny in my gut the first and second and third time around, it's like the words and letters unscramble them-selves before my eyes, forming a clear message.

I know you, Meg. I know you have a reason for everything.

But this baby will have a mom and *a dad.*

Both of those sentences came from me. Absolute, undeni-able, written-down proof that I'm an idiot. I *knew* Meg didn't do anything without a well-thought-out reason. Of course she'd thought of all the possible outcomes and likelihoods. She knew *from the moment she found out she was pregnant* she was probably going to die but still decided having the baby was more important.

She was so insistent Hope have my last name because she

knew all along that Hope *wouldn't* have both a mom and dad. All that "everything is going to be fine" talk was total bullshit. She was lying to me the entire time.

I read through the rest of the journal, this newfound knowledge coloring every word.

☑ Mabel
☐ Alan
☐ Ryden

This checklist *means* something, dammit. I'm even more sure of that now that I know Meg was keeping secrets from me. Lying to me. And I need to find out what.

• • •

I pull up to Alan's. I texted him on my way over, and clearly he didn't have any hot Saturday night plans because he's waiting for me outside. "Hey," I say, getting out of the car.

"What's up?" he asks.

I pull Hope's car seat out of the car, hand it to Alan, and keep moving straight toward his front door.

"Dude, what's going on?" he asks, keeping up with my pace.

"I need to look through your room. Is that cool?" I stop on the stoop and turn to face him.

He stares at me, looking completely freaked. But he holds the door open. "Be my guest."

I know he said there were no journals here, but I need to see for myself. I go straight to his room—I'd been here a couple of times before with Meg, back when she was still strong and barely pregnant. It looks exactly like you'd expect: twin bed covered in a neat blue comforter, books stacked, clothes put away, and hip-hop and Korean movie posters covering almost every inch of wall. There's also a poster of Grace Park in a bikini that is hot as fuck.

I check his bookshelves first. Nothing. Nightstand, dresser… clear. All there is under the bed is a big drawer filled with winter clothes. I rummage through them, but nothing is hidden in the piles. There are a few notebooks lined up spine out on the shelf over his desk, but they're all three-subject books and filled with Alan's class notes. Not a journal in sight.

Alan stands in the doorway, Hope in his arms. She's out of her car seat, awake, blowing little spit bubbles between her lips. She's as happy in his arms as she is in my mom's. The kid loves literally everyone except me.

"I need to check the rest of your house."

Alan wordlessly steps out of the way.

I don't know what I'm doing. I've never been in most parts of his house before. But I can't stop. I'm desperate. I go room to room, looking through bookshelves and under beds and in dresser drawers and in closets. Some part of me knows there's no way Meg would have hidden one of her journals in Alan's dad's underwear drawer, but another part of me says to look *everywhere*.

When I get to the kitchen, I run into Alan's mother. I haven't actually gotten farther than the driveway all the times I stopped by to drop off or pick up Hope this week, so I haven't seen her in a while. "Mrs. Kang," I say, stopping short.

She looks more surprised to see me than I am to see her. Which makes sense. She lives here. It's not that far off that she'd be in her own kitchen. But I'm probably the last person she expected to burst through her kitchen door, red-faced and ransacking her house for my own personal version of the Holy Grail.

"Hello, Ryden! How lovely to see you. Did Alan tell you how much we love having little Hopie spend time with us? She's such a doll."

Hopie? "Yes," I say, trying to calm down. "Thank you so much for taking her in. I really appreciate it."

"Of course! Any time." Her face suddenly loses its glow. "We all miss Meg so very much. It's been quite a comfort to have little Hope around. Don't you agree, Alan?"

I turn to find Alan and Hope standing behind me. "Yeah. I do."

"Mrs. Kang, sorry if this is a weird question, but have you seen any of Meg's journals lying around your house anywhere?"

Her eyebrows crinkle a little. "You mean those notebooks she was always writing in?"

"Yeah."

She thinks for a minute. "No, I haven't seen any. Not in quite a while."

I nod. "Okay. Well, thanks anyway."

Alan walks me back to my car.

"Yeah, so…sorry about all that," I say.

"You going to explain now?"

I take Hope from him, and she immediately starts to whine. "I just thought…I don't know what I thought." I snap Hope's car seat into the base and buckle her in. "I read some stuff in Meg's journal…" I trail off. Suddenly I'm really tired. I close Hope's door and let all my weight collapse against the side of the car.

I feel Alan's eyes on me. "No offense, man, but you're kind of a mess."

I don't say anything. Disagreement takes energy.

"Maybe it's time to let this whole thing go, Ryden. I mean, really, even if she did leave two other journals somewhere—"

"She did." I lift my head sharply and look at him. "I thought you agreed it was something she would do."

"I said it was something she *would* do, not that she actually succeeded in doing it. But even if she did, and even if you do find them, what do you expect to happen? She's still going to be gone, man. You're driving yourself crazy. It's not worth it."

I push off from the side of the car and plant myself in the driver's seat, looking back at Hope through the rearview mirror. "That's where you're wrong."

Chapter 13

Today is Sunday. I don't have to work. Hallelujah, amen. And there's no soccer today either. But that means I'm on Hope duty. I have no excuse.

I got basically no sleep last night, yet again. Between all the crying and feeding and diaper changing, my thoughts were preoccupied with what Alan said. Are the journals really out there? Does the checklist mean anything, or am I so desperate that I'm fabricating some big conspiracy in my head?

No. Even if it turns out the checklist was nothing more than Meg's own little journal-organizing system, even if it doesn't have some *giant, major, world-altering purpose*, it only makes sense that if Meg checked the first box on the checklist and put the red journal in Mabel's room, there are two others for me and Alan. And what harm could it do to keep searching for them?

I call Mabel again.

She answers after four rings. "What's wrong? Are you okay?"

"Yeah, why?"

"It's 7:16 a.m. on a Sunday."

I look at the clock. So it is. "Oh. Sorry. I don't really sleep anymore."

"It's okay." Her voice is softer now. Fuck. I don't want her pity.

I clear my throat and get straight to the point. "So listen, is there any way you can get access to the storage unit where her stuff is?"

There's a pause. "I don't know. I don't know which storage place it's at or the unit number."

"Can't you ask your parents?"

"I don't think you get it. They won't talk about her. Apart from a few photos of me and Meg on the mantel in the living room and the box of ashes on the windowsill—and the massive amounts of wine my dad goes through every night so he's never sober enough in the presence of my mother to actually have a real conversation—it's like she was just passing through, a visitor who moved on at the first sign of something better." Mabel pauses again. "They've never been the lovey, fuzzy kind of parents; we all know that. But now they're… It's like they've decided feeling nothing is better than feeling sad." She sounds bitter and exhausted.

Meg wouldn't want her ashes in a box on a windowsill in that stark, cold house. She would want them scattered at the lake, at our spot.

I wish we could stay here forever, I said once when we were at the lake.

Me too, she whispered back. *It's perfect here.*

I wish I could do that for her. But convincing her parents to let me do that would first require them to acknowledge that Hope and I actually exist. Not gonna happen.

Though the massive amounts of booze actually sounds like a pretty good avoidance tactic—I may have to try that.

"Mabel," I say. "Listen. This book you gave me, it has a list written in the back. Your name, then Alan's, then mine. There's a check in the box next to your name, but not the others. Do you remember seeing it?"

"Yeah, I guess so."

"Do you have any idea what it could mean?"

"Maybe she wanted to leave us each a journal." I can hear the shrug in her voice.

"Yeah, but *why*? Why would she have chosen three journals from the hundreds she had? And why wouldn't she have just given them to us directly?"

"I don't know. Maybe they were more important to her than the others somehow. Hmmm. Was there anything in that book that was different or unusual? I'm trying to remember."

I decide to tell her what I figured out. "I think Meg knew she was going to die."

"Well, yeah, there's that part toward the end of the journal where she says that."

"No, I mean I think she knew a lot earlier than that. Maybe even before she got pregnant. I think that's why she decided to keep the baby."

"I don't understand." Mabel sounds leery now.

I explain the "legacy" thing.

Mabel's silent.

"You there?" I ask.

"Yeah. Just…thinking. She was always so certain that she was going to be okay."

"Turns out maybe she wasn't." And I never picked up on it. Add that to the list of ways I've failed her.

"She kept the baby because she thought she was going to die anyway?" Mabel whispers. "She martyred herself."

"Yeah."

More silence.

"I think," I say, "she wanted us to know that, for some reason. Or at least she wanted you to know that. That's why she left the book in your room."

Mabel gives a small little laugh. "That's my sister. Always planning ahead. She used to write these pro/con lists all the time. Did you ever see her do that? They were about things as stupid as whether she should have Mom buy long grain or short grain brown rice. They would be all over the house. Whenever the cleaning lady came she would collect them and leave them in a little pile on the kitchen table."

I smile. "So now you see why I need to find those other two journals?"

"Let me try to figure out how to get into the storage unit," Mabel says. "I'll call you back."

• • •

Two hours later, Mabel still hasn't called. That's not that long, right? It's fine. It's totally fine.

I toss the phone onto the floor in frustration. It lands in a pile of dirty clothes.

Stop freaking out, man. You'll get your answers when you get them. It's not like Meg's going to magically be brought back to life if you find the other two journals within a certain time frame or anything.

True, but there could be information in those journals that will help me with Hope. Bottom line, if there's a journal out there with a check mark next to *my* name, I want it.

Must distract myself.

I change Hope's diaper, cover her in baby sunscreen, dress her in her onesie with the ladybug pattern, strap her into a carrier on my chest, and grab her diaper bag. She's not crying, exactly, but she's whimpering and fidgeting, like a cat who doesn't want to stay still long enough for the vet to listen to its heart or check its ears or whatever.

Mom's outside, pulling weeds out from between the cracks in the driveway. She's got her earbuds in and is dancing around to the beat of some unheard song. It's probably Alanis Morissette. She *loves* Alanis Morissette. All angry female rockers actually.

I watch her for a second undetected. She looks so happy, like our lives aren't completely fucked. A lot of my mom's friends don't have kids yet. Some of them are married, some aren't, and the ones who have kids, they're little, like a baby or a four-year-old. But most are blissfully child-free. They come over sometimes for "movie night." The living room gets overrun by six or seven thirtysomething women, most of them still pretty hot, drinking frozen margaritas and talking and laughing and not really paying any attention to whatever movie is on the screen. A few times, I've overheard their conversations. They're usually talking about sex or the gorgeous new barista at the Starbucks on Fourth Street or how the men on the online dating sites are hopelessly disappointing. Not mom stuff at all.

And it always hits me, in those moments, how my mother's life would be different if not for me.

The guys she's dated, the ones I've met anyway, are all losers. They seem fine at first, not particularly spectacular but nice enough. Then they find out she has a teenage son and come to the conclusion that they're "not ready for that kind of thing." Now that she's a grandmother too? Forget it.

I've never seen my mother in love. I've seen her hoping desperately for the possibility of love. I've seen her with a tear in her eye and a dreamy smile on her face when she reaches the end of one of her vampire romance books. I've seen her come home the morning after staying at a guy's house, all moon-eyed and floating on air, telling me, "This could be the one, Ry. I *feel* it." I've seen her introduce me to a guy and watch him and me intensely, trying to gauge our reactions to each other, hoping for a "click." But I've never seen her completely, truly in love.

I don't think she's been in love since Michael.

I look down at Hope. She's watching Mom dancing around too, and she's sort of smiling. I wonder if she's old enough to find things funny.

Mom looks up then and sees us standing there. "Hey,

buddy," she says, dumping a handful of weeds in a pile on the side of the driveway and wiping her hands on her jeans. She takes out her earbuds. "Where you off to?"

Anywhere that will distract me from obsessing over Meg's journals. "Dunno. Just need to get out of the house."

She nods. "Well, can we talk tonight? I'll make eggplant parm."

That's my favorite. She only makes it on special occasions or when she's trying to butter me up. I know what this "talk" is going to be about—the same thing she's been trying to get me to talk about seriously for the whole summer. The Great Day Care Dilemma.

"All right," I say. "When do you need me home?"

"Seven-ish?"

"'Kay."

"Have fun!"

I walk past my car, which Mom moved from the driveway to the street to free up space for her weeding, and head out on foot. It's really nice out—not too hot, sunny, quiet, with a little breeze. I kick a rock ahead of me, meet up with it, and kick it again. The continuous impact of the rock against my sneaker is oddly soothing.

Hope's arms and legs dangle from the openings in her carrier, and her head falls against me as she starts to nod off, her little head snuggling into my chest. She's like a miniature space heater, warming up my middle. Tentatively, I lift a hand and brush it lightly across her head, being careful to not press too hard on the soft spot. But then she pulls away and starts whimpering again, her face all scrunched up and cranky.

Fine. Whatever.

As I get to the end of the street and need to make a decision—right toward the lake or left toward downtown—my phone buzzes. It's a text from Joni: What r u doing?

Oh, just walking down the street with my daughter, whom you know nothing about.

Nothin much, I text back. Chillin. You?

Same. Want to do something?

It's been a long time since anyone's texted me to hang out.

I turn toward the lake and look down at Hope. Even if I could concentrate on anything besides whether Mabel's making progress on the storage unit, and even if I didn't have a date with doom scheduled with Mom tonight, I still wouldn't be able to hang out with Joni today. Because I have a kid. How fucking crazy is that? I say the words out loud. Maybe they'll make more sense that way. "I am a parent. I'm a father."

The whole thing makes me want to dive in the lake and never come up for air.

I really need to find those journals. Or Michael. Or both.

Not really having the best day, I type. Not a lie. Need to be alone, I think.

☹   Need me to bring you some candy?

LOL. Noooo. I'm gonna get fat, hanging out with you.

Ummm have you seen you? I think it's genetically impossible for you to get fat.

I pause, my thumbs hovering over the keyboard. This is all getting a little too close to flirting. Need to rein it in. Gotta go. See you at work tomorrow. I type a smiley face but delete it before I hit send.

A few moments later, my feet hit grass and I'm walking directly toward the water. This isn't my favorite part of the lake—it's grassy and there are trees everywhere, not beachy at all—but it's close to home and better than nothing. It's pretty hot out today, probably one of the last summery days of the year. Before long, it will be winter again, and Hope will be too big to carry in the sling, and it'll be like when she was first born and I had to push her around in a stroller through a foot of snow. Uphill both ways.

I sit on the grass, take my shirt off, and lay it on the ground for Hope to lie on. She's sturdier now than she used to be but still all floppy, so I have to be careful whenever I put her down to make sure her head doesn't snap back or anything. I'm not sure what would happen if it did, but it seems like we're better off not finding out. She fusses, making little *ehhhh* baby noises and moving her arms and legs around a lot, but not full on crying. I give her a teething ring to gnaw on. When she's settled, I lean back on my elbows, staring at the water. The surface ripples with the breeze.

I don't know how long I stay like that, staring off into space, but the sun is warm and my mind is blank and my eyes are unfocused, and it feels really good to *not think*. When my phone buzzes again, I snap to attention. The sun is hitting the lake at a different angle now. I have a feeling I was zoned out for a while. Good.

It's another text from Joni—but this one has an audio file attached to it. Thought you might need this. I hit play.

At first I can't identify the sound coming from my phone. It's not a song, I can tell that much. It's not someone talking either. I push the volume as high as it will go, and it finally hits me. It's Joni's room. The street sounds, the fountain. It's the soundtrack of Washington Square Park. I can't help it—I smile. A real smile, the kind only Joni is able to get out of me lately. I place the phone between me and Hope, and I watch, amazed, as it lulls her to sleep. Holy shit. It's like riding in the car but better.

Thank you, I write back. Joni has no idea what a gift she just gave me. One day, I'll tell her.

About twenty feet away, a couple of girls set up a blanket on the grass. A blond and a redhead, both wearing dark sunglasses. They're around my age, but I've never seen them before. Maybe they're in college. They strip out of their shorts and tank tops and stand there in nothing but tiny bikinis, spreading sunscreen on their arms and legs and stomachs and—Jesus—their tits.

I can't look away. My mouth goes dry. They're so incredibly hot.

Then one of them moves her hair aside, and the other girl lotions up her back. I swallow.

I really need to have sex. Not a relationship. *Not* love. Just sex. When was the last time I even…uh…relieved myself? I can't remember. How fucking sad is that.

But really. If I'm not at work, I'm at soccer, and if I'm not at soccer, I'm either in the presence of a crying baby or so exhausted I can barely keep my eyes open. What am I supposed to do, say, "Oh hey, Mom, can you take Hope for ten minutes so I can go jerk off in peace?"

The blond catches me staring, and I look away quickly as she says something to her friend. *Don't stare, you idiot. You used to be smoother than this.* I keep my eyes focused solely on the water ahead of me for as long as I can stand it, and when I finally look back, the girls are coming my way.

Shit.

I sit up straighter, praying to God the crease in my jeans hides my boner.

"Hey," the blond says.

The redhead just smiles.

"Hey," I say.

"We were wondering if you wanted to—omigod, is that a baby?!" Their eyes go all gooey, and they've got these sappy grins on their faces.

Kill me now.

"Yeah. That's Hope. She's my—uh, niece. I'm Ryden."

"I'm Jaime," the blond says. "This is Emory."

Emory gives a little wave and her boobs jiggle.

"So, Ryden," Jaime says, pulling her hair over one shoulder and swaying coyly back and forth. "You want to come hang out with us? We've got plenty of room on our blanket. And we have wine coolers."

Tempting, but no. For about a hundred thousand reasons.

"No, thanks. I'm cool."

Jaime and Emory pout, their expressions so identical I have a sudden hilarious vision of them practicing the look in the mirror together. "Okay, well, we'll be right over there if you change your mind."

I nod.

They turn to go, but Jaime turns back. "By the way, what are you listening to? It's weird."

Hey, don't dis my miracle baby sleep inducer. "It's Washington Square Park," I say and leave it at that. She shrugs and walks away.

A year and a half ago, that whole scenario would have gone *very* differently.

I lie back on the grass, keeping one hand on Hope's belly to make sure she stays where she is, and close my eyes. She grabs my finger in her sleep. It's not very long before the New York sounds pumping from my phone combined with the rise and fall of my hand from Hope's baby breathing and the gentle pressure on my finger from her grip send me off into sleep.

Chapter 14

I'm jolted awake to the sound of crying. I sit up slowly and push my hair back from my eyes. It's almost dark. My face feels weird—I run my hand over it to find there are hundreds of little imprints on my cheek from the grass. The park sounds have stopped. Shit, my phone is dead. Jaime and Emory are gone. Probably long gone. The air is a lot chillier now. And Hope is wailing away.

I lean forward and sniff her butt—yup, she crapped her diaper. Fantastic.

I slap my face a couple of times to wake myself up and go about the disgusting yet depressingly mundane task of changing her.

There's a garbage can about ten yards away, and I move to throw away the reeking diaper but stop. I can't just leave her here on the grass. I've seen *America's Most Wanted*. Babies get snatched like that all the time. A parent turns his head for one second, then *poof*.

Yet another example of how nothing, even something as minute as throwing away a diaper, will ever be easy again. I put the diaper down, pick up the crying baby, and begin the ridiculously complicated process of putting my shirt on while holding her. It involves a lot of shrugging and shifting her from arm to arm, while her arms, legs, and head bobble every which way and she screams in my ears. Then I pack all the diaper stuff back in the bag, secure the baby harness to my chest, and slide Hope inside. She's probably hungry. Actually, so am I. And then I remember—eggplant parm. *Shit, what time is it?*

"We'll get you a bottle soon, baby," I say, picking up the diaper and finally trudging over to the trash can.

Fifteen minutes later, I walk through my front door. The clock on the wall at the top of the stairs says 7:46.

"Mom?"

"In here."

She's in the kitchen, sitting at the set table. She sticks her bookmark in her book. There's a basket of garlic bread in the center of the table and two open beer bottles—a near-empty one at her place setting and a full one at mine, dripping with condensation. I raise an eyebrow. This is new.

Mom follows my gaze. "I thought we could have a beer together, since, you know, you're a dad now, a grown-up for all intents and purposes. But clearly I was wrong."

Oh, now I see it. She's pissed.

"I'm so sorry, Mom. My phone died. And I fell asleep." I pull my phone out of my pocket and slide it across the table as evidence.

She rakes her hands through her hair. Huh. I must get that from her. Never noticed that before. "Where were you?"

"At the lake."

She studies me. I'm just standing there, at the table, like I'm waiting for her invitation to sit down. Like this isn't my house too.

Finally Mom's face changes, and the annoyance and accusation fade away. "Give me that baby," she says, holding out her arms.

I pass Hope over, and Mom shushes and coos at her. "She's hungry," I say. I drop the bag and baby harness in the middle of the floor, heat a bottle for Hope, and pull the eggplant parm out of the oven. It smells amazing. I serve it up, and we all eat. I drink my beer, because warm beer is better than no beer. That was crazy cool of Mom. I look at her, somehow managing to eat her food while also feeding the baby in her arms, and something hits me—something so obvious and *duh* but something I never really thought about before, at least on a conscious level.

"You're a really good mom, Mom," I say.

She looks up, surprised. "Thanks, Ry. I've had practice, you know." She nods to Hope, who's happily chowing down on her formula.

"I know. But it's not only the baby stuff. You've always been a good mom to me, no matter how old I am."

She smiles, and the little lines next to her eyes that none of her friends have yet get all crinkly.

I take another swig. I guess I'm in the mood for talking, because I say, "Meg's parents weren't good parents."

Mom just nods, like she already knew that.

I scrape my plate clean with the side of my fork and lick off the last bits of sauce and cheese. "I'm gonna get more. You want?"

"No, I'm good," Mom says. "Thanks."

When I sit back down, I down the last of my piss-warm beer and say the inevitable. "So, you wanted to talk." Might as well get it over with, so I can call Mabel and see what's going on.

Mom sets Hope's empty bottle on the table and looks at me. "School starts a week from tomorrow, Ryden."

"I know."

"What are we going to do with this little munchkin?"

I stare at my plate. "Alan can take her after school while I'm at soccer, and then I can pick her up and drop her off here before going to work."

Mom shakes her head like she can't believe how thick I'm being. "First of all, it's not fair to rely on Alan like this. You're not paying him, and it's his senior year too, you know. Hope isn't his kid."

I wish she were.

Whoa, where did that thought come from? I mean, if I had it all to do again, obviously I would have put on a fucking condom, pill or no pill. But that's not what the thought was. The thought was I wished Alan were Hope's dad. That would mean everything would be the same—Meg would be gone, Hope would be here. Only, Meg and Alan would have…

No. I do not wish that at all. He's just so much better at taking care of Hope than I am…

"Ryden?" Mom says.

Huh? "What? Sorry, I was spacing out."

"I can see that. Please, we need to focus. This is serious, bud."

"Sorry."

"I think you should really rethink the Alan thing. But the more pressing issue is what we're going to do with Hope during the hours when you—and Alan—are at school."

"I wish Downey High School had a day care center like UCLA does," I say on a sigh.

"Yeah, well, I don't think there's much of a demand for that."

True.

Mom gets up and helps herself to another beer. She doesn't offer me one this time.

"I've tried everything I could think of, Mom. I called Grandma and Grandpa, I went to Meg's parents'…I don't know what else to do."

Mom nods. "Your check from Grandma and Grandpa came yesterday," she says. "I put it on the hall table for you. Did you see it?"

"No." I've been d-i-s-t-r-a-c-t-e-d.

Mom's looking at me, and every time I glance up from my empty plate, I catch sight of her tired eyes and hate myself just a little bit more for putting her through all of this.

Finally she says, "I asked around, did some digging. We have a couple of options."

"You did? We do?"

"Option one: There's a government-subsidized child care

facility downtown that offers a sliding fee scale. I called them, and they would charge us $275 a week."

I'm about to say that sounds amazing—I make about that at Whole Foods. I'm sure Mom will help with other expenses while we figure it out. Maybe I can ask for a raise at work too. But she keeps talking.

"The environment there isn't great though, Ryden. There are a *lot* of children and not enough staff. Hope probably wouldn't get very much, if any, personal attention. And the facilities definitely leave something to be desired. And who knows what kind of germs are being spread around."

"Well, what's option two?"

"My friend Selena offered to share her nanny with us, which was *very* generous. The nanny is wonderful. It would be such a nice place for Hope to go to every day. But they live in Addison, so you'd have to drive more than a half hour each way before and after school."

Which means I wouldn't make it to soccer on time. A half hour there after school, another half hour back to Alan's, then back to school. I'd be almost an hour and a half late to practice every day. Yeah, Coach would stand for that for, oh, about four seconds. And then I'd be gone. Off the team. Sayonara, UCLA.

"And we'd have to contribute to the cost," Mom continues, "because the nanny's rates would go up since she'd be taking care of another child. Selena said two hundred a week should be fine."

So my choice is between handing over my entire paycheck

so Hope can go to an overcrowded, budget day care where she would get ignored and probably catch some nasty ass infectious disease, or quitting soccer and spending a *lot* more time in the car for $75 less a week and for Hope to get a much higher quality of care.

I bang my head on the table. "My brain hurts."

Mom takes a deep breath, clearly about to say something, but the doorbell rings. I look at her. "I'll get it?"

"Yeah, go ahead." She hands Hope back and gets up to start clearing the table.

I open the door. It's Mabel.

My heart suddenly feels like it's on a bike flying down a hill in tenth gear.

She smiles when she sees Hope. "I tried calling you. It kept going to voice mail."

"Phone's dead."

"Oh."

"Did you find something?"

"Can I come in?"

I shake my head and step out onto the stoop, closing the door behind me. I don't want Mom to know about the Great Journal Caper. She'll just give me some line about focusing my attention on all the wrong things. Mabel and I sit on the steps, and I hand her Hope without asking. She takes her happily.

"So?" I ask. "What you got?"

She doesn't answer. She's too preoccupied with the baby in her lap, awake this time.

We sit there, Mabel talking baby talk right up in Hope's face and tapping Hope's little baby nose and putting her pinkie in Hope's fist and laughing when she grasps on.

Get to the point, Mabel.

Finally she looks at me, surprised, like she actually forgot I was sitting here. She reaches into the pocket of her shorts and pulls out a key with a yellow Stor-Fast tag attached to it. The tag reads *#1017*.

"You found it," I whisper, staring at the key like it's that blue diamond from the *Titanic* movie. Meg loved that movie. I never really understood why both of them couldn't fit on the door at the end. There was plenty of room. All they would have needed to do was take off the life vest Kate Winslet was wearing and strap it to the bottom of the door to reinforce the door's buoyancy. Surely they could have found something to use—there was plenty of stuff floating around in the water. Then they wait for an hour, get rescued, and live happily ever after.

I tried to explain that to Meg, and she said that while she admired my mad physics smarts and critical thinking, that wasn't the point. The point was that it was *beautiful* and *romantic* that Leonardo DiCaprio would sacrifice himself for Kate Winslet rather than worry about his own fate. She said it was an "epic love story."

I should have known right then and there that she would also try to go down in a blaze of unnecessary, misguided glory.

"It was in the glove compartment of my mom's car," Mabel says. "Took me forever to find."

"Let's go," I say, standing up. But then I remember Mom. If I bail now, without finishing our conversation, she'll lose whatever scrap of faith in me she has left. "Wait." I sit. "Shit, I can't. Tomorrow? Can you do early? I have practice at nine."

"Yeah, whenever. But it might take a long time to go through all the boxes. There's a lot of stuff in there."

I nod, thinking. "Well, we'll start tomorrow morning and see how far we get. I'll pick you up at seven."

• • •

I take the night to think about the day care options, to show my mom I'm taking this seriously, but come on, there's no question of which one I'm going with. If I go with the nanny, I give up soccer, my scholarship, college, my chances at playing professionally. Which will affect Hope's future too. If I go pro, I'll have all kinds of money to send her to the best schools and all that. But if I don't, I won't. And it's not like the day care downtown is run by knife-wielding Nazis with open wounds on their faces. I'm sure the people there know what they're doing. It will be fine. And anyway, it's only for a year.

Mom's still asleep when I leave early the next morning to go pick up Mabel, so I write her a note.

Had to take care of a few things before practice. See you tonight. Love you. PS—let's go with the day care downtown. Let me know what I need to do.

Chapter 15

M orning," Mabel says as she gets in the car. The curtains at her living room window move a little, then are pulled tightly closed.

"Do your parents know about any of this?" I ask, backing out of the driveway.

"No way."

"But they know you're going somewhere with me."

"They do now."

I give her a side-eyed *you're making no sense* expression, but I'm brought up short when I get a good look at her. She looks different than usual—no makeup, hair pulled up in a floppy loop on the top of her head, hoodie, sneakers. She looks more like Meg than she ever has.

"What's wrong with you?" she asks.

Oh. I was staring. And I guess I took my foot off the gas pedal, because the car is creeping to a stop. I pull my eyes back to the road and shake my head. "There's not enough time in the world to even begin answering that question."

Mabel doesn't say anything.

"Anyway," I say, clearing my throat, "your parents. What

do they think you and I are doing together at seven a.m. on a Monday?"

Mabel shrugs. "I don't know and I don't care."

I squint at the road. "Explain, please."

She sighs. "They've barely blinked at me this entire summer. I could've dyed my hair neon green and I honestly don't think they would have noticed. But then Mom saw your car in the driveway and suddenly started demanding answers. I told her it was too little too late. She doesn't get to know things."

"They probably think I'm gonna get you pregnant too."

Mabel actually laughs really hard at that. "Ryden Brooks's master plan to inseminate all the Reynolds women. Look out, Mom, you're next!"

I laugh a little too. But really, it's not that funny.

We get to the storage center, and I pull up in front of number 1017. We stare at the garage door, neither of us moving.

"Okay, well," Mabel says, unbuckling her seat belt and getting out. "Let's get started."

The storage unit is completely full. I start to feel sick. Meg's bed frame. Her dresser. Her bookshelves. All of it was part of her, part of her life. And now it's junk, thrown haphazardly into a cold metal garage off the highway, left to be forgotten.

There are boxes everywhere—and they're all unlabeled.

I put Hope's car seat on Meg's desk and pull my keys out of my pocket. "Where should we start?" I ask, but Mabel's not really paying attention to me. She's standing near the door, absentmindedly flicking the knobs on Meg's floor lamp back and forth, staring at the room full of stuff. Her eyes look like filled-up fishbowls, and when she blinks, the tears pour down her face.

Don't do it, I tell myself. *Do not cry.*

In one swift move, not giving myself time to think, I pull the nearest box over to me and slice the tape on the top open with my key.

Clothes. T-shirts, actually. The ones she used to wear before her belly swelled to the size of a soccer ball. I push the shirts back into the box and move on to the next. More clothes. Same for the next three boxes.

What the...

Is that *mine*?

I move the pile of Meg's sweats aside—the big, baggy ones she wore in the later stages of her pregnancy—and pull out the thick navy-blue thing. It's my varsity soccer pullover hoodie, complete with the Downey soccer logo, *Brooks*, and my number: 1. I didn't even realize it was missing.

"Hey, Mabel?"

Her face is dry now, and she's sitting on the concrete floor a little ways away, quietly going through a box of books. "Hmm?"

"Did Meg wear this?" I hold up the sweatshirt.

She smiles. "All the time. She slept in it most nights."

"How long did she have it?"

"I don't know. A few months, I guess." She looks confused. "Why, didn't you give it to her?"

I shake my head. "She must have swiped it from my room.

Or maybe I left it at your house and didn't realize it." For some reason, she didn't want me to know she had this sweatshirt, just like I didn't want her to know I had her notebook. Maybe it was the same story. She loved it, it made her feel close to me, and she didn't want it taken away. The thought makes me smile. I'm not crazy—about this, at least. She really did love me too.

I slip the sweatshirt over my head, even though it's getting kinda warm in the storage unit. It still smells like her.

Tears prick the backs of my eyes, but I sniffle and press the sweatshirt-covered heels of my hands into my eyes to push them back. When I open my eyes again and the blurry spots fade, I notice Mabel watching me. She doesn't say anything though.

Hope wakes up then and starts to whine. I put on Joni's Washington Square Park audio file and tuck my phone into the car seat with her. She quiets down immediately.

"What's that?" Mabel asks.

I shrug. "Just some New York sounds. She likes it."

Mabel grins. "So cute."

We go through a couple more boxes until we find some containing journals. That's when the work really slows down, since we have to go through each book, scouring for any sign of a checklist. Mabel says we should just look at the inside back covers, but that's lazy. We don't know Meg put the checklist in the same spot in each book. I don't want to risk having the right journals in our hands and disregarding them.

An hour later, we still haven't found the ones we're looking for.

But honestly, we haven't gotten very far. We're still on the first box. Because we keep stopping to read.

June 1.

This must be the journal that immediately follows the green one, the one from the beginning of our relationship that I've had all along.

Mabel might be happier than I am that Ryden and I are officially going out.

Okay, that's probably not true. But she is super excited about it. She knows how much I like him. She's also beyond thrilled that she knows someone in high school besides me and Alan. Someone "cool," as she puts it. Because she's going to be a freshman in the fall and having a connection to one of the most popular guys in school "will totally up her cred."

I don't know, I think Alan and I are pretty cool.

The only thing Mabel's not happy about is the fact that I haven't told him about the cancer yet. She keeps saying I'm lying to him and it's not right. But I'm not lying. I'm just not giving him the whole truth. There's a difference.

I know I'm going to have to tell him eventually. Once he knows, it's going to change everything, and things are so good right now. Is it really that bad if I'm selfish for a little while longer?

June 12.

I told Alan the miserable truth today: I go back in for round 2 two weeks from Monday.

"Not the best way to start summer vacation," he said over the sound of that god-awful 50 Cent song he's always listening to.

"It's okay. I'm glad it's not happening until school is over. They say the aftereffects will be a lot worse this time. I don't want to have to miss any of my finals."

Her second chemo session. The one that never happened. That's what they were talking about.

I pulled my art history notebook out of my bag and began to copy Alan's notes since I missed class to go to the doctor. Turns out the title Judith Beheading Holofernes isn't exactly a metaphor—yikes.

But Alan was staring at me like he was trying to figure something out.

And then he snapped.

"How can you act like this is all no big deal?" he shouted. I don't know if I've ever heard Alan shout before today. "You have <u>cancer</u>, Meg. And it's getting <u>worse</u>. But you act like all you care about is school."

"You don't get it." I tried to sound tough, but it came out sounding pathetic.

"Well, please, explain it to me. I'm all ears." Alan pushed

a button on his computer, and 50 Cent mercifully vanished. The room was silent. Alan's arms were crossed over his chest.

I took a deep breath and said the things I've been feeling for a while that I never told anyone.

School is important. It's one of the only things in my life that hasn't changed since my diagnosis. And as long as I can go to my classes, learn things, and do my homework, it feels like there's still an order to everything. So the idea of having to miss a bunch of school, the one routine in my life that still feels normal, because of the disease that has made everything else <u>abnormal</u>, is not okay.

Alan spun his cell phone around and around on his desk, letting my words sink in. When he looked up, there were tears in his eyes.

I really, really hated seeing him like that.

He let out a huge, steadying breath. "I didn't mean to yell at you," he said. "Sorry."

"It's okay." It really is.

"But can I say one more thing? Being that I'm your best friend and care about you a lot?"

I smiled at that. "Sure."

"I miss seeing you happy. You're so serious all the time. I know it's for a good reason, but I think that by trying to stay detached from the cancer stuff, you're missing out on other stuff too." He looked at me intently, like he'd just said the most profound thing ever uttered by humankind. And you know what? He had. But I didn't see it yet. I was still clueless.

"Um…what?"

He rolled his eyes. "Does the name Ryden Brooks mean anything to you?"

I felt my face get red.

"You love him." It wasn't a question.

I looked down at my book, but I wasn't looking at the words anymore. I nodded.

"You should tell him. Everything."

He sounded just like Mabel.

I tried to flop back on the bed in exasperation, but I wasn't feeling great, so it ended up being more of a ginger lean-back.

"Live your life, Meg," Alan said.

I've been thinking about that since leaving Alan's house earlier today. And he's right. There are things I want to do before I die. And Ryden's a huge part of that.

I stare at the page, putting the date and context of the entry together with my own memory of that time in my head. The very next day after this was written…

I think I need to have a little chat with Alan.

"We have to go," I say to Mabel, standing up and brushing the storage unit dust off my soccer shorts. "Same time tomorrow?"

"You got it."

• • •

By the time I get to Alan's to drop off Hope, that journal entry has replayed in my mind at least twenty times.

Alan comes outside to meet us. "Hi, Hope!" He opens the back door of the car, unbuckles her car seat from the base, and grabs her diaper bag from the floor. She squeals in delight as he makes a stupid face at her.

I get out of the car. "Hey, Alan, you got a minute?"

"Yeah, sure. What's up?"

We lean against the car, and my words come out all flat and accusing. "Why did you convince Meg to have sex with me?"

Alan sucks in air so fast he starts coughing. *What?*

"I read some of her other journals. Mabel got us into the storage unit. She wrote about a conversation you had, when you told her to 'live her life.' And the *next day,* she told me about the cancer and asked me to have sex with her. She was so intense about it, like if she didn't do it right then and there, she would never get the chance again."

I run my sneaker back and forth over a loose piece of the driveway blacktop. I don't usually talk this directly with my guy friends. We tend—tended, past tense, since, you know, I'm kinda low on the friend supply lately—to stick to more surface conversations. And I *especially* don't talk this way with Alan, who was always Meg's friend first and foremost. But I really could not give less of a shit anymore. "Why did you have to go and put that thought in her head?"

Alan pushes off the car and faces me. "Dude, I never said that. All I said was I wanted her to allow herself to be happy.

Trust me: your sex life is not very high on my list of concerns. I have my own to think about, you know. And let me tell you, it's in desperate need of some attention. I'm starting to feel like Lane Kim."

I stare at him. "You know I have no idea what you're talking about, right?"

Alan sighs. "I miss Meg. She always used to get my references."

There's nothing to say to that, really.

After a short pause, Alan says, "Lane Kim is this Korean character on this old TV show *Gilmore Girls*. She was played by a Japanese actress, which is complete bullshit, but I *guess* I can forgive them because they made the effort to include a Korean character on the show."

"And…um, *why* do you feel like this not-Korean Korean girl?"

"Oh, because she doesn't have sex until she gets married and in the meantime lives vicariously through her friends' recounting of their own experiences. It's completely tragic."

"So what you're saying is, you want a girlfriend."

"That's what I'm saying, yes."

"You could have just said that." A thought hits me, and even though I'm already late for soccer, I say, "Hey, Alan?"

"Yeah?"

"Did you ever feel, uh, *that* way about Meg?"

Alan looks at me sideways, like he's not sure if I'm setting a trap. "Um. Why?"

"I don't know, just wondering, I guess."

"Well…yeah. At times." He steps away. "Don't punch me."

"I'm not going to *punch* you."

"Appreciate it, man, thanks. Don't worry, nothing ever happened between us. I told her once in seventh grade that I liked her. She said, and I quote, she 'didn't want to ruin what we had by trying to make it something it wasn't.'"

"That sounds like something she would say."

Alan smiles. "Yeah. Wise beyond her years, that one."

• • •

Coach is pissed that I was a half hour late to practice again, so he makes me stay late to lug all the equipment back up to the gym by myself.

"Listen, Brooks," he says, walking casually alongside me as I sweat my ass off, dragging a mesh bag of balls up the hill. "I know things are tough for you at home right now, and I know you've had to make some sacrifices, but I need you to know that I've got a lot of interest in you from several D-One schools."

"Several? UCLA is one of them, right?"

"It is. Their recruiter is coming to see you play our third game. I get the impression that if things go well, he'll be ready to make you an offer that night."

"Holy shi—I mean, really?"

"Yes. So if you want a real shot at playing in college and potentially going pro, you need to step it up. That means no more being late, no more dragging your feet during drills, no more spacing out on the field and letting goals go by that you should be stopping no problem. Understood?"

I nod, wiping the sweat from my face as we reach the locker room. "Understood, Coach. One hundred percent."

"Glad to hear it. Don't let him down. And don't let me down either."

"I won't, I promise."

"Hit the showers and go get some rest."

But rest will have to wait. I race across town to Alan's, then my house, then Whole Foods. I'm seventeen minutes late punching in.

Joni's stationed at the register across from me. She shakes her head all mock disappointedly and taps her watch.

"Sorry," I mouth across the aisle.

She smiles and goes right on scanning and packing.

Two hours and countless times of asking "Did you bring your own bags today?" later, Joni turns off her light and comes over to my station.

"Break time?" she asks.

"Yeah, let me finish up here, and I'll meet you in the break room."

She shakes her head. "Meet me out front."

"Why?"

"Don't worry about it," she says, skipping off before I can say anything else. I smile. You can't say Joni doesn't keep things interesting.

I find her a few minutes later, sitting on the curb outside

the exit. I lower myself down next to her—it feels good to sit down—and hand her an aluminum hot/cold bag.

"What's this?"

"Pizza." I open my own bag and pull out a slice.

"You're feeding me?" she asks.

I take a huge pepperoni-filled bite. "You always feed me."

Joni looks at the bag. "Is it pepperoni? I actually don't eat meat…"

"I know." How *did* I know that? I don't think she ever told me. Must have figured it out from being around her, I guess. "Yours has broccoli and shit on it."

"You know, I don't usually eat shit," she says, grinning. "But the broccoli part is good. Thanks, Ryden," she says through a mouthful of veggies and cheese. "That was very…maternal of you."

I almost choke on my food.

Joni looks at me. "What?"

"Nothing." I swallow slowly, making sure it goes down the correct pipe this time. "So why did you want to meet out here?"

She points straight ahead, past the trees, to the horizon. "Sunset. Pretty, no?"

I look down at my sneakers. "Yeah." Pretty, sure, yeah, whatever. Also, say, the number one most clichéd romantic thing in the world.

Joni nudges me with her shoulder. "Oh, don't get your panties in a twist. I'm not hitting on you. I just didn't want to stay inside all day. We only have so much summer left. We'll be back at *school* next week."

"Yeah. Senior year."

"Woooo! Seniors! Kings of the school! Paaaaar-tay!" She waves her hands over her head. I know her well enough to know she's being sarcastic.

I laugh, and she calms down, giving me an eye-rolling grin.

"I found out the recruiter from UCLA is coming to watch me play in a few weeks, and he's bringing a contract with him."

"Really? That's awesome!"

"Yeah. I've been working pretty much my whole life for this."

Joni starts talking about what she thinks she might want to do after high school. I catch the gist of it—she's still trying to decide between college, traveling the world, or going to work at her family's doggie day care business. But what I'm thinking about is everything I'm not telling her. I still like the idea of keeping her separate from all the shit. She's kind of my salvation that way. But I'm also starting to feel bad about lying to her, or omitting the truth, or whatever.

Somehow, this weirdo girl has become my best friend.

But then I look at her, really look at her, her face lit up and glowing in the pink-orange-purple light from the sunset, her nose ring shimmering, her hair falling in her eyes, and I don't want to ruin it. She doesn't even like kids. Why should I take her down with my sad story?

Besides, Meg and I were actually *together* together, and she clearly had all sorts of stuff she didn't tell me. And we were happy. Mostly.

I think back to Meg's journal from this morning.

But I'm not lying. I'm just not giving him the whole truth. Once he knows, it's going to change everything. Is it really that bad if I'm selfish for a little while longer?

If Meg can keep a secret from me, I can keep a secret from Joni. It's not hurting anyone. If anything, it's making our friendship better.

• • •

I pull into the driveway and walk up to my house. It's a quiet, warm night, and Mom has the windows and screen door open. She's talking to someone. At first I think she's on the phone, but as I get closer to the front door, I know she's talking to Hope because she's got that *you're such a cutie face sweet munch-kin* baby voice going on.

"Who's the most ticklish baby in the world?" Mom says. "Hope is!" She makes tickly noises and, I think it's safe to assume, tickles Hope's belly or feet. "Hope is the most ticklish baby in the world!" More tickle noises, and then—

A laugh. A gurgling little baby giggle. Hope's *happy*.

I sink to the stoop's top step and listen. The two of them are having so much fun in there, laughing and playing and bonding, like they're the mom and daughter in a Cheerios commercial.

I look at the sky. I really hope Meg is witnessing this, wherever she is now. We made that laugh together. Even with all the other shit, everything I did, all the mistakes I made, that laugh is one twinkling star in a blanket of darkness.

"Your daddy's going to be home from work any minute, little girl," Mom says. "Isn't that great news? We get to see Daddy soon!"

The joy in my gut twists into trepidation. If I go in, I'll ruin it. Hope will get all anxious again, and clueless, fumbling me will take over for Mom, and the magical moment will be over.

Mom must tickle Hope or do something funny, because there's that laugh again. "That's right! Can you say Daddy?"

Guess that's my cue.

"Guess what?" I say to Mom as I open the door and take the stairs two at a time.

She smiles. Hope smiles too, from her perch on Mom's hip. Her eyes look different today. A brighter blue. "What?"

"The recruiter from UCLA is coming to see me play in a couple of weeks."

The smile vanishes from Mom's face. "He is?"

"Yeah, game three. What's the matter? This is *it*, Mom. He's flying here from California to see *me*. They don't do that for everyone. He's going to offer me a full ride."

Mom shakes her head a little. "That's wonderful, Ryden. A real testament to your talent."

"So…?"

"So…" She pointedly looks down at Hope, who's still smiling, unaware the mood in the house has shifted. "What about her?"

"She'll come with me. They have the day care place there, remember?"

Mom raises an eyebrow. "Yes, but—"

"Mom." Why does she have to ruin this for me? "There's no way in hell I'm turning down this opportunity. UCLA was always the plan. And I need *one* thing to stick to the plan, okay? So it has to work out, because there's no other option." She opens her mouth to say something, but I keep talking. "This is for Hope too, you know. If I go to UCLA, I'm securing a future for her. For us. You too. We'll have money. Opportunities we wouldn't have otherwise. You know it's true."

Part of my brain pipes up and reminds me that I need to find the journals before I leave for California. Once I find out whatever Meg had to say to me, the new-better-good stuff will have room to flood in.

"Okay. Fine," Mom says. But the way she says it, it's not really fine at all.

Chapter 16

Three days later, Mabel and I still haven't found either of the other two journals. We spend Thursday morning going through the remaining two boxes. Zilch.

"Maybe they don't exist," Mabel says, wiping an arm over her sweaty forehead and sitting back on her heels.

I shake my head. "They exist," I insist. "They have to. She wouldn't write that list and put that book in your room without there being two others out there that she wanted us to find. She wouldn't fuck with us like that."

Mabel just watches me through sad eyes.

"*No*," I say. "Don't look at me like that. Don't pity me, Mabel."

"I'm not pitying you. She was my sister. I miss her as much as you do."

"Yeah, but you weren't the one who killed—"

Mabel leaps to her feet. "Seriously, Ryden, enough with that. Just *stop*."

I stare back at her indignantly. I don't care what she thinks. She thinks she knows everything because Meg's journal entry said she didn't blame me, or there was nothing to blame me for, or whatever. But Mabel wasn't there. She wasn't part of any of it. She has *no* idea what she's talking about. But I'll stop saying it around her if that's what she wants.

"Well, either way," I say, "Meg knew what she was doing with the journal. She wanted us to find it because she wanted us to know the truth. Without that first one, we wouldn't know that she knew she was going to die all along. I think there was something else she wanted us to know, and I think we owe it to her to find out what."

Mabel stares at me. "We *owe* it to her? Since when is *that* the reason we're searching for these journals? I thought it was because we wanted the answers for ourselves. So we could move on."

"There are lots of reasons." I stand up too. Now I'm the one looking down on her. I lift Hope out of her car seat, balance her on my hip, and give her a pacifier. She'd be on my side about this if she were old enough to understand. I'm beginning to think she's the only one. "We can't give up."

"But what if they *don't exist*? We'll be chasing a ghost for the rest of our lives."

"They do."

She crosses her arms and speaks more softly. "They don't, Ryden. They're not here. Maybe she never got the chance to mark the other two and put them where we would find them. Or maybe she forgot about it. Or maybe she died before she could finish them. She was really weak and totally out of it toward the end, you know."

What, she thinks I don't remember *exactly* what Meg was

like in those final days? Her body thin and brittle, her stomach round and looking more like a tumor than any of the actual tumors inside of her. Her lips dry, her eyes unclear. Asleep most of the time, and the rest of the time too exhausted to do much more than walk the short distance to the bathroom. But still looking at me with more love than I've ever known in my life.

And then, one day, gone.

"She finished the journals," I say. "I know it. And I'm going to find them."

Mabel pushes the boxes against the storage room walls, picks up Hope's car seat, and walks to the car. I follow, closing and locking the garage door.

The drive back to her house is silent. Before she gets out of the car, she turns to me and says, "I'm done, Ryden. You're on your own. I have to move on."

I nod. I guess I kinda knew that was coming. "Call me whenever you want to see Hope."

"Thanks. See you at school on Monday."

She walks up the path toward her giant, cold house.

The thing is, now I'm even more determined to track down the journals. There was something Meg wanted us to know, *me* to know, and now I'm the only one left who wants to hear what she said just as desperately as she wanted to say it.

. . .

"Brooks!" Coach shouts as I run onto the field. "That little conversation we had on Monday wasn't for my health. That's it. You're sitting out next Friday."

"But, Coach! That's the first game of the season!"

"I'm aware of that. Two miles. Go."

Fuck. Fuck fuck fuck! My teammates have stopped what they were doing and stare at me as I switch from cleats to sneakers and start my eight laps around the track. Most of them are looking at me like Coach is looking at me—pissed off for my being late again and for forcing Coach to take me out of the game, which means we'll probably lose. Well, guess what? I'm pissed too. But some of the guys, like Dave, are looking at me like they feel *sorry* for me, the same way Mabel looked at me earlier this morning. Poor Ryden Brooks. His life is so fucked that he can't even keep his head straight.

And the saddest part is, they don't know the half of it.

The track is like a belt around the soccer field—on my left, inside the belt, the team is practicing. On my right are the stands. I pass by the home stands, then the visitors' stands, again and again. As I approach the home team side for the third time, my eyes land where Meg and Mabel sat during the championship game last December. Meg was six months pregnant and looked like a shell of her former self. But she pushed herself out of the house and cheered so much during that game that if you didn't look at her, just listened, you would never know how sick she really was.

She was my good luck charm. Downey won its fourth state championship in a row last year, and Meg was there for all of it.

You know, that may have been the last moment things were truly great.

• • •

There is one place I haven't checked yet.

A few days later, I get up early and drive to Meg's and my secret spot at the beach. I haven't been here since she got too sick to come with me. It looks exactly the same, right down to the half-empty Sprite bottle stuck in the sand that we must have forgotten to take home with us last time.

I scan the area for a journal peeking out of the sand or sitting in the grass. I even look up at the trees to see if there's anything nestled in the branches. There's nothing here. I don't know what I was expecting. Even if there had been a journal here, the weather would have gotten to it by now.

Hope sits in her harness on my chest. Her wails feel all wrong here; they don't mix with the serenity of this place. But then, this moment is strange for lots of reasons. This is the spot where she went from being a whole lot of nothing to the smallest beginnings of a *something*.

I bounce her up and down to try to keep her calm. It sort of works.

I sit in the sand and close my eyes, letting the sounds and smells and memories of the place fill every empty part of me. It all happened right here. It's still happening right here, like one of those weird sci-fi movies where time is stuck in a loop, and the people in it are trapped, destined to repeat a moment over and over without ever moving forward.

May 24…

"Turn left up here," Meg said. It was the night of the dance—the one we were skipping. I'd just picked her up from her giant house and met her pod people parents for the first time. They hadn't been very welcoming.

"Uh, why?"

She gave me a sly smile. "Just do it."

"Yes, ma'am."

We drove on for a while, Meg dictating the turns, me having no clue where she could be taking us.

"Okay, now slow down," she said when we got to an isolated one-lane road surrounded by woods. It was still light out, but everything got really dim as we continued driving under the leafy branches. "There's a turn soon, but I can never remember exactly where it is."

"A turnoff *here*?" I asked. "That leads to what? There's nothing here but trees."

"Ah, ye of little faith. Oh, there it is! Right past that weird branch that's sticking out. Turn right."

Sure enough, there was a tiny dirt road just wide enough for my car. I maneuvered us onto the path and inched the car forward at about three miles per hour. The road, if you could call it that, was really curvy and rocky. I had to lean forward over the steering wheel as we crept along, being extra careful not to drive over any tire-puncturing rocks or cute, furry forest creatures. The Sable wasn't exactly made for off-roading. Low hanging tree limbs and rogue, leaf-covered branches snapped against the windows—I felt like I was going through some sort of prehistoric car wash.

And then Meg was telling me to park and we were out of the car and walking through the woods.

"Are you taking me somewhere to murder me?" I asked. "Whatever I did to piss you off, I'm sorry."

Meg rolled her eyes. "Where's your sense of adventure, Ryden Brooks?"

The thick of trees opened onto a tiny, secluded beach, complete with sand and a shore. It was amazing. No one would ever find us here.

"How did you find this place?" I asked.

"I came here with Alan's family a long time ago. His dad knew about it somehow. I was, like, eight or nine at the time, but I loved it so much that I remembered where it was, and I started coming back when I was old enough to drive."

Meg pulled a sheet from her bag, spread it on the sand, and grabbed my hand, pulling me down with her.

"Have you decided what author you're going to do?" I asked after a minute of our joined hands being the only thing my brain seemed capable of focusing on. Mr. Wheeler had given us this assignment to pick an American author to give a presentation on before the end of the year, and it seemed like as good a thing to talk about as any.

"I think I'm doing Harper Lee," she said. "You?"

"Toni Morrison."

"Really?"

"Yeah, why? She's great."

"I know she is. I just…" She shook her head. "You're full of surprises, Ryden Brooks."

"Why do you always call me that?"

"Why do I always call you what?" she asked.

"Ryden Brooks. My whole name. You do that a lot."

"I do? Oh. Um…if I tell you, do you promise not to laugh at me?"

"Uh, yeah?"

"Okay, well…you know how when you talk about movie stars, you always say their first and last names? Like, it's always 'Matt Damon' and never just 'Matt'?"

"I guess…"

"Well, you're kind of like that, a celebrity in our school. You're the guy who's so perfect and untouchable that it feels weird to only call you by your first name."

I shook my head. "I'm not a *celebrity*. Jesus. I'm just Ryden. And you're Meg. And I like you."

She nodded, her cheeks coloring. Her hair fell in her face, and I reached forward and brushed it back.

"And…you like me too?" I asked.

She laughed. "You could say that."

And then I pulled our still-clasped hands toward me so that she fell against me, and I crushed my mouth to hers.

June 13…

We'd been together only a few weeks, but already it seemed like we'd known each other forever. We'd hung out with Alan a bunch of times, both in and out of school, and my mom had had Meg and Mabel over for dinner twice so far. But mostly we spent time at the beach. School was almost out—we just had to get through finals—and it felt like the days were endless. Sometimes Meg would write in her journals while I read a book or went swimming, or we'd study for exams together, or we would lie on our backs and *talk*. Our family shit, what it was like growing up with money (her) versus without (me), what was better: sweet (me) or salty (her).

And we made out a lot.

She acted a lot older than sixteen, and you could almost see her mind thinking, but she was also fun and laidback and nonjudgy. Meg was the only person I could just *be* with. I never felt antsy on those quiet afternoons together, like we had to be *doing* something to fill the space. She made me feel real.

"I have to tell you something," she said as soon as we spread the blanket on the sand that afternoon.

"What's up?" I asked, cracking open a Sprite and handing it to her so she could have the first sip.

She shook her head at the Sprite. "Actually, I have to tell you a few somethings."

I grinned at her, the idiot that I am, still not picking up that anything was wrong. "I have to tell you something too. Can I go first?"

She lowered her eyes and nodded. "Sure, go ahead."

I grabbed her beautiful, pale hand and brought it to my lips. "I love you."

Meg looked at me, her eyes sorta shimmery. But she didn't say anything.

"I know we haven't known each other that long, but I've never felt like this in my life. And before you go thinking I say this to all my girlfriends, I don't. I've never said it to anyone before. Except my mom. And that's, you know, different. But I wanted to say it to you because it's true and it's not fully real until you say it out loud."

Her lips parted, and here's what she said: "I love you too, Ryden Brooks."

Those words, coming from Meg's mouth, felt so fucking good, I can't even tell you. I felt indestructible. We toppled over on the blanket and made out for, like, ever.

"I wish we could stay here forever," I whispered against her mouth.

"Me too," she whispered back. "It's perfect here." But then she pulled away. "Wait, I still have to tell you something."

"Anything."

She sat up and pulled me with her. "I haven't told you this yet because I didn't want to freak you out, and things have been going so well with us and we've been having so much fun that I didn't want to ruin it. But I went to the doctor today—"

"Doctor?" I repeated. "What's wrong, are you still sick?"

She hesitated. "Yeah, I am. Um…" She peeked at me through her jet-black eyelashes. "I…well…I have cancer."

What?

I didn't know if I said the word out loud or not, but suddenly all the warm, happy, floaty feelings from the *I love you*s were gone, gone, gone.

"It's melanoma." Meg picked at a pilly part of the blanket. "Or it started that way. There was this tiny mole on the back of my leg that I didn't notice had changed. And I started feeling really bad all the time, so about four months ago, I finally went to get checked out, and it turned out that the melanoma had metastasized to my liver, gallbladder, and kidneys."

I was listening, soaking up every single word, trying to understand, but it all felt like a dream. Like I was watching some *very special episode* of a primetime drama during February sweeps, and the writers had thrown this curveball for one of the main characters, but don't worry, you know she'll be cancer free by the end of the season, because, after all, she's the show's star.

"The treatments make things tricky. It makes me feel really gross, and it's why my skin is so pale and why I couldn't go to the dance—I have to stick to low-key activities."

Her skin. The skin I thought was so pretty was actually cancer skin.

"I went in for a week of chemotherapy in April, so I was out of school for a couple of weeks. I don't know if you noticed." I shook my head, and she shrugged. "They do it in rounds, giving your body time to recover a bit before they go back and do it again, so I'm on break now. I still get sick from it sometimes though, as you've seen."

So *that's* what that was. She didn't have the flu. She was sick because of fucking *chemotherapy*.

"But I have to go back in soon. So, um…I thought I should tell you."

I didn't know what to say or do or feel. The best I could come up with—God, I'm such an idiot—was, "But you still have your hair."

That made her smile at least. "Yeah, I was lucky. I didn't lose my hair in the first round. It got a little thinner, which is why I stopped blow-drying it. I figured I might as well be good to it, stop trying to wrangle it into something it's not, and maybe I'd get to keep it longer. But my doctor told me yesterday that they're upping the dose the next time around…so I'm probably going to lose it then."

"But…" I mumbled. "I love your hair."

Meg looked sad. "Me too."

I knew I needed to say something else, something better. So I forced my brain to clear itself and said, "Will you be okay?"

"I think so. The doctor said the first round of chemo was somewhat successful, and the masses have started to show indications of shrinking. But there's still a long way to go." She looked me straight in the eye. "The survival rates for this kind of thing aren't great. You should know that, but…I just have this feeling everything will be fine."

Everything will be fine. Yes! Good! Okay then! I grabbed her hands, suddenly needing to touch her, to remind myself that she was still here, that even though she had this disease, it didn't mean she was going to die. "Promise?"

"Promise." She gave a little smile. "Do you want to take back what you said earlier?"

I blinked. "That I love you?" I shook my head. "Why would you even think that?"

"Okay, good. Because I have something else I need to tell you."

"Oh God, now what?" I asked before I could stop myself.

Meg laughed. "Don't worry, this one is better. At least, I hope you'll think so."

I waited.

"I want to have sex," she said. Just like that, all direct and to the point.

"What?"

"I want to have sex," she repeated. "With you. Today."

It wasn't the sexiest proposition I'd ever gotten, but damn if I wasn't immediately on board. "Are you sure? I mean, *can* you?"

"I'm completely sure. And yes, of course I can. I'm not on my deathbed." She paused. "Do you? Want to, I mean?" Her face was all red, embarrassed. As if she really thought I was going to say no.

I leaned forward and kissed her with everything I had. Soon we were horizontal, me hovering over Meg, looking down into her excited, trusting face. I kissed her again, gently, wanting to show her how much I loved her. "Does that answer your question?"

She giggled.

But there was a problem. "Did you bring a condom? I don't have one on me." *Stupid, stupid, stupid.*

"Don't worry, I'm on the pill."

That surprised me. "Have you done this before?"

"No, but I've been on the pill since last year. Helps with cramps."

"Oh."

"Have *you* done it before?"

I cleared my throat a little. "Uh…well…yeah. Is that okay?"

"Of course. I figured as much anyway."

I was still hovering over her, paused in suspended animation, waiting for her to press play. But there were still more things to say. "The pill only prevents pregnancy, not…you know, other stuff. Not that I have any of that stuff," I amended quickly. "I don't. I swear."

She smiled. "I may not have ever done this before, but I know how it works. Ryden, I have *cancer*. I'm in chemotherapy. My whole life is a guessing game. All I want is to do this, with you, before it's too late. Please. If you say you're fine, I believe you."

I gazed down at her beautiful, pink mouth. "I wish I had waited for you," I whispered and brought my lips to hers.

June 28…

"Ryden," Meg said.

I almost didn't hear her at first. I was tracing my fingers up her leg, slowly, up, up, up, almost at the bottom of her shorts. I definitely didn't notice the shake in her voice until she said my name again, louder.

My hand stopped where it was.

"You okay?" I asked, starting to get scared. We'd already had one enormous, way-too-serious, life-changing conversation a couple of weeks ago. I really wasn't ready for another one yet.

"I…um…" She couldn't get her words out, which was rare for her. And she wouldn't look at me.

"What is it?" I sat up and grabbed both her hands, relieved at the way she held on tight.

She took a shallow, trembling breath. "I'm pregnant."

Moments like those don't mean anything while they're happening. I mean, they mean *everything*, but at the time, your brain is completely fucked. I know because I've experienced a lot of those mind-blowing moments recently. You can't remember your own name, let alone make sense of whatever you've learned. That comes later.

In the moment, *nothing* makes sense. So really, even though it's probably the biggest moment of your life, it's also a nonmoment. Instead of an exclamation point, there's a gaping black hole.

As Meg studied me, waiting for me to respond, time started ticking again. The only thing going through my head was *fuuuuuuuuck*. But I couldn't very well say that, could I?

So I went for the brilliant, "But you're on the pill."

To which she answered, "Yeah."

"Guess it didn't work."

"Guess not."

Neither of us was going to win an award for Ability to Conduct Intelligent Conversations While Under Severe Emotional Stress.

We got quiet again, and I squeezed her hands tighter, not wanting to let go, as the bigger picture started to form. Of course. She couldn't keep it. Duh. There were other factors in play here. I started to breathe a little bit easier.

"I'll come up with the money," I said. "I'll go to the appointment with you and everything. We'll get through this. Everything will be fine."

She shook her head. "It's not that simple."

"What do you mean? You start back with chemo on Monday." Shit—the chemo. That was probably why the pill didn't work. Why hadn't I thought of that two weeks ago?

"I know. That's how I found out I'm pregnant. I had to go in for pre-chemo blood work yesterday."

"So…? They're not gonna let you go back to chemo if you're *pregnant*, Meg."

"I know." She kept her eyes down. I hated not being able to see them. "But…I need to figure out what's more important to me."

I couldn't believe what I was hearing. For a nerdy smart girl, she was being pretty goddamn stupid. She *had* to go back to chemo. It was the only way she'd get better.

"Well," I said, unable to stop the biting tone from creeping into my voice, "I know what's important to *me*. There's no choice here."

She looked up finally, and the second her dark eyes met mine, I knew she'd already made her decision.

And that's when the fighting started.

Chapter 17

On Friday after work, I finally give in and tell Mom what I'm looking for.

She blinks a few times, like she's thinking really hard. There's a Sandra Bullock movie paused on the TV. It's not *The Lake House*. "And the one you found has a checked box next to Mabel's name?" she repeats.

"Yeah. Why, you know something about it?"

She shakes her head. "No. What did it say?"

I tell her what the first journal revealed, and she says, "I'm not surprised."

"What do you mean? What are you not surprised about?"

"That she wanted to have the baby even though she knew she might not make it."

"*What?*"

"It makes sense, Ry. Think about it. She wanted to feel like she had done something important with her life. That's how I felt when I was pregnant with you, even after I knew your father wasn't going to be around to help me. Suddenly it was as if my life was so much bigger than just me. And I can only imagine how much stronger that feeling must be when you don't think you have much time left."

I drop my head back against the couch and stare up at the ceiling. "But she didn't *tell* anyone she didn't think she had much time left! She kept saying how she would go back to treatment after the baby was born. She made me believe she thought everything would be fine! She *lied*, Mom."

Mom doesn't say anything. She's probably trying to figure out what she could possibly say that won't make me more upset.

I shake my head. "So you're saying you haven't seen any journals around anywhere."

Mom sighs. "No. I'm sorry."

• • •

"Want to play a game?" Joni asks me at work on Saturday.

"A game?"

"A game. You know, for to have fun?" She crosses her eyes and sticks her tongue out at me.

I laugh. "Um. Sure."

"Right this way, sir."

I walk beside her as she walks slowly up and down the aisles. She seems to be paying more attention to the people in the store than the items on the shelves, which is kind of the opposite of what we usually do at work.

I lean forward and whisper in her ear. Her hair smells like Sour Patch Kids. Weird, but oddly appealing. "What are you doing?"

"Just wait for it." We see an old, white-haired man in a

mechanical wheelchair. "Okay. See that guy?" she whispers to me as we pass him. "He's ninety-four years old, and he has a twenty-three-year-old wife. Her name is Brenda, and she's had not one but *two* breast enhancement procedures. She married him for his money, of course, but he doesn't care. Today's his birthday, and he has big plans for tonight, involving whipped cream and chocolate syrup."

Sure enough, the shopping basket on the old man's lap contains whipped cream and chocolate syrup, as well as a container of cherries.

I turn to face her. "How the hell did you know that?"

She laughs. "I didn't. I made it up. The guy's probably making ice cream sundaes with his grandkids. But that's not nearly as much fun as my version, is it?"

I feel a smile spreading across my face. "This kinda reminds me of this game I play with my mom. She creates customized event invitations and shows me her materials, then I try to guess the kind of people who've ordered the invitations."

Joni raises her eyebrows. "I'll have to meet this mom of yours. She sounds like my kind of chick."

I'm about to say, "Oh, sure, anytime," but that wouldn't work, would it? She'd find out about Meg and Hope in about a second and a half.

I give a noncommittal shrug instead.

"This game is a little different though," she says. "The point is to come up with a ridiculous story, not try to guess the truth."

I nod.

"Give it a try."

"I don't think I'll be very good at it." Especially the way my brain's been lately.

"I'm not taking no for an answer, buddy." A lady walks past pushing a cart filled with nothing but tofu. Joni nods at her. "Perfect. Go."

"Umm…she was just diagnosed with heart disease and her doctor told her she needs to eat healthier."

She shakes her head. "Nope. Try again."

"What do you mean, 'nope'? There's no correct answer—I thought the point was to make something up."

"The point is to use your *imagination*. Try again."

I study the woman. She's got frizzy, gray-streaked hair and is wearing a lot of clunky metal jewelry that looks like it was made with a hammer. Actually, it's a lot like the top of Joni's stepbrother's tree sculpture.

Got it.

"She's an avant-garde artist," I whisper, watching the woman push her cart toward the checkout. "She spent the '70s and '80s in New York City but had enough of that scene and moved to New Hampshire after Andy Warhol died. She's semiretired now but has been commissioned to create a sculpture made solely out of tofu for a PETA fund-raiser."

I look back at Joni. She stares at me with a crooked smile. "Ladies and gentlemen, the student has become the teacher!" she shouts, skipping around the rest of the shoppers in the aisle.

We keep the game up for over an hour, whispering stories

about a guy who refuses to eat anything but foods that start with the letters C, R, or W, because those are his initials, the couple who's planning to fill their swimming pool with rice pudding to celebrate their anniversary, and the frazzled woman who's buying enough hot dogs and hamburgers to feed her husband's entire extended family—who arrived, unannounced, from the Czech Republic earlier this morning.

We get zero work done, but we move from aisle to aisle enough that no one notices.

I don't realize until later that it's the first time in over a week my thoughts aren't entirely consumed with journals.

Chapter 18

Monday morning, Mom gets up early to go with me to drop Hope at the day care downtown. It's in a municipal-type building, and you have to go through security to get in. We have to take Hope out of her car seat so it can go through the X-ray machine. Mom carries her as she walks through the metal detector.

Mom hasn't said much about my decision to go with this place. It seemed like she'd been pulling for the nanny option, but ever since I made my choice, she's been all business about the downtown day care, like it was the plan all along. She's probably just glad I made a decision at all.

We walk down a few different cinder block corridors, following the handwritten signs for the child care room. Harried parents in badly fitting suits and various uniforms hurry past us.

The day care is a large room with mismatched tiles and area rugs and crayon drawings on the walls. It seems clean enough, but the furniture is old and worn. Freestanding shelving units and cubby bins divide the room into sections. Signs hang from the ceiling over each area: 6 Weeks–1 Year. 1–3. 3–5.

And it's really, really loud. There are kids everywhere. Each section is more crowded than I imagined. Kids crying, screaming for their mommies, running around, squealing, fighting over blocks and books and markers. I have an instant headache.

Mom and I head over to the front desk. The woman sitting there is holding a cup of coffee with both hands and guzzling it as if it's Gatorade at halftime.

"Excuse me," Mom says, but the woman holds up a finger for us to wait while she takes one last gulp.

"Mondays," she says, shaking her head.

Mom makes a kind of commiserating *I totally hear ya* chuckle that I have never heard her make before. She doesn't work in an office. And she loves her job. She doesn't care about Mondays. I raise an eyebrow at her, and she shrugs.

"We're here to drop off Hope Brooks," Mom says to the woman. "Today's her first day."

The woman punches some buttons on her computer's keyboard with her way-too-long nails. "Right. Brooks. Full days, seven a.m. through three p.m., Monday through Friday, is that correct?"

"Yes," Mom says, and the woman pushes some forms across the counter at her.

"Make sure all the contact information is correct, fill out the rest. Don't leave anything blank. And sign."

Mom slides the papers to me and hands me a pen.

I look at her. "Can't you do it?"

"You're the parent, Ryden. I'm not her legal guardian."

I let out a little groan and complete the forms as quickly as possible. Name, address, emergency contact, allergy information, feeding information, insurance, blah, blah, blah. I hand them back.

"We send our bills every two weeks. Payment is due within five days." She waves a hand, gesturing that we should bring Hope over to join the chaos.

The 6 Weeks–1 Year section is actually the calmest. The kids aren't old enough to be fighting or playing with each other much, so there's just a lot of crying and sitting around and stuff. But there're a lot of kids here—at least twenty—and there're only two teachers or whatever you call them.

I feel Mom tense beside me, but she keeps a smile on her face and introduces us to one of the teachers. In a matter of seconds, she's handing over Hope and we're waving good-bye, and then we're out in the hallway.

Mom and I look at each other as the door swings closed and the noise from the day care is somewhat dimmed.

What just happened?

And why does it feel weird?

Mom's eyes get watery, and she swallows a couple of times to keep her emotions in check.

"You okay?" I ask.

She sniffles and shrugs. "That was harder than I thought it would be."

Sort of, yeah, for me too. But that's stupid. I've left Hope with my mom and Alan a zillion times. This isn't any different, except now I have to pay for it. I get to go back to school and go back to normal, and Hope gets to be around other babies and do, I don't know, *baby* stuff. So what's the fucking problem?

"*You* okay?" she asks, and I realize I'm staring off into nowhere.

I'm fine. It's all fine. But I can't seem to find the words, so I nod.

Mom puts her arm around my shoulder as we walk back to the car.

• • •

School.

Friends. Lunch. Homeroom. Report cards.

It's all back.

The first clue that the normal world is still spinning—and that it now actually expects me to get back on board—is how everyone comes up to me like I'm their long-lost brother or something.

"Ryden, omigod, *hi*!"

"What's up, Brooks?"

"State champions fifth year in a row, man! Eastbay is going *down*!"

"How was your summer?! I went to France—it was *amaaaazing*."

I guess, unlike that day at the lake, because I don't have Hope with me, they've forgotten about her. Or maybe they're avoiding the subject on purpose. I smile and laugh and hug and fist-bump everyone, like life's totally great.

No one mentions Meg. I guess it makes sense. She stopped

school in November of last year, so everyone's used to seeing me without her. I wish *I* were used to seeing me without her.

My locker is the second sign that nothing has changed in the Bizarro World that is Downey High School. I don't even know which one is mine until we're given our assignments in homeroom, but clearly someone got the memo before I did, because my locker is decorated. It's covered in Puma blue and white, with a paper soccer ball with a giant *#1* painted on it and lots and lots of streamers and silver glitter. I look down the hall—there are a few other lockers that look like mine, all belonging to my fellow varsity soccer team members. Clearly whoever went to the trouble to find out my locker assignment and get here early to decorate it hasn't heard that I'm benched for Friday's game.

I don't have any books yet, and though it's almost fall, it's not really cold enough outside for a coat, so I don't have anything to put in the locker. So I just close it and go to AP English.

And there she is. Meg Reynolds, dark hair all wild and flowing around her shoulders and down her back, pale face resting on her pale arm sprawled across the desk, vigorously scribbling in a notebook. She looks up and gives me the brightest, most beautiful smile in the whole world. I stop dead in my tracks. The memory is so real, so vivid, I have to fight to get air. And then I blink.

She's gone. All that's left is an empty desk with the class syllabus sitting on it. There are plenty of other seats, but I sit there.

Shoshanna walks into class just as the bell rings, so I'm saved from having to talk to her, but she keeps throwing me grins throughout the period.

As soon as the class ends, I hear, "Ryden!" Shoshanna throws her arms around me and keeps the hug going way too long. I try to pull back twice, but she just holds on tighter.

Finally she lets me go, and we exit the classroom together to find Dave waiting for Sho in the hall. I give him a fist bump. "What's up, guys?"

Shoshanna's still beaming at me. "What did you think of your locker? Did you love it?"

"Um, yeah. That was you?"

"Yup." She claps her hands excitedly. "You're my player!"

Oh God, no. There's this tradition at Downey where the varsity cheerleaders are each assigned a soccer player during the fall and a basketball player during the spring. All season, the cheerleader wears his number, cheers his name during the roll-call cheers, brings him cookies and little gifts and stuff on game days, and on and on and on. Last year, this girl named Madelyne Binder was my cheerleader. She moved away a few weeks into the season—I think her mom lost her job or something—and I was cheerleaderless. But I had Meg, so I didn't care. Now it seems I have Shoshanna. At least in this one way. I know she means well, but I really don't have the energy for this.

"Shouldn't Dave be your player, since you guys are together now?" I ask.

"That's what I said!" Dave replies. "But Sho insisted that

you're the team's star, and she won't accept anyone less than the best as her player." He laughs as he says this, like, *Isn't she so cute?* so I guess he doesn't care that his girlfriend basically told him he's a shitty player and not good enough for her. Well, whatever.

"The locker was great," I say. "Thanks."

"There's more where that came from, mister!" Shoshanna giggles, and she and Dave continue on to their next class.

A few periods later, I'm making my way to the cafeteria when I'm hit with another hallucination. Meg's smiling face flickers in and out of view through the gaps in the passing stream of students. Unlike the last hallucination, this one doesn't bring me to a halt. Instead, I pick up speed and push past arms and shoulders and backpacks, desperate to get close to her. I blink once, twice, but she doesn't disappear this time.

"Meg," I whisper through my clogged throat.

Meg's eleventh-grade class photo, blown up to the size of a thirty-two-inch flat screen and framed in light-colored wood, hangs on the wall. She's not a hallucination. But she's not real either.

Under the photo is a plaque that reads, *Megan Elizabeth Reynolds. In our hearts forever.*

I want to claw the stupid plaque with its stupid message down with my bare hands. I would too, if it weren't screwed into the cinder block. *In our hearts forever.* On this wall forever.

They think they knew her. They think they'll miss her. They think they're mourning her.

They know nothing.

I see Alan at lunch. He's sitting with a few people I don't recognize. When Meg was in school, I sat with her and Alan most days. But it was just us then. Whoever these other friends of Alan's are, they must be new.

I carry my tray over. "Hey."

"Hey."

"You see the picture?"

He nods. "I thought it was nice."

"Nice. Yeah," I say.

"You wanna sit?" He slides down, making room for me.

I look across the cafeteria toward where Dave and Shoshanna and Matt Boyd and a bunch of the other guys from the team are sitting. Dave's shotgunning a Dr Pepper, and everyone's cheering him on. He breaks away from the empty can, face red, and gives Shoshanna a sloppy, wet Dr Pepper kiss.

I look back at Alan and his quiet group of nerds. With the exception of Alan, everyone here is staring at me like I've got a dick growing out the side of my head.

I don't know what the hell to do. I don't feel like sitting with a bunch of people I don't know, who I surely don't have anything in common with, but I also don't feel like I belong at that other table either. They'd take me back no question, but that's not the problem. It would require a massive effort on my part to try to blend in. I'm so tired. I don't care about arm wrestling tournaments or betting Dave a dollar that he wouldn't eat his fries if they were smothered in a mayo, Tabasco, pickle juice, and A.1. concoction.

But I'm not gonna sit by myself either.

"I think I'll go sit with them," I tell Alan, nodding over to the soccer table. At least I *know* them. "See you later?"

Alan nods. "You bringing Hope by after school?"

"I have to pick her up at day care. But then I'll bring her to your house, yeah."

"I can pick her up if you want," Alan says, shrugging.

"Dude. Really?"

"Sure."

"That would be fucking amazing. Then I wouldn't be late to practice. I'll text you the address of the place."

"Cool."

Oh shit, wait. "I'll need to switch her car seat to your car somehow. Maybe I can do that now—give me your keys."

"No need. I have a car seat in my car already."

I blink. "You do?"

"My mom got it when Hope first started coming over. So we can go to the park and stuff."

I shake my head, amazed. "I owe you one, Alan."

"Ryden, you owe me about a billion."

• • •

I'm in the locker room changing for practice when my phone rings. It's Alan.

"They won't let me take Hope home," he says when I pick up. "Something about me not being on an approved list."

Oh, you've got to be kidding me. "Put the lady on, I'll talk to her."

The woman from the front desk comes on the line. "This is Sonya."

"Yeah, hi, this is Ryden Brooks. Hope's father?" A few of the guys in the locker room pause what they're doing and look my way. I duck behind my open locker door and lower my voice.

"Yes, Mr. Brooks."

"Listen, you can send Hope home with Alan Kang. He's her babysitter. It's fine."

"Mr. Brooks, we can't do that. You need to come in and add Mr. Kang to the approved pickup list and sign the form."

"I will, tomorrow. But can you just send her home with him today? Just this once? I'm telling you it's okay."

"I understand, but I still can't do that. We need to have it in writing, for legal reasons."

I kick the row of lockers, and the clang reverberates throughout the room. "I was in this morning filling out all your paperwork and there was nothing about an approved pickup list."

"You have to ask for that separately."

I can't deal with this woman. "Can my mother pick her up?"

I hear the clack of Sonya's typing, and a second later, she comes back on the line. "Is your mother Deanna Brooks?"

"Yes."

"Yes, she's fine. She's listed as an emergency contact."

I exhale. "Thanks." I hang up and call Mom. She doesn't answer the house phone. Her music in her office is probably too loud. I try her cell. Four rings and then voice mail. I redial. Same. *Fuck.*

Five minutes and countless calls later, I still have no idea where my mother is.

The guys are all leaving the locker room and on their way to the field.

"You coming, Brooks?" Andrew, one of our fullbacks, asks, filling his water bottle at the fountain and screwing the lid back on.

"Yeah. In a minute," I say. He gives me a wary look but shrugs and leaves.

I rest my forehead against the cool metal of the lockers and try to think. Hope can't stay there until I'm done with practice. If I don't get her before three, I'll be charged extra. And I don't have anything extra to give.

I have no choice. I have to go.

I shoot Alan a quick text that I'll meet him at the day care, grab my keys, and start to run, still in my cleats and shin guards. When I get to my car, the clock on the dashboard says two fifteen p.m. Practice is starting now. And I'm on my way out of the parking lot. Coach is gonna have my ass.

Alan's waiting outside the day care building, leaning against a brick column with a sign that says *No loitering*.

"Why are you out here?" I ask.

"They made me leave. Said people without kids aren't allowed in there. I think they thought I was some sort of creeper or something."

I sigh. "Be right back."

There's a line at the metal detectors, and the security people don't seem to be in any rush, chatting with each person who comes through. My heart is pounding, every second feeling like an hour. Finally I cut to the front of the line and say, "Sorry, I'm in a rush. I have to pick up my kid."

The middle-aged woman at the front of the line with '80s hair—you know, the kind with the bangs that are hair sprayed to look like they're flying in every possible direction—stares at me, appalled. She takes in my soccer gear and my long hair and my sweaty face and looks like she's trying to decide if she feels bad for me, "poor teenage dad, what a shame," or if she wants to tell me to go to the end of the line and wait my turn like everyone else, that it's not *her* problem I have a baby at seventeen.

"She's sick," I add. "Really sick." I toss my keys in the bin and go through the metal detector before anyone can stop me.

I sprint down the halls, sliding a little in my cleats, and finally reach the day care.

"Ryden Brooks, Hope's dad," I call out to Sonya as I bypass the front desk and head directly to the baby area. Hope's in a crib, crying. No one's paying attention to her. The two teachers are busy changing and feeding other babies. Goddammit. I lift my baby from her crib, hold her securely to my chest, grab her bag, and leave without saying anything to the teachers. No time.

I only stop to fill out the form that says Alan can pick up Hope from now on, and then I'm on my way again, though I have to take it a little slower on my way out of the building—can't go sliding in my cleats with a baby in my arms. I retrieve my keys from where I left them at the security station and meet Alan outside.

"She's crying," Alan says.

"No shit, man."

"Does she need to be changed?"

"Probably." I hold Hope toward him. "Do you mind taking care of it? I really need to get back to practice."

Alan's mouth presses into a hard line for about a second, but he looks at Hope and starts making those idiotic smiley faces people do at babies and takes her into his arms. "No problem. See you after practice."

By the time I make it to the soccer field, it's close to three o'clock. I'm forty-fucking-five minutes late. Again.

This time no one even looks at me when I arrive. That's worse than them all staring, because it means they're getting used to me being unreliable. *I'm so not that guy*, I want to shout at them. I'm the guy who puts in extra time at practice, who gets there early and stays late. I'm the guy who runs five miles on Saturday morning even when we don't have practice. I'm the guy who's pulled a W in every single game played for the past two years, the guy with the lowest goals allowed average Downey High School has ever seen, the guy who's ranked in the top five high school goalies in the country, for Christ's sake. I'm the guy who's going pro.

Coach calls me over to the sidelines. His voice is pretty level, considering, but I already know this is going to be bad.

"I'm so sorry, Coach," I begin. "I had an emergency. It won't happen again."

"I've heard that before, Ryden."

Ryden? He never calls me Ryden. He always calls me Brooks.

"I mean it this time. There was a problem at the day care—"

Coach O'Toole nods, still watching the drills out on the field. "I have kids too, Ryden. Four of them. And their mother and I are divorced. I know what it's like. There're times when they're with me that I just don't know how to handle them. Someone's always sick or getting her period or needs to be picked up from somewhere or needs help with some science project or decides she's a vegan and won't eat anything I've made for dinner. I know, Ryden. I get it."

Why the hell is he telling me all of this?

"Lots of people get it. Anyone with kids gets it. Being a parent is the hardest thing in the world." He claps a hand on my shoulder and finally turns to looks at me. "But the world is full of single parents, and we all have jobs to do, apart from being parents. And my job is to get this team another state championship and keep producing players who go on to play D-One. And your job is to be part of the team and do what's expected of you, what's expected of everyone here. And if you can't do that, I understand…but then you're off the team. I can't hold you to a different set of rules than everyone else."

My heart stops dead in my chest. I shake my head fiercely, trying to find the magic words that will turn this conversation back around. "I know. You're absolutely right. I know I've been undependable, but I've finally got it figured out. I swear. Give me one more chance, Coach, please. I won't let you down again. *Please*." I know I'm begging, but I don't give a shit. I'll get down on my hands and knees and kiss his sneakers if it would make him change his mind. I *can't* get kicked off the team.

Coach considers me a minute, arms crossed, chewing on a huge wad of gum.

"Please," I say again.

Finally his shoulders relax a little. "One more chance. If you are even one minute late to a practice or game from here on out, that's it."

I nod like crazy. "Yes, of course. I understand."

"And you're still benched Friday."

"Got it."

"All right, go join the rest of the team."

I resist the overwhelming urge to hug him and jog out onto the field.

Chapter 19

Mom's sitting on the front stoop with a glass of white wine when I stop by to drop off Hope before work. "Everything go okay getting Hope from day care?"

"Actually, no. They wouldn't let Alan pick her up because he wasn't on some list, so I had to get her. I was late to practice."

Mom nods. "Those places have to be really careful about who they release the kids to."

"I called you."

"You did? I'm sorry, bud—I had my ringer off."

"I called the house phone too. Where were you?"

"I was out."

I narrow my eyes at her. Something's off. "Where'd you go?"

"I had a date."

"A *date*?"

"I'm allowed to date, you know," she says.

"Yeah, but on a Monday afternoon? That's just weird."

She shrugs. "You're not the only one whose schedule has been crazy since Hope was born. We've all been struggling to find time for stuff, Ryden." She says it softly, not bitter at all.

I scoot closer to her and rest my head on her shoulder. "I

know. I'm sorry, Mom. You know I love you, right? And that I appreciate everything you've done for us?"

She smoothes my hair. "I know, buddy."

"So you wanna tell me about the guy?"

"No, I'm not really sure what it is yet. But I like him."

"Well, as long as he's good to you, I like him too." I stand up. "Gotta go to work."

"Have fun."

• • •

I search the whole store but don't see Joni anywhere. Maybe she's off? She usually works Mondays, but maybe she switched with someone.

It's not until I take my fifteen that I discover she actually is here. She's in the break room, curled up on the little couch, red-eyed and crying, a box of Whole Foods brand recycled tissues tucked in the crook of her arm.

Before I allow myself time to think about what I'm doing, I'm by her side and pulling her close to me. She starts crying harder, burying her face into my shirt. I just hold her tight and let her get it out. I have absolutely zero idea what I'm supposed to say. Joni's always so happy. Strong. What could have made her like this?

People come in to the break room, take one look our way, and turn right back around. So apart from a few brief entrances and exits, we're alone.

Eventually she pulls away. She's not crying anymore, but her face is all splotchy, and her eyelashes are clumped together with moisture. I'm supposed to be back out on the floor by now. But fuck it. I'm not gonna leave her. I'm not a *total* asshole.

"I got your shirt all wet," she whispers.

I shrug. "It'll dry."

"I'm so sorry," she says, blowing her nose. "I don't know why I'm acting like this."

"Just a guess, but probably because something is wrong?"

She looks at me through bloodshot eyes. "I didn't tell you this, because I didn't want you to think I'm one of those stupid girls who makes drama out of everything—"

"I don't think that."

She nods and takes in a shuddering breath. "My dickwad ex-boyfriend and my best friend have been hooking up all summer."

Ex-boyfriend? What ex-boyfriend? Okay, focus on the best friend. "Carrie, right? Or Karen?"

"Karen. Yeah."

"Not cool." She's crying about her friend getting together with her ex? Does that mean she still has feelings for him?

"Well, I knew about it," she continues. "She told me a while ago. I was trying to be cool with it. Even though it felt like shit. But it turns out they've been talking about me a lot. Like, comparing notes on personal stuff I've told them. And apparently he's told her pretty much every detail about the times we had sex. Stuff that even I didn't tell her. And we've been friends forever."

Thinking about Joni having sex with some dude makes me feel like I just ate a bad hunk of meat. Plus, it's like she has this whole other life that I had no idea about. "What kind of stuff?"

"What I liked to do, what I didn't like to do. He even told her about when we lost our virginity to each other. All the graphic, gory details."

"I'll kill him," I say, and for a second, I actually mean it. I fucking hate this guy, whoever he is. "Tell me his name and I'll go kick his ass right now."

Joni sort of smiles at that. "You're sweet."

I wasn't exactly going for sweet, but whatever. "How'd you find out?" I ask.

"That's the worst part. They've been having these conversations in front of other people. Like, drunk at parties or on Facebook or whatever—places I haven't really been, because I didn't particularly want to see them being all kissy and gross with each other. They had a code name for me, but everyone obviously knew who they were talking about. I'm his only ex-girlfriend. And when I walked into school today, all these people started calling me *Jog*." She shakes her head and coughs a little.

"Jog? What does that mean?"

"Apparently 'Jeff's Old Girlfriend.' I finally got one of my other friends to tell me what was going on. But even she'd known for months and didn't think to tell me about it until today." She shakes her head. "Jog. So stupid. It's not even *clever*." She's trying to joke, but the crack in her voice gives her away.

I pull her into my arms again. She melts into me a little. "I'll kill all of them," I whisper into her hair.

"Yeah, don't do that. Then you'd have to go to prison, and I'd be left without any friends at all." She sniffles.

"Hey, don't forget about Julio in the deli, and the tattoo shop girl."

"No, they're just people I've met. It's easy to meet people. Real friends are harder to come by."

With Joni in my arms like this, I think we must be the real kind of friends. We might actually be each other's only friends.

But then she asks, "Your ex-girlfriend wouldn't do anything like that to you, would she?" and I know she might be my real friend but I'm not being one to her. Why should I feel weird about this other part of her life when I'm keeping a World Cup stadium full of secrets from her? I'm still just another "person she's met," even if she doesn't know it.

"No," I say. That's true, at least Meg wouldn't do anything anymore.

"Good. Though, you're a boy. It would probably be different for you anyway."

I don't say anything. I just squeeze her tight and hope she doesn't notice that she's being held by the arms of a liar.

"I'll be fine," she whispers.

"I know you will."

Then she starts crying all over again.

• • •

Joni and I stay in the break room until our shift is over. No one comes looking for us. The manager must have heard something was going on and decided to let us be. Or maybe we weren't missed. It's one of the benefits of working in a place with so many employees.

At ten o'clock, we walk out to the parking lot together.

"Let me drive you home," I say.

"You don't have to do that."

"There's no way I'm letting you get on a bus right now." I unlock my car doors. "Get in."

We don't talk about the fact that Joni has to go to school tomorrow—and the day after that and the day after that—knowing everyone knows the intimate details of her life. Instead, I tell her about Mom's mysterious midafternoon date. She tells me about the fifth book in the *Bahamas Bikers* series, which she just finished. We talk about her family some more.

"I want to tell you something," she says, sounding like she's thinking it through as she goes along. "Something nobody else knows. I feel like that would make me feel better, as if I've still got some control over who knows things about me."

I glance at her. "You sure?"

She nods. "I can trust you, right?"

My breathing feels spiky all of a sudden. I mean, yes, she can trust me in *that* way—I won't tell anyone else. But I haven't been truthful with her. But what am I supposed to say? *Nope, you can't trust me. Sorry. Want to choose a radio station?*

"Yes," I say before the silence goes on too long. "Of course you can."

She smiles. "When I was really little, and my dad and step-mom first got married, I had a crush on Elijah."

"Your stepbrother?" I say. "Gross."

"I know, right?" she says, laughing. I like it a lot better when she laughs than when she cries. "I think he was the first crush I ever had. I was four and drawing family pictures that looked more like misshapen balloons than people, and he was seven and sculpting perfect likenesses of our dog Tito. His room was filled with real art supplies, and I would just sit in the doorway and watch him work for hours. Witnessing his art take shape was like seeing into his thoughts. And something about that fascinated me." She laughs again. "Plus, I liked his blond hair and dark brown skin. I'd never seen anyone like him before."

"Does *he* know about this?"

"No way! I'd never hear the end of it. It only lasted a couple of months at the most. By the time I was five, he was officially in the brother-only column." She looks over at me. "Repeat that and you're dead."

I do some sort of made-up hand signal, grinning. "Your secret's safe with me. Scout's honor."

"*You* were a boy scout?"

I give her a look. "Hell no. I was way too cool for that shit."

That makes her laugh again.

We pull up in front of her house, and I flick off the ignition and turn in my seat to face her. "You gonna be okay?"

"Yeah. After this year, I won't have to see any of these people ever again, right?"

"Right. Call me if you need anything, okay?"

"Thanks, Ryden." Joni leans toward me, and for a split second, I think she's going to kiss me again. And for an even smaller fraction of a second, I think maybe I *want* her to. But her head veers to the side, and she gives me a quick peck on the cheek. I breathe out in relief. Yes. Much better.

"See you tomorrow."

"Yeah," I say. "See ya."

Chapter 20

The rest of the week goes by pretty problem-less, now that we've figured out the whole day care routine. Alan's been picking up Hope after school, and I haven't been late to practice. Coach seems relieved I've gotten my shit together.

Now that school's in full swing and I'm getting piles of work thrown my way, I'm beginning to understand what my mom meant about school being harder when you have a crapload of other responsibilities—not that I would admit that to her. I'm only managing to get about half my homework done, and a couple of times, I've been called out by a teacher for dozing in class. But it's not too bad. For the most part, my teachers are going easy on me, giving me extra time to complete assignments and not calling on me except for when I have my hand raised. I know it's because they feel sorry for me, but hey, I'll take it. My economics teacher, Mrs. Schonhorn, is being especially awesome and told me that as long as I come to class and don't sleep, I'll get full participation credit. Plus, she excused me from the field trip to the Concord Chamber of Commerce, which was a total fucking godsend.

Joni is doing way better too. She's still shaken about the

rumors, obviously, but there hasn't been any more crying at work. On Thursday, she even brings me a pumpkin cheesecake that she baked *herself*.

"For being you," she says, and I feel another stab of guilt. You know, 'cause I'm not *actually* being me around her. Not really.

"Joni…" I begin. I want to tell her the truth. I want to invite her over to hang out at my house so we can share the cake. I want her to meet my mom and Hope and know everything there is to know about my crazy, fucked-up life. But then she'd know I lied to her, and that would make me the same as her dickwad ex-boyfriend and her stupid friends.

"What's up?" she asks.

Nope. Can't tell her.

"Thanks for the cake," I say. "Looks amazing."

I'm going to suggest to Mom that we have the cake after dinner on Friday, but when I get home from the game (the one where all I did was sit on the sidelines and watch ball after ball get past the depressingly incompetent backup goal-keeper), she's dressed in her skinny jeans and high-heeled boots. She only wears the skinny jeans on special occasions—she says she'd rather breathe than look hot. But I guess that's not the case tonight.

"Date?" I ask, taking the cake out of the fridge.

"Actually, yeah." She's smiling.

"Where you going?"

"Dinner. Drinks. Maybe back to his place." She winks.

I really don't need to hear that. "Have fun," I say.

• • •

So it's just me and Hope and a giant pumpkin cheesecake.

This is too depressing.

I grab my phone and call Alan. "Wanna come over?"

"Why, your mom can't watch Hope?"

"What are you talking about? *I'm* watching Hope."

"Oh." A pause. "So you don't need a babysitter?"

"No. I just wanted to see if you want to hang out."

"Really?" he asks. "Like, as friends?"

"Dude, you're starting to make me regret calling you at all."

Alan laughs. "Yeah, I'll be over in a few."

"Cool." I hang up and call Mabel. "I know you're probably busy," I tell her, "but Alan's coming over to hang out if you want to join us. Hope will be here."

"Sounds awesome," she says. "I'll bring wine."

"Where you gonna get wine?"

"Um, have you *met* my dad? We've got it stockpiled in the garage."

A half hour later, Alan, Mabel, and I are sitting around the kitchen table, drinking wine and eating pumpkin cheesecake. Well, Alan and I are eating the cake. Mabel had a tiny slice and claimed to be full. Hope's in her swing in the middle of the kitchen.

"No more updates on the journal search?" Mabel asks, pouring herself a second glass.

I shake my head.

"That's 'cause they don't exist," she says.

"I'd have to agree," Alan says through a mouthful of cake. "Where the hell did you get this cake from, anyway? It's glorious."

"A friend," I say. "But you're wrong—the journals are out there."

"You know, Ry," Alan says, his voice taking on a tone of *I'm about to say something genius, so listen up.* "There's this song by Eminem and Rihanna called 'Love the Way You Lie.' It's about domestic abuse, so not *entirely* applicable here, but there's this line where Eminem says he can't tell you what it really *is*. All he can do is tell you what it *feels* like."

I wait for him to start making sense. "And?"

"That's you, man. I think you're living a completely different version of Meg's life and death than the rest of us are. But it's real to you, because that's how it feels."

"I have no idea what you're talking about."

"Think about it—you're convinced there are two other journals that hold magical answers to everything."

"Not *everything*—just to tell me how to be a better father." Is that really too much to ask?

"Wait—you're trying to find the journals so you can be a *better dad*?"

I nod.

"But how? I mean, why? I mean...huh?"

I tell them how I know Hope hates me, and how I attempted to find Michael but failed miserably, and how I was hoping Meg would have left clues that would make this whole parenting thing click.

"For a smart guy, Ryden," Alan says, "you're being pretty moronic."

"Dude. Not cool."

"Don't you think the way to do a good job with Hope is to forget all this other stuff and just work on *being a good dad*?" He holds up his bracelet. "What would Sandra Oh do, man? You're focusing on the wrong thing."

"*You're* focusing on the wrong thing!" I down half the glass of wine in one gigantic swallow. "The checklists. They mean something. I don't know why you're ignoring them."

"Don't you think it's possible it was a note Meg wrote to remind herself of something? Or, like Mabel says, even if she did plan to leave behind two other books for us to find, that she got too sick to finish whatever it was she meant to do? Maybe *that's* the real truth."

I gulp the rest of my wine and pour more. "I knew her. I *know* she left those journals for us. It's the least we can do to find them."

"Just like you *know* you're responsible for her death?" Mabel asks, slurring her words a little.

I glare at her. "Yes. Exactly like that."

"Wait, *what*?" Alan asks, palms braced on the table.

"Oh, you didn't know?" Mabel says. "Ryden is convinced he killed Meg and ruined all our lives because he got her pregnant."

"That is such bullshit, man. That's exactly what I'm talking about. Your version is warped. You made her life *better* for that last year, not worse."

"Oh, totally," Mabel says. "Hey, Alan, remember how she got you to convince our parents to let her go out with Ryden in the first place? Didn't you get them to admit it would be good for her to do some normal high school stuff, and when they finally said yes, you casually slipped it in that it wasn't *you* she'd be doing that normal high school stuff with but Ryden?"

Alan laughs. "How badass was that?! That was some John Cho, Daniel Dae Kim shit right there."

"Most badass Korean ever," Mabel says, clinking glasses with him.

I really don't feel the need to join this conversation. I've heard this story before, and none of it matters now anyway. But Mabel and Alan don't seem to notice. They're drunk and haven't seen each other in a while apart from in passing at school, and they happily tra-la-la on their journey down memory lane.

I tune them out and focus on the wine in my glass. *Red wine* is totally a misnomer. It's not red. It's more like crimson. No, maroon. Or burgundy. Wait, isn't Burgundy a *kind* of wine? Is that what Ron Burgundy is named after? There are little swirly shapes floating in the top of the wine from the grease in my ChapStick. It looks like a solar system. Not our solar system. A different one.

"Ryden!"

I snap out of it and blink at Mabel. I think I'm drunk. "What?"

"Did you know Alan has a *girlfriend*?"

"Dude, you have a girlfriend? No more Lane-whoever? From that show?"

"She's not my girlfriend," Alan says quickly. "Not yet, anyway. So at the moment I am still Lane Kim. Virginal and tragic." He bangs his head lightly against the tabletop. "But I do like her. It's Aimee Nam—you know her? She's in our year."

"I don't think so. She's Korean?"

"Yeah, but that's not *why* I like her," he says all defensive-like.

"Yeah, sure," Mabel and I say at the exact same time. She fist-bumps me.

"No, really! Meg wasn't Korean, and I was in love with *her*, wasn't I?" Suddenly Alan's eyes get huge and he clamps his mouth shut.

"Whoa, dude. Back up," I say, holding up my hands. "When were you in *love* with Meg?"

"I already told you about this…" he says.

"You said you liked her in seventh grade and she turned you down."

"Yeah."

"So…?"

Alan exhales in a huff. His breath carries all the way across the table to me. It smells like wine. And pumpkin cheesecake. "So, okay, maybe it was more than 'like.' And maybe it was longer than seventh grade. But I don't think she knew. And it didn't last forever—by the time we hit sophomore year, I was completely over her. My self-preservation instincts kicked in."

I glare at him. I'm allowed to be mad that he was in love with my dead girlfriend before I knew her, right?

"Well, she might not have known you were in love with

her, but the rest of us sure as hell did," Mabel says as she opens another bottle.

"Shut up, Mabel. You did not," Alan says.

"Did so."

"Did—"

"All right, all right," I say. "Tell us about Aimee Nam."

"Dude, she's gorgeous. She looks like Yunjin Kim. She runs the yearbook staff. She wants me to join, but I watch Hope after school, so, you know, that wouldn't work."

I'm probably supposed to say, *Oh, that's cool, man. You don't have to watch Hope anymore. Live long and prosper.* But there's no way. I need Alan to watch her after school. He's the sole bridge connecting me and UCLA.

"But you like hanging out with Hope, right? Because she makes you feel close to Meg? Isn't that what you said?" I know I'm a dick for playing that card. But right now, I don't really care.

"Yeah." He looks over at Hope, sleeping in her swing. "You're not wrong about that."

We drink the rest of the wine (four bottles total…we're *wrecked*), and Alan and I eat the rest of the cake and decide that wasn't enough, so we order a pizza.

My mom comes home Saturday morning to find us sprawled across the living room, surrounded by empty wine glasses and a half box of congealing pizza.

"Looks like you guys had a fun night," she says. She doesn't sound thrilled, but she doesn't sound super mad either.

"Yeah. You too," I mumble into the throw pillow I was

sleeping on. Nothing like seeing your mom come home at eight in the morning on a Saturday in the same clothes she left the house in the night before. I have a sudden vision of me and Hope in a frighteningly similar situation seventeen years from now. Ugh.

Mom smiles. "Most fun I've had in years."

"Glad to hear it. Love you."

"Love you too, buddy."

And I close my eyes again.

Chapter 21

Shoshanna was *pissed* on Friday when she found out she couldn't cheer my name because I was on a one-game suspension. She was more pissed when Addison beat our pathetic asses by six goals. And she was even *more* pissed when I told her I wasn't going to her postgame party. But by Monday morning, it's like she's forgotten about all that.

She meets me at my locker, smiling and upbeat, her cheek painted with a sparkly blue *#1*. She holds out a cookie tin.

"You know there's no game today, right?" I stash my gym bag in my locker and pull out a couple of books.

"I know that, silly," she says, bouncing on the balls of her feet, her ponytail swinging back and forth behind her. Even her eyelashes are glittery. "Today is the first day of a brand-new week, and as your cheerleader, it's my job to make sure you're pumped and ready to kick some Clinton Central ass come Friday."

"Actually, that's kinda *my* job," I say.

"Every little bit helps, Ryden." She hands me the cookie tin.

"What's this?"

"Brownies. Happy Monday!" She rises to her tippy toes, gives me a quick kiss on the cheek, and goes to class.

What is it with girls giving me food lately? Am I emitting some sort of "feed me" signal on a frequency only women can hear?

In homeroom, I try one of the brownies. They're pretty good. But not nearly as good as the stuff Joni's given me. I never thought I'd say this, but I'd take Joni's dad's vegetarian empanada over one of Shoshanna's brownies any day.

I pass the tin around homeroom, and by the time it gets back to me, it's empty.

Shoshanna's little Monday Morning Cheerleader Surprise did get me thinking though…

At work that afternoon, I locate Joni in the bread aisle, restocking the pumpernickel and cinnamon raisin.

"Wassup, homie?" she asks. She's wearing a tank top that has a picture of the Spice Girls on it. I think she's wearing it ironically, but you can never be sure with her. One of her earrings is in the shape of a question mark. The other is an exclamation point. I guess the stud in her nose could be considered a period.

"Hey."

She holds up a bag of bread with a grin. "Look, this is your bread."

I glance at the loaf and then back at her, trying to figure out what the hell she's talking about. "Huh?"

She points to the writing on the package. "Rye bread. See? *Ry* bread? Your name is Ry. This is your bread."

I shake my head. "You do realize you're nuts, right?"

She points to a different loaf of bread with a dorky grin.

It's banana nut bread. Nuts for the nut. I roll my eyes, and she laughs and shelves the package of rye. "Yeah, so I've been told."

"Good. As long as you're aware, then it won't be too much of a surprise when someone finally has you committed."

"Noted."

"So we're playing Clinton Central on Friday," I say. "It's an away game, so we'll be on your home turf. Want to come?"

Joni purses her lips. "I don't know, Ryden. I'm trying to stay away from school-oriented social events. It's bad enough I have to spend all day with a building full of people who know every embarrassing detail of my life. Spending after hours with them too? Not so much."

I nod. "Makes sense. Okay, well, just thought I'd ask."

I walk away but feel her eyes on my back right up until the moment I round the corner.

Chapter 22

As the scout's visit looms closer and the promise of UCLA grows clearer, the possibility that I might not find the other journals before leaving town next year starts to become real. I feel myself panicking just a little more each day.

My house and Alan's house have been completely scoured from top to bottom. I'm clearly not able to search Meg's house, but Mabel swears she's looked and looked and there's nothing else, and I've even been to the storage unit a couple of days this week before dropping Hope at day care, just to check again.

Meg didn't really have any other friends besides Alan, and her aunts and uncles and cousins are all scattered around the country, so there's no one else I can think of who she would have left the journals with. But they've got to be *somewhere*, goddammit.

On Thursday, I skip lunch and drive to Meg's oncologist. He's the only other person who she saw on a regular basis during those last months. Yeah, I'll admit it: we've gone way past desperate.

I try to ignore the waiting room full of sick-looking people and explain to the receptionist that I need to see Dr. Maldonado.

"Do you have an appointment?" she asks.

"No. I don't have canc—I mean, I'm not here for anything medical. I just need to talk to him for a couple of minutes."

She studies me over the top of her glasses. "What is this in reference to?"

"That's private."

"Well, I'm sorry, sir, but I can't let you in to see the doctor without a reason. He's very busy." She leans back in her chair and crosses her arms as if she's a bouncer at a club.

I run my hand through my hair. "Fine. It's about Meg Reynolds. Can you tell him that, please? He'll know who she is." I nod to the phone. The sooner she calls the doctor, the sooner I'll leave her the hell alone.

Her face gets softer. "Meg Reynolds? My goodness, I never thought I'd hear that name again. We miss her so much around here. Were you a friend of hers?"

She looks at me so kindly, one side of her mouth turned up in a half smile brought on by some memory, and I suddenly don't want to tell her who I am. Clearly this woman liked Meg—loved her even. I can't tell her I'm the guy who single-handedly brought on her demise.

"Yeah, we were friends," I say. "I'm…uh…Alan." I clear my throat. "Can I speak with the doctor for a minute or two? I promise it won't take long."

She nods. "Of course, dear. Have a seat. I'll call you in as soon as he's finished with his current patient."

Twenty minutes later, I'm following the receptionist down a small corridor and into an office. Meg's doctor—I assume he was Meg's doctor; I've never actually met him before—is sitting at his desk, typing away. He's an older guy, but really well put together, with slicked-to-the-side white hair, a close shave, and a perfectly knotted tie.

"Dr. Maldonado, this is Alan," the receptionist says and then leaves us.

Dr. Maldonado looks up. "Have a seat, young man. I hear you were a friend of Megan Reynolds."

"Yeah. I mean, yes, sir."

He nods thoughtfully. "Such a bright young woman, she was."

"Yes."

"What can I do for you, son?"

Son? I've never been called that by anyone before. Not even my mom. It's weird as fuck. "I…um…well, I know this is kind of strange, but I was wondering…did Meg ever leave a journal here? It would have been a regular, one-subject notebook."

Dr. Maldonado thinks for a minute. "I do recall her carrying around a notebook or two. But I don't think she ever left anything here." He picks up his phone and pushes a button. "Ann, did Megan Reynolds ever leave a notebook here that you know of?" There are a few seconds of silence and then he says, "Thanks," and hangs up. "I'm sorry, Alan, there's nothing here."

I nod and stand. It was a long shot. I knew that going in. "Thank you, sir." I hold out my hand and he shakes it. "And thank you for…taking care of her."

"Of course, son. That's my job."

I'm halfway out the door when a thought hits me. I turn back. "Um, Dr. Maldonado?"

"Yes?"

"Would Meg have lived? You know, if she hadn't gotten pregnant and didn't have to stop her chemotherapy? Would she have gotten better?"

The doctor's lips press into a thin line. It's the first sign I've seen that this guy is ever anything but cool, calm, and in control. "I'm afraid I'm unable to discuss specifics of my patients' cases."

Oh, come on.

"But I'm her…best friend. And she's gone. What difference does it make now?"

"I'm sorry. Even after death, I'm still bound by a confidentiality clause." His fingers are steepled under his nose, and he looks at me with apology in his eyes.

I nod and move to leave. My shoulders feel like they're weighted with all the boxes in Meg's storage unit.

"Alan."

I turn.

He sighs and lowers his voice. There's no way anyone outside the office would be able to hear him. *I* can barely hear him. "Her cancer was very advanced."

That's not really an answer to my question, but it seems like he's okay with breaking the rules now, so I ask another one. "But you wanted to keep doing the treatment? Before she got pregnant, I mean?"

"Yes."

"So that means you thought there was a chance it could work, right? It wasn't completely hopeless?"

He looks at me, his gaze clear. "There was a chance, yes. A small chance. But a chance."

"That's all I needed to know."

Chapter 23

It feels good to finally be back on the soccer pitch, playing in an actual game.

The air is a little bit cool, the lights are a little bit warm, the crowd is wild, and I am on fire. I feel like Spider-Man, anticipating every shot before it comes my way, knowing where the ball is going even before the kicker does. I block each goal attempt like it's nothing, like the goal is the size of a Whole Foods shopping basket.

I briefly wish the UCLA recruiter were at this game to see me play, but next week's is going to be even better, on our home turf, with everyone in the stands cheering my name. This week is only the warm-up.

A huge grin splits my face as the buzzer sounds, indicating game over. Downey Pumas: 2, Clinton Central Pioneers: 0. I run out to the middle of the field to join my teammates in the celebration. They meet me in a frenzy of hugging and cheering and jumping up and down, and I pull my shirt off and swing it around over my head, screaming along with the crowd. After we shake hands with the other team (*losers*) and get a verbal pat on the back from Coach, half the team runs to the sidelines to make out with their cheerleader girlfriends. Dave and Shoshanna are the worst—she leaps up on him and wraps her legs around his middle, practically shoving her tongue down his throat. His hands grip her ass, under her skirt.

I grab my water bottle and towel from the sidelines and am crossing the field on my way to the visitors' locker room when I hear my name. "Ryden!" It's a girl's voice. I look back at the cheerleaders. They're all occupied. So I shift my glance over to the stands, scanning the crowd for a familiar face. Who could it be? Some random girl from school? Mabel? My mom didn't come tonight, did she?

"Whole Foods boy!"

And then I see her—Joni. She's in the guest stands, a few rows back, waving and trying to get past all the celebrating Downey kids. I can't believe it. She came.

I toss my towel over my shoulder and run over to her. We meet at the bottom of the bleachers. Her face is red and flushed from the cool air, and she's got on a pair of purple earmuffs. She's grinning the grin I've seen on a million fans but never thought I'd see on her: the "holy shit, sports are fucking awesome, especially when your team wins" look.

"You're here," I say, unable to keep the dopey ass smile off my face.

"I wanted to see you play. I figured no one I know would see me if I sat on this side."

I glance around. No one's paying us any attention. "I think you're safe."

"Dude, you're crazy good," she says. "I mean, I don't know anything about soccer, but I know your job is to make sure the ball doesn't go into the net, right? And you, like, *really* did that."

I laugh. "You sound surprised."

She shakes her head. "That's not what I meant. I meant—"

"Joni," I say. "I know."

She nods quickly. "Okay. Good."

"It means a lot to me that you came tonight."

She looks up at me. Her nose ring glistens in the field lights. "It does?"

I hold her gaze. Why *does* it feel so good that she came to see me play? Why should it matter to me? "Yeah."

We stare at each other a minute longer. The sweat on the back of my neck is cooling, and I get a chill. I'm still shirtless, and it's not exactly warm out here. But the only movement I make is to shift my gaze from her eyes down to her lips. Her tongue darts out to moisten them, almost in anticipation...

"Brooks!" The sound of my name snaps me out of it. Most of the guys are already making their way to the locker room. Coach is waving me over, pointing at his watch. "Bus leaves in ten. Go hit the showers!"

I look back to Joni. The stands are a lot emptier now, the sounds of cheering Downey fans and rowdy, drunk, grumbling Clinton Central fans fading in whatever direction the party is at.

"I should be getting home anyway," she says. "See you at work tomorrow?"

"Yeah."

She turns to go, and I know I should let her. That would be the right thing to do, the fair thing to do. But then my hand is shooting out and grabbing her wrist. She turns. I catch a fleeting glimpse of her confusion before I pull her to me and press my lips against hers. She melts into me, as if her body was ready, even if her mind wasn't expecting it at all. I feel exactly the same way.

I know I must taste like sweat, and I'm certain I don't smell awesome, but Joni doesn't seem to care. As our mouths move together, our tongues tangling, she reaches up and gently pulls the rubber band from my hair, slipping it around her wrist and threading both her hands through my damp, sweaty, knotty hair. It feels so good I actually let out an involuntary groan and pull her closer.

"Brooks!" Coach calls out again. "Hate to interrupt, Casanova, but we've got to *go*."

Unlike the last time Joni and I kissed, I don't want to stop. I want to stay here forever, to lose myself in her soft, sugary, sexy-as-all-hell Joni world.

But I pull away. "I have to go," I whisper.

She nods, her hands still playing with the hair at the back of my neck. "I know."

"I'll see you tomorrow."

"You better."

• • •

Since I was too late getting to the locker rooms to shower, that's the first thing I do when I get home. Tonight must be my lucky night, because Mom and Hope are asleep on the couch when I get home, a movie flickering away on the TV. I sneak past them and go straight to the bathroom.

I think of Joni the entire time I'm in the shower.

The taste of her mouth, the confident possessiveness of her tongue, the way she rubbed her body against mine as we kissed.

I wonder what she looks like naked.

I wonder what else that tongue of hers can do…

• • •

I barely sleep that night.

After my, um, *shower*, my head is a little clearer.

What do I do when I see her at work tomorrow? We can't just pick up where we left off. Of course we can't. Nothing has changed. Meg is still dead. It's still my fault. I still miss her more than I could have thought possible. I still *love* her more than I could have thought possible.

Joni doesn't even know me. I've been lying to her the whole time.

Kissing her was amazing, yes, and she's incredibly beautiful, yes, but we're still just friends. That's all I want us to be. I'm not ready for anything else. Fuck. I have to tell her that.

She'll probably hate me when I do. She has every right to,

after the way I've been dicking her around. So maybe we won't end up being friends at all.

Which is good, I guess, because damn if I don't keep thinking about her in a very *non-friend* kind of way.

Chapter 24

I punch in at ten a.m. and take a deep breath, psyching myself up to go find Joni and put an end to whatever started last night.

But before I can even put my hand on the break room doorknob, the door swings open, and she steps inside and closes it behind her.

She's wearing black jeans, huge, chunky boots, a black tank top, and a blue belt. Her lips are bright red and her hair is falling over one eye. She looks like some sort of futuristic, ass-kicking warrior.

"Hey," she whispers, taking a step toward me.

"Hey back," I hear myself say, suddenly glad there's no one else in the break room.

Dude. No. Wake the fuck up. I have a plan. A speech, actually. It starts with, "Joni, thank you for coming to my game last night," and ends with, "And that's why it's best if we are just friends." But I can't for the life of me remember the middle part.

Just friends? Force myself to be around her all the time, staring at that body, watching those lips, laughing at whatever happy-making thing she's saying or doing, but no more kissing? No chance for anything else? *Jesus Christ, man, haven't you been through enough torture?*

"Well…" she says, blowing her hair out of her eye. Her lower lip juts out a little with the motion, and next thing I know, that lip is between my own, and I have Joni pressed up against the wall next to the break room door. She matches my intensity point-for-point, and our hands are *everywhere*. I know she feels my boner pressing against her hip, but I'm too lost in her to be embarrassed.

Joni runs her hands through my hair like she did last night, and it feels so good, like her fingertips are working delicious magic and pushing all the negative energy out through the ends of my hair.

She tastes like Skittles today.

We break apart for air but hold each other's gazes, breathing heavily.

I hook a finger into her belt loop and pull her hips close to mine while one of my other fingers traces the line where the top of her pants meets the bottom of her shirt. I graze her stomach skin, but she doesn't flinch. Doesn't move away. Doesn't react at all, really. She just stares into my eyes, trusting, almost challenging, as if she's waiting to see what I'll do next.

I take that challenge.

I turn my hand so my palm is flat against her stomach, my fingers pointing down, and inch them slowly, meeting the top of her jeans and plunging farther, underneath the fabric. The farther down my hand travels, the more labored Joni's breathing becomes—her chest is rising and falling visibly now.

But I don't stop.

I can't believe this is happening. At work. At all.

She's so fucking sexy. How did I not see it from day one?

Joni makes everything better.

She makes it easy to forget.

I close the gap between us and kiss her with everything I have. Everything the old Ryden had. Everything I had no idea was still in me. She wraps her arms around me, slipping her tongue into my mouth, hitching one leg around my ass as I loosen her belt and undo the button of her jeans for easier access. My breath catches as the tips of my fingers hit the point of no return and Joni lets out a soft, encouraging moan.

And then the door swings open, hitting my back, making me lose my balance and stumble into her, which of course makes her lose *her* footing, since she was standing on one leg to begin with. I catch a glimpse of her horror and panic as she turns toward the corner to right her clothing. I can't ask her if she's okay because I need to deal with the fucker who just interrupted the best damn moment I've had in months.

Some dude from the seafood department walks to the fridge, looking at us over his shoulder, eyebrows raised, a smart-ass, know-it-all grin on his stupid face.

I don't know what exactly he saw, but this isn't good. I need this job. I can't get fired. "Oh, hey, man," I say as coolly as I can. I shove my hands in my pockets in an attempt to hide the evidence of what we were just doing. "We were, uh…I was checking Joni for ticks. She…went camping last night. Lyme disease is serious stuff, ya know? Can never be too careful." God, I'm a fucking loser.

The seafood guy grabs an iced tea from the fridge and heads back to the door, shaking his head and chuckling. "Whatever, man." He leans in close as he passes. "Nice work." He holds his hand out for a fist bump, which I return after a few seconds. Anything to get him out of here. "Your secret's safe with me." He winks and leaves.

I turn back to Joni. She's leaning against the wall, arms crossed, all traces of her earlier daringness gone.

I gently put my hands on her shoulders. "Are you okay?"

She nods, staring at the floor. "I'm fine."

"Are you sure? You don't look fine. Don't worry—he's not going to tell anyone. I don't think he saw much anyway."

"I don't know what I was thinking, climbing all over you like that here, where anyone could walk in at any time. After everything that's been going on at school, why the hell would I invite that same shit into the place where I work?" Her voice is hard.

She's right. I shouldn't have let it go as far as it did, especially knowing what she's been through lately. "I'm sorry, Joni."

Finally she looks up at me. "Don't be sorry. It's my fault as much as yours. We got carried away. We just can't let it happen again."

I drop my hands and take a tiny step back. "Yeah. Carried

away. Totally." *So she doesn't want it to happen again.* Okay, yeah. That's probably better. That's what I wanted—want—anyway. Clean break. Mutual agreement. Couldn't have worked out more perfectly.

I take a couple more steps backward and am about to head out the door when her voice stops me.

"We'll have to stick to more private places from now on. Bedrooms and the like." She smiles, and her eyes show some of that fire again.

Oh thank God.

Chapter 25

I can't stop thinking about her.

I also can't stop thinking about how the "her" is a different "her" than it should be. I don't know what I think or what I feel or what's right or wrong.

So I take the easiest, smoothest, straightest road. Which, okay, are usually the roads that lead you straight to danger. But how much worse could it possibly get?

Sunday afternoon, I drop Hope at Alan's. Mom knows it's my day off from work, and I know better than to ask her to be on grandma duty. Last thing I need right now is a "you're her father" lecture. But Alan doesn't know my work schedule, and what Alan doesn't know won't hurt him. Hope will be happier spending the day with him anyway.

I tell Alan I'll pick her up by six and speed toward Clinton as fast as the Sable will take me.

If this were some stupid, teenage, romantic comedy, I would be pulled over by the cops, and they would have mustaches and mirrored sunglasses, and they'd demand to know why I was in such a rush.

"I'm going to see a girl, officers."

"A girl*friend*?" they would ask, giving each other a knowing we-were-young-once smirk.

"I…I don't know, sirs."

"Well, do you *want* her to be your girlfriend?"

"I don't know."

"Well, do you *love* her?"

"I don't think so, sirs."

"Then you better keep it in your pants. No good can come of this."

"I know, officers. You're right. You're absolutely right. But I can't seem to stop myself. Any advice?"

"Who do you think we are? Some sort of psychiatrists? You need professional help, boy. Now turn that car around and go along home."

I press harder on the gas and make it to Clinton in record time.

Joni and Elijah are in the garage. She's sitting Indian style, elbows on her knees, chin in her palms, on an overturned garbage can. He's painting a portrait of her. It's all shades of black and white and gray. It's not anywhere near done yet, but he's already managed to capture her aura of awesome.

I glance at Elijah. I'm pretty sure he's what most girls would consider hot. His blond dreads are tied back from his face with some sort of leather shoelace, his arms are covered in tattoos—artsy ones he probably designed himself, not the lame generic ones you pick off a wall—and he's built. He must lift. No one gets like that by flinging around a paintbrush.

Joni admitted she used to have a crush on him. I know

it was when she was really little and he wasn't her *brother* yet, but…they're not *actually* related. I wonder if there's any part of her that still likes him that way. I hate the idea. And I hate that I hate it. I am *not* going to become too attached to this girl. I like her, sure, and kissing her is amazing, but I know there are levels of *like*. And this isn't going to get past a simmer.

Joni's eyes flicker to where I'm standing off to the side of the garage, and her face lights up. She hops off the garbage can.

"Heya," she says, skipping over to me. She stops about a half foot away.

"Hey."

"You remember Elijah, right?"

"Yeah. What's up, man?"

Elijah doesn't take his eyes off his painting. "Hi, Ryden," he says as his brush flicks across the canvas.

Huh. I don't think I told him my name the last time I was here. Joni must have told him about me.

"Joni, can you sit for me again tonight?"

"Sure thing." She grabs my hand and leads me into the house. It's quiet.

"Where is everybody?"

"My parents took the kids to the water park. We're all alone." She smiles and pushes open the door to her magic room.

God, I love this place. It immediately calms the jitters from my mad dash over here.

I sit down in the middle of the AstroTurf floor and lie back, staring up at the sky beyond the glass ceiling. I take a few long, deep breaths, letting the magic seep into me.

"You okay?" Joni asks quietly, lying down next to me.

"Yeah."

She gently rests her hand on mine. "Anything you want to talk about?"

I turn my head and find my face just a couple of inches from hers. "No. Definitely not. No talking." And I make those two inches of space disappear.

She responds, pulling me on top of her, wrapping her legs around me. Her lips feel like they were made to be on mine. I would be completely happy to kiss her forever.

But Joni clearly has other ideas, and her hands travel slowly but determinedly down toward the fly of my jeans. The second her hands graze me down there, all reason dissipates and all romantic notions of simply kissing fade away into Washington Square Park. I want her. Right now, I actually think I might need her.

At least I remembered to bring a condom this time.

Chapter 26

I bury my face in Joni's hair, inhale deeply, and chuckle to myself.
"What's so funny?" she asks, lifting her head from my sweaty chest and looking at me.

"When I first met you, I thought you were gay."

Joni laughs. "You did? Why?"

"'Cause of your hair."

She nods, mock seriously. "Short hair on a girl means she's a lesbian. I see. In that case, what does long hair on a boy mean?" She lifts a few strands of my hair and raises an eyebrow.

This time I'm the one to laugh. "Shut up." I roll on top of her again and show her exactly how not-gay I am.

• • •

The sun is low in the sky, and I trace the patterns the warm light shining through the blinds makes on Joni's skin. When I get down to her hip, my hands linger on her tattoo. Now that we've seen every inch of each other, she can't keep it a secret anymore. It's a tiny unicorn next to her right hip bone.

She sighs. "You know my secret."

I smile. "Yup."

"Are you going to tell me yours?"

My hand halts and my heart jumps. "What do you mean?"

She brushes her finger against my eyebrow scar. *Oh. Right. That.* "I told you—it was a soccer injury."

Joni lets out her frustration in a growl and takes my lower lip between her teeth, nipping gently.

"Come here," I say, pulling her to standing and leading her over to her big, white bed. "The AstroTurf is badass, but not exactly conducive to rolling around naked, you know?"

I sit on the bed and Joni climbs into my lap. She doesn't seem self-conscious about being naked in front of me at all. Not that she has anything to feel self-conscious about.

"Conducive," she says. "Nice. I love when you use words like that."

"Why?"

"It's…unexpected, coming from you."

"Why?" I ask again. For a conversation about my vocab, I sure am at a loss for words.

"Um, because of the way you look?" Joni says, like, *duh.*

"What do you mean?"

"Look at yourself, Ryden. You're sex on a stick. Even that mysterious scar across your eyebrow makes you hotter."

I stare at her. "I mean, yeah, I've been told that girls find me attractive—"

Joni shakes her head. "It goes way beyond 'attractive.' I bet my *dad* would have sex with you."

"Um. Thanks?"

"My point is, with all of *this* going on"—she waves a hand around my face and body—"plus the whole jock thing, people don't expect you to be smart too. So when you bust out the million-dollar SAT words, it's kind of a shock."

"I'm not nearly as smart as M—" I stop myself. Shit. I was just going to say Meg. "As some of my friends." Jesus. That could have been bad. Even if I didn't go into the whole story, Joni would still want to know who Meg is and why the hell I was bringing up my ex-girlfriend five minutes after we had sex for the second time. Amazing, super hot sex. During which I did not once think about Meg. Actually, now that I think about it, since things turned the corner with Joni, the gaps between my obsessing-about-Meg stints seem to have been lengthening. So why *was* I about to bring her up?

Great. Now all I can think about is Meg. Is she watching me right now? Does she hate me for having sex with someone else? Why don't I ever seem to know what the right thing is?

I hate you, brain.

"Well, I don't really care about your friends," Joni says, apparently having missed my mental moment. "I care about you. And you're going to get into UCLA, I know it."

I pull her closer and brush my lips across her forehead. "I care about you too."

And you know what? It's the truth.

• • •

The rest of the week is one of the best I've had in a really long time. Because of school and practice and work and Hope (though Joni doesn't know about that last factor), we don't get any more "bedroom" time. And we don't really talk on the phone much at night since Hope's always around then and Joni would probably want to know what's up with the crying baby in the background. But we text constantly, even during school, and spend all our work hours together, sneaking off to my car during breaks to make out.

It's like this one thing—being with Joni—has somehow started fixing all the other shit in my life too.

Practice has been awesome.

Shoshanna seemed satisfied with my level of enthusiasm for the shirt she wore to school with a *#1* on the back and an action shot of me blocking a goal on the front.

Alan introduced me to Aimee Nam as his *girlfriend*, and I was genuinely happy for him.

Ms. Genovese pulled me aside after AP U.S. history to thank me for participating in class more this week and to tell me if I keep up the good work, she doesn't see any reason why I wouldn't get a five on the AP exam at the end of the year.

My mom told me it's great to see me smiling again. And she had the hugest smile on *her* face when she said it.

I know it sounds crazy, but Hope hasn't been crying as much. She finally has one full tooth, right in the front, so maybe it's not hurting so much anymore? Whatever the reason, she's let me hold her a couple of times without putting up a fuss. And her little chubby fingers have been reaching toward my face more than they used to, like she's trying to tell me she wants me around.

I've been feeling good. Sturdy. Which is saying a lot. So of course I let my guard down.

Seriously, how is it that I've waded this far through waist-high shit and *still* haven't learned there's no such thing as a happy ending?

Chapter 27

Friday afternoon, I pick up Hope at day care and go straight home to rest before I have to be back on the field for the biggest game of my life. Coach confirmed the UCLA recruiter is in fact in town to watch me play, so all I have to do is put up a good showing—hopefully as good as last week's—and I'll be golden.

I actually manage to get in a half-hour nap, thanks to Hope's new cooperative attitude. I get up when my alarm goes off at five-fifteen, change Hope's diaper, and head into the kitchen to make her a bottle. Mom's there, stirring sauce into a pot of pasta.

"What's this?" I ask, swapping the baby for a bowl. She slides the baby harness over her chest and lowers Hope into it. "I thought you'd still be working."

"I cut out early today. Thought you might want to fuel up on carbs before the big game." She starts mixing some baby formula, and I plop into a kitchen chair.

I take a bite. God, I was really hungry. I take another. "Thanks, Mama," I say through a mouthful of food. "But I thought you didn't want me to go to UCLA anymore."

"It's not a matter of whether I want you to go or not, bud." She kisses Hope's little baby nose, and Hope giggles and squeals and waves her arms and legs around. "It's more complicated now. But that doesn't mean I don't want you to impress the pants off that recruiter."

"Mom. Gross."

She laughs. "You know what I mean."

"Yeah." I finish off the contents of the bowl and chug a bottle of water. "I gotta go. Have to be at school by six."

Mom nods. "Hey, I wanted to ask you if it's okay if I bring Declan tonight."

"Who the hell is Declan?"

"My boyfriend." She grabs Hope's hand and waltzes around the tiny kitchen.

"Whoa, whoa, whoa. First of all, since when is he your *boyfriend*?" Mom getting a boyfriend? Alan getting a girlfriend? The world is a strange and remarkable place. "Second of all, his name is *Declan*? What the hell kind of a name is that?"

"It's Irish, you doofus. What the hell kind of a name is *Ryden*?"

Good point. "A weird-ass name my weird-ass mother made up."

She sticks her tongue out at me. "And he hasn't been my boyfriend for very long, but I think he will be. And I want you to meet him."

I raise an eyebrow. "He knows about me?"

Mom rolls her eyes. "Obviously he knows about you if he's coming to your game tonight."

"And he knows about Hope?"

"He knows about Hope."

"And he's okay with it?"

Mom looks me dead in the eye. "I wouldn't be with someone who wasn't."

"All right, then I guess it's okay if he comes. Game starts at seven. You should get there early to get good seats."

"Thanks, bud. Is your, um, friend coming tonight too?"

"My, um, friend?"

Mom's suddenly super occupied with smoothing Hope's hair. Which is ridiculous, because her hair sticks up every which way no matter what. "The girl from work you've been spending time with."

I clear my throat. "Her name is Joni."

"Joni," Mom repeats, nodding.

"She has to work tonight, so no, she's not coming." That's true, though Joni wanted to switch her schedule so she could make the game. I told her not to, that I'd be too nervous with her there, that I'd call her after to let her know how it went. Which was code for, "No, don't come, 'cause if you do, you'll talk to my friends and find out everything I've been hiding from you, and that would be very, very bad."

"Bummer," Mom says.

"Yeah." It *is* a bummer. I would have liked Joni to be there. I always played better when I knew Meg was in the stands, watching. Oh well.

"Has she met Hope yet?"

"No."

"You going to bring her around here? She's welcome any-time, you know."

"I know." I nod. "Well, see you at the game. Love you."

"Love you too. Have fun."

• • •

On the drive to school, my phone keeps ringing, but it's in my gym bag in the backseat, so I ignore it. I pull into the parking lot and am getting my gear out of the car when I hear some-one call my name. Alan sprints toward me from the school's entrance, waving his arms.

"Jesus, man. What's wrong?" I ask as he reaches me. I sling my bag over my shoulder and start toward the locker room entrance on the side of the school.

"Ryden," he says, gasping a little but keeping stride with me. Poor guy needs to get more exercise. He sounds like my grandpa. "I've been looking everywhere for you. I called you, like, ten times."

"I was home, dude."

"I thought you had a game tonight."

"I do. Hence me being here now. What's wrong with you?"

"I found something," he says.

I stop. Only now do I notice the expression on his face—he looks kinda freaked out. "What? What did you find?"

He reaches into his backpack and pulls out a notebook.

Purple. Single subject. Pristine. There's a folded piece of paper taped to the cover.

Alan holds it out to me, but I can't take it. I can't seem to move at all. "What. Is. That."

"It's exactly what you think it is. Well, not exactly. It's different from the others. But it's definitely Meg's."

"But we looked everywhere!" I hate that my voice sounds frantic, but that's pretty much how I'm feeling. I've barely thought about the journals this week. Why did it have to appear now, when life was finally starting to make sense? When I finally stopped looking back and started looking forward? "Where did you find it?"

"It was in my old camping backpack, in the back of my closet. I was looking for a bag to bring to the game. Aimee's into sports, so I was going to pack us some snacks and hot chocolate and stuff and come with her tonight—" He stops when he realizes I don't give a shit about his romantic picnic with his girlfriend. "Anyway, this was in the bag."

"Did you read it?"

A pause. "Yes. But if I had known what it said, I never would have—"

"Does it have a checklist in the back?"

Alan thrusts the book toward me again. "Just take it, Ryden."

I still can't move my arm. I feel cold and hot and sick and sad and nervous and so, so mixed up. I don't trust my own eyes. It's easier to hear it from him. "Alan. Please. Does it have a checklist in the back?"

He nods once. "Yes."

I suck in a breath. "What's checked off?"

"*Mabel* and *Alan*."

I fucking *knew* it. Those two were sooooo sure the other journals didn't exist. But I knew Meg. I know Meg.

"Ryden…" Alan says, starting to look a little uncomfortable. "Please, take it. There are things in there…I'm sorry, man."

What? He's sorry? What does that mean?

I don't move, and he drops the book. It lands with a soft thud at my feet. Then he walks away almost dejectedly, the opposite of the frenzy he was when he first arrived.

When Alan's gone, my body starts to work again. I crouch and pick up the book, opening the note stuck to the cover.

Alan,

If you find this before Ryden has read the first journal, please don't give it to him. Only let him see this if he's already looking for it. You'll know what that means when the time comes.

Love always,

Meg

What the hell?

I'm about to tear open the book, but the parking lot is filling up, and there are more and more people walking past as it gets closer to game time. "Hey, Number One! Kick some ass tonight!" one guy says as he passes. I nod numbly and go inside. The halls are quiet and dark; it's a nice night out, so no one's taking the shortcut through school on their way to the field. I turn a few corners until I'm deep in the middle of the school, away from the people and the locker room, and I sit on the floor next to a water fountain.

I take a deep breath and flip quickly through the book. Sure enough,

- ☑ Mabel
- ☑ Alan
- ☐ Ryden

is written on the inside back cover. What catches me off guard is that most of the book is blank. There are only a few pages with writing on them, right at the beginning. Maybe Meg really did run out of time before she could finish it.

February 5.

Ten days before she died.

I've been thinking about calendars a lot lately. I used to fill them with school assignments and plans and college visits and application deadlines. Doctor appointments too. But now planning, dates, schedules mean nothing to me anymore. I only have two things left to do: give birth to my baby and die. And I think I can remember that easily enough. No need to write it down.

Now that I don't have many calendar boxes left to check off, I'm left wondering if the boxes I had were <u>full</u> enough. And every time, I come up with the same answer: yes.

I haven't written about this yet, maybe because I had to

get to this point in order to look back clearly. Or maybe I didn't want to risk anyone—Ryden especially—finding out while I was still healthy enough to get mad at. We've finally gotten back to <u>us</u> these last few months—no more fighting. It's been really nice. But I'm out of time. I have to write it down, otherwise no one will ever know, and it will be like it never happened. And it did happen. And I don't regret it one bit.

So here goes:

I got pregnant on purpose.

I'm sorry, what? *WHAT?!?*

There, I said it. Or wrote it. Whatever. Whoever's reading this, please don't hate me. Just listen. Or read, I guess.

I didn't even know if it would work, to be honest. I'd already done one round of chemo, and Dr. Maldonado said chemo can mess with your reproductive system. I wanted to try anyway. Because I knew when I got my diagnosis that I was going to die. Dr. Maldonado doesn't sugarcoat this stuff. The cancer was advanced. It had spread. The odds were not good. Yes, there was a small amount of shrinkage after the first round of chemo, but not enough to matter. It's my body, and I know it well. I've known from the beginning I was going to end up here, staring at an empty calendar. It sucks, but it's the truth.

I wanted to take the time I had and really do something

with it. I wanted to make my life matter, to leave behind a legacy. And after Alan said I should "live my life" that day in his room, it all clicked. I'm not an artist or a filmmaker or even a very good writer, but there was something I could create that would be important and make a difference in the world. A baby. I could use what was left of my life to give life to someone else. Like magic. And I actually had a boyfriend for the first time in my life. An amazing boyfriend who I wanted to be with on every possible level. It couldn't have been more perfect.

So we did it. We had sex. And then we did it a few more times. We never used a condom, because as far as Ryden knew, I was on the pill, though I've never taken the pill in my life.

Ryden would never talk to me again if he knew I got pregnant on purpose. He didn't want to keep the baby. I hate that I've been lying to him, but I can't lose him. I need him. I love him so much. And I love our baby so much, even though I haven't met her yet.

There are only three truly important things left in my life: My baby. Ryden. And the cancer. We're all so intertwined that I can't imagine any of them without the others.

Because even before the pregnancy, even before Ryden and I were together, he was part of it.

I liked him so much freshman and sophomore years that I couldn't concentrate. I could barely sleep. I didn't have an appetite. All I ever thought about was Ryden and how *utterly convinced I was that we were meant to be together. Even when I started feeling really terrible midway through sophomore year with the fatigue, the unexplained bruising, the constant feeling that I couldn't get enough air, Ryden was still the primary occupant of my thoughts.*

As this is the time for the truth, there's something else I want to get out there, something else I've never told anyone: while I sat there in that oversized chair during my first chemotherapy treatment, shivering and sick, I wondered if maybe I would have picked up on the warning signs earlier if I hadn't been so infatuated with Ryden. Turns out the symptoms of an unchecked melanoma that has metastasized to your liver, gallbladder, and kidneys are remarkably similar to those of lovelornness.

Would things have been different if I hadn't had a crush on him? Would I have noticed that the mole on my leg, the one that had been there as long as I could remember, had changed? Would I have gone to the doctor sooner? Would I be less sick now?

I don't have answers to these questions, and I never will.

But I don't care.

I got to be with the guy I love, against all the odds. And he loves me too. And I get to take all that love and energy and joy and pass it on to my daughter. My legacy.

Though I may not have many boxes left, the ones I have are pretty damn perfect.

Chapter 28

Pretty damn perfect?!" I slam the book against the face of the locker across from me. The sound of my voice reverberates down the empty hallway. I thrust my hands through my hair, pulling hard, feeling the skin of my scalp tugging away from my skull, and let out the longest, loudest scream I can.

Full sentences are beyond me right now. All I've got are words. Tiny phrases. Like my head is one giant keyword infographic.

On purpose.

Legacy.

Love.

Lying to him.

Need.

Perfect.

Symptoms.

Lovelornness.

Blame.

My fault.

Her fault.

On. Fucking. Purpose.

Oh God oh God oh God. I pace the dark hall like a crazy person, raking my hands down my face over and over again, trying to make sense of all this.

The funny thing is it *makes* sense. It makes perfect sense, actually. I can think clearly enough to know that if I weren't me, if I were some random person watching the movie of my life, I would get it. The picture is clear now. But it's not making the right kind of sense, the sense that's been in my head for the past year.

Here's what I knew for certain: this whole mess was my fault.

Here's what I know now: Meg believed that too, but not in the way I thought. And not in a way that makes me feel any better at all. She was so obsessed with me sophomore year that she didn't go to the doctor when she started getting sick? Her cancer got bad just because I fucking *existed*? Are you fucking kidding me? Why would she ever write that? Why would she leave it in a journal for Alan to find? How cruel could she possibly be?

I can't believe I used to *like* knowing that Meg had a crush on me before we got together. That was the first secret I learned from her journal, the green one before the checklists. Now I wish I didn't know any of it. I wish I'd never laid eyes on her notebooks.

And the pregnancy, the one thing I *knew* I was to blame for—turns out it wasn't my fault at all. Meg lied to me from day one. Used me, manipulated me, made me love her, let me fight for the abortion when she knew her decision all along, destroyed me just so she could leave something meaningful behind. *Seriously, are you fucking kidding me?*

Well, guess what you left behind, Meg? Nothing but misery and pain and regret.

I will hate you forever.

Chapter 29

M y phone's been going crazy. I sort of hear it ringing and beeping, but it's far away, like I've got on noise-canceling headphones.

It's not until someone slams their hand on the driver's side window of my car, right in my face, that the noise rushes in.

I blink at Dave through the glass. *Wait, how did I end up in my car? How much time has passed?* It's almost dark out now.

He tries the door handle. It's locked. "What are you doing? The game is about to start. You missed warm-up."

Oh shit. The game. The recruiter.

I should fling open the car door, change into my uniform, and book it to the field with Dave. Maybe that's what alternate-universe Ryden Brooks is doing right now. Or maybe he's already there, warming up, because he never met Meg Reynolds in the first place. But all I do is slowly rest my head on the steering wheel.

Why did I think the journals would actually contain good news? A cheat sheet of parenting tips? Really, Ryden? What the hell is wrong with you? You should have left well enough alone.

Dave pounds on the window again. "Ryden! What the f!"

Ha. Dave doesn't curse. Forgot about that. It's annoying. Sometimes a situation really calls for a *shit goddamn fuck motherfucker*, you know? Like right now, for example.

"Why is everything so hard?" I ask. I'm still face-to-steering-wheel, so I'm pretty much talking to my crotch, but I know Dave can hear me.

"What do you mean?" he asks, sounding a little less pissed off.

"Why does everything suck so bad? Even when you think it's getting better, it's not. Life's building up suckiness, getting ready to hit you again, at the worst possible moment."

"Dude." Dave's voice is way lower. I can barely hear him, so I lift my head and roll down the window a little. "Is this about Meg? I…uh…I've been meaning to tell you how sorry I am about…you know, for your loss—"

I hold up a hand to stop him. "Don't. Just don't, okay? I can't talk about this right now." *Not without breaking a few car windows and hand bones anyway.*

Dave nods, all relieved-like. "Well, I don't know what's going on, but you need to play, man. That recruiter is here to see *you*. Besides, we have no chance of winning without you."

The recruiter *is* here to see me. No one else, only me. And that's who I need to be thinking about now—me.

I squeeze my eyes shut for three seconds, promising myself that by the time I open them, I'll be ready to play. One. Two. Two and a half. Three.

I open my eyes.

Everything's the same as it was earlier today before I laid eyes on that godforsaken journal, I tell myself. Just because the *whys* have changed doesn't mean the *whats* have. Everything's fine.

Yeah right. Nice try, brain.

But I can still do this. I need to.

Don't let her win.

I unlock the door.

"Okay. Let's go." I throw on my uniform right there in the parking lot, right in front of the stragglers who are still making their way to the stands. At this point, I don't give a shit if people see me in my underwear. Dave and I break into a run.

The stands are completely packed with fans dressed in Puma blue and white, the lights are on, and the guys are out on the field, ready to start. Coach O'Toole is standing next to a middle-aged guy in a blue-and-gold jacket. *UCLA Bruins* is written on the back. Walter Paddock. I remember him from my visit to the school.

The energy of the place pushes into me. Yes. This is exactly where I need to be.

"Thanks, Dave," I say, clapping him on the back. He raises his eyebrows in a *good luck—you're going to need it* look and runs out onto the pitch.

Fuck luck. I don't need luck. This is soccer. I'm good at this.

Just don't think about her.

I approach the sidelines. "Coach," I say, trying desperately to clear my head. I secure my hair back in a rubber band and pull my socks up over my shin guards. "I'm sorry I'm late. I had a…family emergency."

Coach looks like he would love nothing more than to punch my lights out. But he knows how important this game is to me—he's got to know I wouldn't have been this late unless something major went down. You know, like finding out your dead girlfriend was a lying, selfish, cruel bitch.

Goddammit, Meg.

Don't. Think. About. It.

"Ryden, this is Walter Paddock, the head recruiter for the UCLA men's soccer team," Coach says simply, letting his eyes do the real talking. Even if I kill it tonight, I'll be lucky to see any more game time the rest of the season.

I shake Walter's hand. "Mr. Paddock, of course, I remember. Nice to see you again, sir. Thank you so much for coming all this way. My team is waiting for me, but I'd love to speak with you more after the game."

Walter nods enthusiastically. "Looking forward to it. And I'm looking forward to seeing more of what you can do out there in front of the goal. If your stats and game film are any indication, I'm in for quite a show tonight."

"Thank you, sir." I pull my gloves on and run out to rousing cheers.

"Wooooo! Go, Ryden! Number One forever!" Shoshanna shouts, waving her pom-poms and shaking her ass.

The ref flips the coin, and the Hornets win the toss. They choose their side, I head off to the goal, and the Pumas kick off. While the action is happening at the other end of the field, I let my attention drift toward the stands. Alan and Aimee are sitting toward the top of the bleachers, off to the left, huddled together under a blanket. Mom and I guess that's Declan—he looks like he belongs on the cover of one of Joni's romance novels with his dark hair, short beard, and leather jacket—are sitting along the halfway line down front. They're sitting as close to each other as Alan and Aimee, smiling like there's no place they'd rather be and no one they'd rather be with. Everyone's all coupled up and blissed out. *Don't get comfortable*, I want to shout at them. *It doesn't last forever.*

And then there's Hope. She's bundled in her hat and puffy jacket and propped up in Mom's lap, bouncing up and down as Mom jiggles her legs. Declan makes a stupid face at her, and she laughs and reaches out toward him, trying to grab his beard. She looks happy.

Out of nowhere, even though I look at Hope every day, it's like I'm seeing her for the first time.

Her face is almost perfectly round, except for a tiny little chin jutting out. She's got dimples on either side of her mouth, and the way her little eyebrows arch reminds me of the way my eyebrows look in my baby pictures—long before I got my scar.

Her hair is still like Meg's—dark and wild—but really, her face has changed so much in the months since she was born. She doesn't look as much like Meg anymore. She looks like me. The baby girl version of me.

Holy shit. It doesn't matter that Hope hasn't said "Daddy" yet—I'm a dad *already*. It's happening, with or without my permission and even though I don't have a single clue how to do it right. That kid is going to grow up and go to school and get into trouble and break bones and have her heart broken, and I'm going to be there for all of it.

Suddenly, the entire world is like an hourglass that's been flipped over, the sand running back through the narrow hole in the opposite direction as before.

It's not about what I did to Meg anymore. The journal made sure of that. It's about what *she* did to *me*.

She blamed me—not for her pregnancy, but for her cancer. By writing about it in her journal and leaving it where she knew someone would find it, she made sure I would feel that guilt forever. Even though *I didn't even know who she was* when she was diagnosed.

And because she blamed me, she felt I was hers to do whatever she wanted with. So she used me as an unwilling means to her own selfish end. She left me sad and alone and with a baby. She never thought what my life would be like once the baby was born and she was gone. She knew she *would* be gone, and she didn't even do me the courtesy of talking about it. She only thought about herself and how to fill her remaining calendar squares.

I didn't take her life away from her.

She took mine.

The ball whizzes past my head and into the net. I feel it and hear it, but I don't see it because I'm still watching Hope.

The crowd is on their feet and booing, waving at me to wake the fuck up.

I wrench my eyes back to the field in front of me, where all the players—from both teams—are just standing there, staring at me. I don't know what expression is on my face, but it must be pretty scary, because no one's coming over to talk to me, to find out why I didn't attempt to block that goal.

I make myself move, though I feel like I'm walking through a wall of thick, gooey plasma, and return the ball to the ref.

"You all right, Brooks?" he asks, low enough so that no one else hears.

"Yeah," I say. "Fine."

All this time, I've been trying to make the best of this awful situation, trying desperately to be a good father (and failing miserably), trying to reconcile my life now with the part I played in taking Meg's from her. And it turns out *I* was the one being played all along.

The ref returns the ball to the center of the field, and the Hornets kick off.

I try to get my head in the game, I really do. At least my feet aren't nailed to the ground anymore, but the rest of the half doesn't improve much. I manage to block one shot, but I let three others go by.

By the time halftime hits, the mood in the stands is somber, and my team won't talk to me. The only one who says anything is Shoshanna. "You're joking, right?" she bites out as I make my way to the sidelines, her hands on her hips, a dark scowl marring her beautiful face. I pretend I don't hear her.

I sit on the bench for the entire fifteen minutes, alone,

thinking, trying to regroup. I'm not confused anymore. Everything is more clear than it's been in months.

The fact that Coach hasn't pulled me out of the game yet means the recruiter is still here. The guy came all the way across the country to see me play, and Coach has to honor that, even though *no one* wants to watch me play right now.

I have to get my shit together. Show the recruiter what I can really do.

Don't let her win. Go to UCLA and prove your life is not *over.*

When halftime ends, I calmly get up and take my place at the opposite goal.

For the entirety of the second half, I do not look at the stands once. I do not think the M-word. I do not think the H-word. I don't even think about UCLA. The only thing I think about is BLOCKING THE FUCK OUT OF EVERY GOAL THE HORNETS ATTEMPT.

It's like therapy.

And it's even better than last week.

Gradually, the mood in the stands lifts. The cacophony of sounds coming from the crowd becomes higher pitched and more amped up. My moves become sharper. My name is chanted with rising enthusiasm each time I make a clutch save. My teammates start high-fiving me. My blood is pulsing with adrenaline and defiance.

Final score: 6–4 Pumas.

• • •

I head straight to Coach O'Toole and Walter Paddock like a man on a date with destiny.

Walter extends his hand. "I'm not sure what was going on in the first half, but boy am I glad I stuck around for the second. That was quite an impressive comeback, Ryden. I don't think I've ever seen anything quite like it."

"Thank you, sir. I know it's not an excuse, but I got some bad news right before I arrived tonight and it affected my game. But I'm glad I was able to pull it together and show you some of what I can do. And if you allow me to come play for you, I will bring one hundred and ten percent every single day."

Walter's glance cuts to Coach. Coach doesn't look nearly as happy as he should after winning a game like that. What am I missing?

Walter looks back at me. "Ryden." He says it in a way that sounds less like my name and a whole lot more like, *You might want to take a seat, young man. I'm afraid I have some more bad news.* "You're an excellent player, and UCLA would be honored to have your kind of talent on our team."

I hold my breath. "Thank you, sir."

"But Coach O'Toole here has filled me in on your…personal situation." He *what*? "I wish I had been informed before coming out here. In fact, I wish our department had been notified as soon as your situation changed." He looks kind of annoyed. "If this were just about your skill, it would be a much different story. But unfortunately, we cannot offer you a spot on the UCLA team at this time."

My head is on the verge of exploding. "If this is about the way I played in the first half, it was an extenuating circumstance," I manage to eke out. "Please, let me have another chance."

Walter shakes his head. "Division One athletics are an incredibly demanding commitment, Ryden. It's hard enough for our players to manage a healthy balance between academics and athletics. There's simply no way for someone to manage that while also being the primary parent to a young child. Which, it seems"—he looks at Coach O'Toole—"has already been proven during your season. Your coach said today is not the first time you've been late or distracted by personal issues. Plus, we require all our first-year athletes to live on campus, and the university does not offer family housing." He pauses and looks right in my eyes, like he really wants me to know how much he regrets having to tell me this. "Unless you've made some other arrangements? Will the child be staying with her grandparents during the academic year?" He sounds almost hopeful.

I glance at the stands, where Mom is still sitting with Hope and Declan. They look like a perfect little family. My throat suddenly feels swollen. If I left Hope with Mom—if Mom even agreed to it, I mean—they would be fine. But I can't. Whether I wanted it or not, I have a daughter now. And I'm not going to let her grow up with *no* parents.

I shake my head.

"Then I'm sorry," Walter says. "There's simply no way it could work." He gives a nod of acknowledgment to Coach and then walks away.

I stare at Coach. He looks uncomfortable, pursing his lips and shifting his weight from one foot to the other. "How could you do this?" I shout. "Do you realize you've just ruined everything?"

"I'm sorry, Brooks, but I had to tell him. Especially after you showed up late—again—and completely blew the first half of the game. I've kept quiet during my dealings with the UCLA recruitment office all summer because I'm expected to see my players off to good colleges. My job is on the line here too. But I could no longer in good conscience recommend you for his team without him knowing your situation. The truth is, you're distracted and your playing has suffered. That's the long and short of it, Brooks. I know you think things will be different once you get to college, but they won't. You'll be facing the same set of challenges you are now, constantly trying to find the time for everything and coming up short. Mr. Paddock needed to be informed. And since you clearly weren't going to tell him…" He drifts off. I know the rest.

"Don't even think about saying 'this hurts me more than it hurts you,'" I say, each word dripping with poison. "My life is none of your business. And you had no right to tell him anything about me."

Coach shakes his head sadly. "Then you shouldn't have put me in a position where I felt I had to."

"You know what, Coach? I quit."

I storm toward the locker room. It feels like it should be raining. Thunder, lightning, torrential downpours. Big, fat raindrops saturating every last inch of every last thing in the world with cold, clammy bleakness.

But it's not raining. The weather is perfectly crisp and dry and autumn-y, which means the number of things that make sense in my life is officially zero.

Mom and her boyfriend and Hope intercept my path. Mom gives me a one-armed squeeze. "You were awesome, Ry! What did the recruiter say?"

I just stare at her.

She must get the message that the news isn't good, because she quickly moves on to, "Ryden, this is Declan."

"Ryden, it's great to meet you." He holds his hand out to me, but I ignore it. Eventually he drops it. "I've heard a lot about you," he tries. "You're a hell of a goalkeeper, man."

I turn back to Mom without acknowledging his existence. Something inside of me is breaking. It's like hundreds of hairline fractures sprouted throughout my body when I read that purple journal—or maybe earlier than that, I don't know—and there's been more and more pressure placed on them throughout the night. I'm about to fall apart.

I wrap my arms around myself, trying to hold myself together a little bit longer. "She did it on purpose," I say to Mom.

Her eyes narrow. "Who?" she asks.

"You know who. I found the second journal today. She got pregnant on purpose. She did this to me on purpose. She—" My voice is dangerously shaky.

Mom hands the baby to Declan and is about to pull me

into her arms, but I know if I let her, I'll collapse into a million pieces. I step away. "I have to go."

"Where are you going?" Mom asks, worry written all over her.

I glance at the emptying stands, at Alan and Aimee and Dave and Shoshanna joining the mass exodus, working their way up toward the school, the locker room, the parking lot. "A party," I say. "Shoshanna's house."

Chapter 30

I need to get fucked up.

I push past the crowd at Shoshanna's already full house and make my way to the downstairs bathroom. It's where the keg is always kept, in a bathtub full of ice.

"What's up, Number One?" Matt Boyd asks as I enter the room. He's in there with a group of sophomore girls. One of them—a girl with feathers dangling from her earrings—hands me a cup. I help myself to a second and fill them both. "Awesome comeback tonight, dude."

I chug one beer and hold it out to be refilled as I down the second one.

"When do you hear from UCLA?" Matt asks.

"I heard," I say halfway through my third beer. "Not gonna happen."

"Oh, dude, that sucks. Well, you'll get in somewhere, man. I know Coach has other recruiters coming to watch some games later in the season."

My head is getting cloudy. The girls aren't joining in on the conversation. They stand there, pretending to be interested in everything we're saying.

"Nope. I'm done. I quit the team." I refill my cup again.

Matt gapes at me. "You *quit?*"

"Yup. Not playing for that asshole O'Toole ever again. I have absolutely no chance of playing D-One or going pro, so there's no point in sticking around. Like everyone keeps reminding me, I have *bigger responsibilities* now."

I leave the bathroom, full cups in my hands.

The whole downstairs is packed. You'd think coming to this same house after every single game would get old, but Shoshanna has made it something of a tradition. Her parents don't care, there is always more than enough beer, and her house is on this huge piece of property with no neighbors within hearing distance, so we can be as loud as we want. It's actually the perfect party situation.

I glide in a daze past couples making out and girls dancing in little groups and what appears to be a pretty intense game of flip cup and search for a place to sit down. All the couches are taken. I stop in front of a love seat where a guy from the JV soccer team is sitting with some girl I've never seen before. She's got braces and huge boobs.

"Hey, Ryden!" the guy says. I have no idea what his name is. "Great game tonight!"

"Up," I say, jerking my thumb over my shoulder.

He looks at the girl and back at me. "Uh. Okay." The two of them leave.

Nice to know I still have some power.

I collapse into the love seat and work on beers four and five.

Or is it five and six? Whatever it is, I'm not anywhere near drunk enough yet.

My phone buzzes with a text from Joni: How'd the game go???

I put the phone back in my pocket.

Time goes by, and it's like I'm in one of those movies where the guy's at a party but he's really depressed or on drugs and the camera is focused on him sitting, unmoving, staring at nothing, while the rest of the party happens in blurred fast motion around him.

I must ask someone to get me another drink at some point, because one minute my cups are empty, and the next they're full again.

I'm vaguely aware of people talking to me, sitting beside me, but I'm pretty sure whatever they have to say is not worth the energy it takes to engage. Because engaging equals effort and effort equals cognizance and cognizance equals pain.

Then Shoshanna comes over. She stands right in front of me and doesn't move until I make eye contact. Her eyes are glassy, her cheeks flushed with a boozy glow. But her lipstick and ponytail are as perfect as ever.

"This is a party, Ryden," she says. "The point is to have *fun*. So cheer the fuck up or go home."

"S-sorry, Sho," I slur. Hmm. Guess I'm drunker than I thought. Excellent.

She sighs and sits next to me, her thigh against mine. "Here." She hands me an orange Fanta bottle.

I shake my head. "That shit's gross."

She raises an eyebrow. "Just try it."

Whatever. I unscrew the cap and take a sip. The liquid bites my tongue and scorches the back of my throat. I look at Shoshanna. "Is this vodka?"

She smiles. "You know I don't like beer. But don't tell anyone—that's my parents' one rule: beer only. It's like they think there's a limit to how drunk beer can get you or something."

I laugh. "You know what? They might be right." I take another long swig of the vodka. It tastes better now that I'm prepared for it.

We sit there, sharing the "Fanta" until it's all gone and I'm wasted out of my mind. My face feels hot and cold at the same time, and my hands feel like they're made of pipe cleaners and putty. I move the empty bottle around in front of my face, trying to make my eyes focus. The conclusion of my very scientific experiment is that four inches away from my nose is the sweet spot. Any closer or farther and the bottle becomes a jumbled blob of orange.

Shoshanna rests her head on my shoulder and drapes a leg across my lap. Her hair smells like hair spray.

I run my putty hand over her leg. She's wearing a skirt, and I'm able to travel all the way to the top of her thigh without touching any fabric. When I get to the bottom of the skirt, I keep going, underneath, and cup her ass. She rolls into me so she's almost on my lap and presses her mouth to mine.

Oh yes. This is exactly what I need. The best feelings in the world, without having to feel anything emotional. Shoshanna's a nice person, but, you know, she's not someone I'll ever fall in love with. We make out like crazy people for a while, then Shoshanna grabs my hand and pulls me up off the love seat. "Come on." She leads me in the direction of her bedroom.

When we get there, she pulls her shirt over her head, pushes me down onto the bed, and crawls on top of me. It may not be very manly, but I'm perfectly okay with her taking the reins on this whole thing. My brain synapses are so delayed that it seems like it takes about a year for my body to respond to anything my brain tells it to do.

Shoshanna presses her body against me and kisses me again. "I've wanted this for so long, Ryden," she whispers against my lips. "I've missed you so much. I knew we'd get back here eventually."

She pulls my shirt off and unbuttons my jeans, leaving a trail of kisses down my chest, going farther and farther south. Good feelings. Only good feelings.

Her mouth is just at the top of my boxers when the door to her bedroom opens.

I don't look to see who it is. I don't care at this point. I'm so blasted the house could be on fire and the only thing I'd be able to focus on is the feel of Shoshanna's tongue on my skin.

"I can't freaking believe this," Dave says. I finally cut my eyes to the doorway. He's silhouetted in the dim light of the hallway so I can't see his face—and let's be honest, I wouldn't be able to focus on his face right now even if this place were lit up like Times Square. But his voice sounds pretty messed up.

Like, half heartbroken and half wasted and half pissed as all hell. Wait, I think that's too many halves.

"Dave, shit." Shoshanna climbs off me and puts her shirt back on. "I…we're really drunk. I'm sorry…I didn't mean…" She starts walking toward him, but he backs away.

"Oh, I'm pretty sure you knew exactly what you were doing, Shoshanna," he says. "I want to speak with Ryden."

I've managed to sit up, but it's the staying upright part that's giving me a problem. Forget about trying to put my shirt back on. Why are shirts so complicated, anyway? So many holes for your arms and your head.

"Dave, don't…" I hear Shoshanna say, but he pushes past her and marches over to me.

"Stand up," he commands.

"Uh…"

"Stand *up*, Ryden."

"Not…sure…I can," I say.

Dave sighs. "Fine." And he punches me. Actually *punches* me, right in the fucking face. My cheek explodes, and I fall back on the bed, clutching my face, but my putty hands aren't doing a damn thing to ease the pain.

"Dave!" Shoshanna screams and tries to pull him away.

"Get off me, Shoshanna. Ryden and I have some stuff to work out."

"Well, can you at least do it outside?" she asks. "Leave my poor room out of it!"

Gee, thanks for the support, Sho.

"Be out front in three minutes," Dave tells me.

The one eye that's not radiating in excruciating pain follows him out the door. Oh look, there's a crowd hovering around the door and in the hallway. Fantastic.

"You don't have to go out there, you know," Shoshanna whispers to me once he's gone. But the way she says it, I'm pretty sure she's all kinds of elated that two guys are fighting over her.

What she doesn't get is that we aren't fighting over her. Well, maybe Dave is, but I'm not.

My face hurts like a bitch, but it's actually kinda *good*.

I thought sex was what I needed—only good feelings—but it turns out pain is way better. It's like whatever's happening to me on the outside finally matches all the shit that's on the inside.

Okay. New plan.

"Pull me up," I tell Shoshanna.

She helps me to standing, and I stagger out the door, followed by the crowd of people in the hallway. Somehow I make it out to the front lawn. My eye must be swelling because I can't see out of it too well.

It's cold out here with no shirt. Even with a shirt, I guess. It's almost October.

Dave's pacing the lawn, waiting for me. "Wow, look at that," he says. "Ryden Brooks actually keeping a freaking commitment for once."

"Just say 'fucking,' Dave. Be a man."

"Be a *man*? Okay, how's this?" He punches me again.

I don't know how the hell I manage to stay standing, but I do.

The crowd has grown, and they start chanting, "Fight! Fight! Fight!" What a cliché. I wonder if people chant that during fight scenes in movies because that's what people do in real life, or if people do it in real life because that's what they've seen in the movies.

Anyway.

"You think you can do whatever you want," Dave says, his voice and face—what I can see of it—wild. "You think that because you've had some bad luck that gives you the right to treat everyone else like crap."

That makes me laugh. Or at least I'm laughing in my head. I'm not sure what my face is doing. *Bad luck.* It's a bit more than that, buddy.

"You don't show up to things," he continues, "you're late to practice, you only put in an effort during games when it's convenient for you, you don't call anyone anymore, and you almost have sex with my fucking girlfriend!"

"Good job," I say, egging him on. "You said a grown-up word." *Hit me again, Dave. Do it.*

"You were my best friend once, Ryden."

"Yeah, well. Shit happens. Not like you ever called me either, you know."

He ducks and charges at me, ramming his shoulder into my stomach, tackling me to the ground. He backs off pretty quickly when he realizes I'm not fighting back, but his last few blows are enough. I'm shattered in every possible way.

I keel over and puke into a pile of leaves. And then I just stay there, curled in the fetal position, waiting for my breath and my sanity to return. My eyes are closed—one swollen shut and the other just trying to shut out the light—but I can tell by the drifting noise that most people are filtering back into the house. Dave must be gone. Good riddance.

Someone kneels beside me. "Are you okay?" It's Shoshanna.

"Go away," I mumble into the grass.

After a few more seconds, I feel her leave.

Finally, I'm alone.

So, so alone.

The tears start before I know what's happening. I don't know if it's because of the physical pain or because everything that's happened today—and over the last year—is finally catching up with me, but I'm officially in breakdown mode.

I should hide or leave before I embarrass myself any more, but I'm sobbing and dry heaving and tearing up clumps of the earth with my stupid, useless drunk hands, and I need to get it out. I can't hold on any longer.

I force air into my lungs and scream into the dirt like it's a sponge that will soak up all my misery and carry it far, far away.

I scream until my voice is shot, and then I cry and cry and cry like I never have before. Not even when Meg died.

A few minutes or hours or seconds later, I feel the ground pulsing as someone runs toward me. Unless it's Meg, back from the dead to tell me "Ha! Just kidding!" I don't want them here.

"Ryden!"

"Go away," I force out, my voice hoarse.

"Ryden, it's me. It's Alan. We just got here—what happened?"

"Everything happened."

"Did you get into a *fight*? Why aren't you wearing a shirt?"

"Dave. Shoshanna."

"No, it's *Alan*. Alan and Aimee. Ryden, open your eyes."

"No. Shoshanna took my shirt. Dave hit me. I wanted him to."

"Why the hell would you want him to hit you?"

"Because. Hurt is good." The fragments inside me ache. "She did it on purpose. She blamed me and she wanted to punish me and said she loved me but she really hated me. And I hate her too. I *hate* her. She ruined everything."

Alan hesitates for a minute. "I'm calling your mom."

"No." I force my good eye open. "No. Don't." I try to sit up, to show him I'm fine, that he doesn't need to call my mother, but the whole world tilts and the ground meets my face with a crash.

"Ryden, it's Aimee," Aimee says. "Let us help you."

"Aimee Nam. Did you know Alan here was in *looove* with Meg Reynolds? She made everyone love her."

I hear the sound of someone pushing buttons on a phone. "Deanna? It's Alan Kang…I'm fine, how are you? Listen, I'm calling because of Ryden. I just got to this party at Shoshanna Harvey's and he's here and got in a fight with Dave, and he's really upset and I don't really know what to do…yeah, I think so… yeah…I can try to get him in my car, or maybe you can come—"

"No!" I shout, stopping him.

"What?"

"No way." I shake my head. It hurts like hell. "I'm not going anywhere. I'm staying right here."

"Ryden, you can't stay here. You're hurt. And you're going to freeze to death."

"Tell my mother she is abslo…I mean ab*so*lutely not allowed to come here." I turn my face into the ground. Smells like dirt. "Hope can't see this. And she better not leave her with that Deckland guy."

"Did you hear that?" Alan says into the phone. "Yeah, so… oh. No, I think he'll be fine. He's conscious, obviously… What? Who…? Okay…okay, I will. I'll call you back."

Alan grabs my phone from my pocket. This time he walks away to make his call. He's probably calling an ambulance and doesn't want me to hear. Or the mental institution people to have them take me away and lock me up.

"Aimee?" I ask. "You still here?"

"Yeah," she says.

"Can you go away please?" *Everyone, just go away.*

There's a pause. "Sure, Ryden." She walks away. "I'm going to wait in the car, Alan."

"I'll meet you there," he calls back.

Hallelujah. Now I can wallow in my self-pity without interruption.

It's quiet. Or as quiet as it can be with a rager inside the house a few yards away. But this little spot on the ground near the bushes is peaceful. I have nothing left—no more tears, no more words, no more booze or food or puke. I'm done.

It's cold, but cold is nothing. I wrap my arms around myself and drift off to sleep.

• • •

I wake to someone's hands on my face. Someone's speaking, but I can't make out the words. My good eye flies open, and the whole left side of my face pulsates with agony. *Damn, Dave really got me good.* The cool hands on my cheek feel nice though.

I try to focus through the dark. I don't think I'm drunk anymore. I blink a few times, and the face in front of me becomes clear. Her nose ring is a tiny gold hoop today.

Joni.

Chapter 31

J oni?" I sit up.

Her fingers graze lightly across my bruises. "What happened?" she whispers.

For the time it takes me to suck in one long, deep breath and let it out slowly, everything's okay.

And then the situation becomes real.

Holy shit. Joni cannot be here.

I glance to my left, where Alan and Aimee are standing a few feet away, watching. I thought they left. But no, of course they didn't. My mom told Alan to call Joni. That's why he needed my phone. They were just letting me sleep while they waited for her to show up.

"How did you get here?" I ask, stalling.

"I borrowed Elijah's car. What's going on?"

"It's a long story," I say, grabbing her hand and removing it from my face.

"Well, lucky for you, I've got nothing but time," she says. She sits on the ground next to me and rummages through her giant bag, producing an oversized scarf. She wraps it around my shoulders. I'm instantly warmer.

"What did Alan say when he called you?" I ask.

"He said you were drunk and got in a fight and wouldn't leave. He said your mom said if anyone could talk sense into you, it would be me. I don't know why she thought that; she doesn't even know me."

"She was right though," Alan says. "He's already acting more normal."

I sigh. "Joni, this is Alan. And that's Aimee."

"We met," Joni says.

"Right."

There are a few moments of silence.

I wish I could stand up, take Joni's hand, and transport her far away from here without saying a word. But there are three pairs of eyes on me, and they want answers. Joni wants to know what's going on, and Alan surely wants to know who the hell Joni is and why my mom thought she would be the answer to all my problems. I don't know what Aimee wants. Probably to go home.

Okay, easy part first.

"Joni and I work together at Whole Foods. She goes to Clinton Central. We're…uh…friends."

Joni's eyes are flat. "Friends. Sure. We'll go with that."

"You know what I mean," I say to her, trying to lower my voice but knowing Alan and Aimee can hear every word. I lace my fingers through hers. "We never talked about…"

"You guys are going out?" Alan asks. He doesn't sound amused. "Isn't that, you know, kind of soon?"

I close my eyes. Guess we've come to the hard part already. "Alan, please, shut up."

"Soon?" Joni asks. "Soon after what?"

I open my eyes to find Alan staring at me like I've got salamanders crawling out of my ears. "She doesn't *know*?"

"Ohh, is he talking about your ex?" Joni asks, trying to catch up. "I guess I knew about that. How long ago did you guys break up, anyway?"

"Jesus, Ryden," Alan says. "Does she even know about Hope?"

"Who's Hope?" Joni looks back and forth between us. "Is that your ex?"

Alan groans and looks to the sky in exasperation. "I can't believe this. No," he says. "Meg is his ex. And she's not his *ex*, she's dead. Hope is their daughter. Come on, Aimee, we've wasted enough time here. Let's go." He drops my phone at my feet.

The whole time Alan is giving his rather succinct little speech, I watch Joni. Her eyes don't leave mine, so I have a perfect view of the betrayal taking hold with each revelation.

I squeeze her hand and beg her, silently, to stay, to please just hear me out.

But then Alan backtracks to us. "Oh, also, I'm not going to pick up Hope from day care or watch her after school anymore. I know you've been taking advantage of me wanting to know Hope, and for a while, I didn't care because it made me feel close to Meg, but I'm not putting up with it anymore. I'm joining yearbook, and from now on, I'm going to live my own life."

"Go ahead," I mutter. "I'm done with soccer anyway."

Alan stares at me, openmouthed. "You're unbelievable."

Then he and Aimee leave—for good this time—and Joni yanks her hand from mine and scoots back so no parts of our bodies are touching. But she stays.

It's just me and Joni, sitting on the grass on Shoshanna's front lawn.

"Start at the beginning," she says levelly. "And don't leave anything out."

I nod.

I know under more normal circumstances, I'd be feeling all kinds of stuff. But we passed normal a long time ago, and now I'm numb. (Emotionally numb, anyway. Physically—my face is killing me.) I've got nothing left, which is probably why I'm able to tell her the story in such detail. It's a book report, not an analysis—only facts, no feelings. It's amazingly simple.

I tell Joni about Meg and the cancer and the pregnancy and how she died and how I thought it was my fault and how I have a baby whom I don't quite know what to do with. I tell her about Mabel and Meg's parents and the journals and what I found out today. I tell her about the game and UCLA. I tell her what happened with Shoshanna and how Dave beat the crap out of me and how I know I deserved so much worse.

When I'm done, I wait. Joni's face is blank, like her brain is overloaded with data and has been forced into shutdown mode.

I wish she would put her hand on my face again.

People start to leave the party. It must be late. I wonder how long I slept.

Eventually Joni stands. She doesn't reach down to help me up, but she waits for me to join her. "Let's go," she says once I'm on two feet again. "I'm driving you home."

"My car is here."

"And you're in no shape to drive it."

True. "Let me just get something out of it." I walk over to my car, each step sending shooting pain through my body, and grab my soccer bag. I don't really need my cleats and dirty uniform, but the purple journal is in there. As much as I never want to read it ever again, I still want to keep it close. I can't explain why.

We get into Elijah's car and drive in silence, except for me telling her what streets to take. I check my phone—there's a ton of texts from my mom asking if I'm okay and telling me she spoke to Alan and she knows that Joni came and that I'm not dead but that it would be nice if I called or texted her myself.

I'm ok, I text. On my way home. Love u. Sorry.

I watch the dotted line in the middle of the road skip by.

Why won't Joni say anything?

"It's that house. Second one on the right."

She pulls into the spot in the driveway usually reserved for the Sable.

Should I get out? Is this it? Is she not going to acknowledge anything I told her?

"Um, so, thanks," I say.

She stares at the house. I'm about to open the car door when she asks, "Which window is yours?"

"That one." I point to the window over the garage. "Why?"

She shrugs. "I'm trying to picture where you've been going to sleep every night, thinking it's perfectly okay to lie to me like this."

"Joni, I—"

"Nothing you can say to me right now will help your case, so you should really quit while you're ahead."

"I'm sorry. I know I should have told you. I just…I needed you, okay?" Amazingly, I must have some small amount of pride left, because it's embarrassing to admit this. And yes, I know how ridiculous that sounds, after getting the shit beaten out of me and sobbing like a baby in front of a houseful of my classmates and having to go home wearing a unicorn-patterned scarf. "I knew I would lose you if you found out the truth, and I couldn't risk it."

Joni looks really tired. "You think I wouldn't have liked you if I knew you had a baby and that your girlfriend died? Last I checked, those aren't crimes."

"You said you don't like kids."

Her face crinkles like she can't believe I said that. All right, I can't believe I said that either—obviously that's not the real reason I didn't tell her. "Jesus, Ryden." She sighs. "It would have been a lot to deal with, but it would have been okay."

A match is struck inside me, producing a tiny flame of hope. "Really?"

"Really."

"So…you're not mad?"

She sort of laughs and looks back at my bedroom window. "Oh, I'm so mad I can't see straight."

The match is snuffed out. "I'm confused."

"Ryden, you're not stupid. So don't pretend to be. I'm mad because you *lied* to me, you asshole. I was honest with you about *everything*. I told you stuff I would never tell anyone, and you made a mockery of that."

"I'm so sor—"

"Don't, okay? I'm not looking for an apology. What I need is an explanation. Why? Why did you lie?"

I hesitate.

"You owe it to me to be honest about this, at least," she says.

Maybe so. But it's not going to sound good.

"Ryden."

I pull the scarf tight around my shoulders. It's pretty warm in the car, but the scarf is like a security blanket. I open my mouth, and this is what comes out: "I wanted a chance to be *me* again. I guess I saw that chance in you."

Joni nods. "So you used me. My feelings never factored in at all, did they? You're no better than Jeff and Karen."

"That's not exactly—" I stop there. She's right. I used her. I lied to her and had sex with her but didn't really think about *her* during any of it. Like I was about to do with Shoshanna tonight. And exactly the way Meg used me—as a means to an end.

There's a long stretch of silence. Minutes and minutes go by, and I still don't know what to say. Joni picks at the stitching on Elijah's seat cover.

I need to go inside soon and let Joni leave. So eventually I say, "I hope someday you can forgive me."

A beat goes by, and then she says, pissed off and dejected all at once, "You really need to figure out a way to make peace with your life, Ryden." She starts the car engine. "And please, don't drag me or anyone else into it until you do."

Chapter 32

Mom is sitting on the stairs when I enter the house, her head resting on the banister. If I thought Joni looked tired, Mom looks as if she hasn't slept in a year. Her eyes are strained, the skin around them dry and taut. All the worry she's been hiding for the past year has finally sprung free.

She doesn't say anything, but she watches me, really *looks* at me, like whatever she's seeing is just as bad and just as new as what I see on her.

I sit on the step below her, put my head in her lap, and hug her legs. Her arms go around me, and she strokes my hair.

"I'm sorry," I mumble.

"Shhh," she says. "All that matters is that you're okay. *Are you okay, bud?*"

I nod.

"Good."

"Where's Declan?"

"I asked him to go home."

I lift my head. "Because of me? Mom, I'm so—"

"It's fine, Ryden. He'll be back. I thought it should be you and me when you got home, in case you wanted to talk."

I lean my head back against the wall. Suddenly it's hard to support my own weight. I feel like absolute shit. "I can't talk tonight," I tell her.

She nods and stands up. "Come on. Bedtime."

I follow her up the stairs and down the hall, dragging my feet and using the walls as support. We part ways at our respective doors, but I pause.

"Where's Hope?"

"She's asleep in my room. I figured that would probably be best tonight."

Wow. That's the first time Mom has taken Hope at night. Like, ever. I consider telling her that she doesn't have to. In a weird way, I've actually gotten used to Hope sleeping—and crying—in my room every night.

But all I say is, "'Kay. Thanks. 'Night."

• • •

I open my eyes and know immediately something's off. But my head is pounding and my face is sore and my mouth tastes like I swallowed a handful of sand and I don't have to look to know that my stomach is bruised. So I can't quite place it at first. But then I realize: a *lot* of somethings are off.

The room is quiet. I didn't wake up to the sound of crying. In fact, Hope isn't in her crib or in the room at all.

The sunlight coming through the blinds is different than it should be. It's brighter and hitting my bed at a weird angle. It must be late in the day. I check the clock. Two p.m. Holy shit.

I'm supposed to be at work.

I get up as fast as I can, which isn't very fast at all, grab some clothes, and head to the bathroom to jump—okay, inch slowly and carefully—into the shower. I meet Mom in the hall. Hope is saddled to her chest, looking alert and happy and curious, going "Da-da-da-da" like the world is just aces.

"You're up," Mom says.

"I'm late."

She shakes her head. "I called in for you. I told them you got injured at the game last night and need a few days off."

I blink. "We need the money."

"I know. But you need some time off, Ry." She looks at me seriously.

"Is my face really that bad?" I reach up to touch the tender flesh around my eye.

"It's not your best look. But that's not what I meant. I meant you need some time off *emotionally*."

Truer words…

Since I apparently don't have anywhere to be, I head to the living room and fall onto the couch. Mom follows and moves my feet aside so she can sit too.

"Hey, Ryden?"

"Yeah?" I say into the couch cushion.

"Wanna fill me in?"

Nope, don't particularly feel like rehashing the Shakespearean tragedy that is my life. But she took the baby all night and let me sleep until two, so she's kind of my hero. I owe her one.

I roll over to face her and stick to the highlight reel: the journal, quitting the team, the fight with Dave, all that shit with Joni. The end.

She sits there, nodding to herself, like she expected most of it. Alan must have told her more than I thought.

Then she says, so quietly I almost think she's talking to herself, "You found the second journal."

"Um, yeah. Didn't I just tell you I did?"

"No, I know, but…" She trails off, as if she's putting together some sort of mental puzzle.

"What? What's going on?"

She lets out a long, resigned sigh, gets up, and walks down the hall to her room. A few moments later, she reappears, holding a notebook.

I bolt upright, causing my head to feel like it's punching itself from the inside out.

As she comes closer, the notebook fills every corner of my vision. Thin. Single subject. New-looking. Pink. I'm absolutely positive I've never seen this one before.

"Tell me that is not what I think it is." My voice cracks.

Mom's face is sad and apologetic. "She gave it to me a couple of days before she died," she says. "When I was over visiting."

I feel like my heart has stopped. I didn't check my mom's room because I thought there was no way…I mean, I trusted…I thought surely if she had one of Meg's notebooks, she would tell me. What the fuck!

"I *asked* you if you had one," I yell. "I was going crazy looking for these things, and you *swore* you hadn't seen any."

"She made me promise," Mom whispers. "She said I could only give you this one if you already had the other two. She seemed really serious about it. But apart from that..." She takes a breath. "I...I didn't know what was in it, so I figured waiting a little while, until you...got a handle on things might be a smart idea. Maybe I was wrong. I don't know. I'm so sorry, bud." She gently sets the book on the cushion between us. Then, after a few moments' hesitation, she leaves the room.

This is un-fucking-believable.

I stare at the glossy pink cover like it's dripping with blood. Nothing good ever comes from these things. Whatever's inside will only make matters worse. I don't know how the situation could get any worse, but it always does.

I should burn the book without reading it.

But of course I won't. 'Cause I'm a fucking idiot.

I open to the back cover.

☑ Mabel
☑ Alan
☑ Ryden

I take a deep breath. Whatever is in here, I know it will be the last thing Meg will ever tell me.

I flip back to the beginning. Like the last book, most of the pages are empty, with just the first few pages filled in with Meg's small, messy handwriting. But unlike the last journal or any of the others, this one begins with two insanely improbable words:

Dear Ryden

This isn't a journal. This is a letter. To me. From Meg.

My heart starts beating again, pumping overtime to make up for lost time.

There's no date at the top, but it was most likely written after ~~Alan~~ *Alan*, which means it was written sometime between February 5 and February 15—the day she died. No, it had to have been before February 15, because she would have needed time to get it to my mom.

Dear Ryden,

If you're reading this, you've read the other two journals by now. It also means you probably hate me.

Truth.

I want you to know that I'm sorry. Not for having Hope, but for so much else. For letting you come into my life without warning you about my cancer, for lying to you about the pregnancy, for making you a father far too young and in the worst possible way, and for being too chicken to tell you the truth about all of it. And for dying. I'm really sorry about that.

But one thing that I never lied about was how I love you.

You know that movie your mom likes, The Lake House? I've been thinking about that movie a lot lately. Remember how we talked about it in school that day with Alan? As I look back, with all the supposed wisdom of someone facing the end of her life, that conversation was when I fell in love with you. Until then, I'd loved the idea of you. But that day, I knew I could never let you go, even though holding on to you was the most selfish thing I could do.

Anyway, in the movie, they're so in love, but they're at the mercy of time. Like us. We never had enough time. It's not fair. But if I had it to do over again, I'd do everything the same. Because these months with you have been the best of my life.

I know you probably feel differently right about now, after everything you've found out. But even so, I wanted you to find these journals, to know everything there is to know about me, about us. I knew you had that journal of mine—the one I forgot at your house when we first got together. I had come to hang out at your place and your mom let me in. I was going to surprise you, but when I peeked my head around your bedroom door, I saw you sitting on your bed reading my journal. It's a green one, right? You were so into it. That gave me an idea, later, after the baby became a reality and I started getting sicker. I knew if I could find a way to leave you my journals after I was gone, you'd read them just as closely. You'd listen to what I had to tell you more than any video message or letter, because you'd believe the journal was entirely uncensored—a true glimpse into my thoughts. And you'd be right.

But I had to figure out a way to do it so you'd only get the information when you were ready for it. So I left the first one with Mabel, the one that says I never thought the chemo was working. I'd written those entries even before I decided on my plan, and I knew you'd see that message in those pages, when Mabel probably wouldn't. I figured that notebook would be the easiest to find, though it would take time to get to you. Time is good. The checklists in the back of the books were the clue that there were other journals, other things to be said—if you wanted to look for them.

The fact that you've gotten this far, that you're reading this, means (to my muddled, failing brain at least) that you were actively looking for the second journal when you found it and therefore ready to know the whole truth.

But it also means you haven't moved on. You're still looking backward. I don't know how long it's been since I've been gone, but you have to move on. If not today, then someday soon.

I love you, Ryden, I will always love you, but I'm not here anymore.

Her handwriting becomes shakier, less fluid, as I read on.

I hope you'll find great love in your life, the kind that lasts a lot longer than ours. If I still have the right to ask for anything at this point, that's what I want—I want you to move on and be happy.

I've enclosed a letter for Hope. Please give it to her when she's old enough to understand it. Maybe when she's seventeen, so you can tell her that's how old I was when I wrote it. And please make sure she knows I love her, that I wanted her more than anything, and that I wish I didn't have to leave her.

Aaaand there it is. I *knew* she would have included something for Hope. Some sort of mother/daughter thing. I guess her letter won't help me any, since it's all secret and shit, but I think I already gave up on that anyway.

Along those lines, I have something else for you.

I know you don't like to talk about your father; I'm not even sure how much you think about him. But I've had a lot of time on my hands while you've been at school, so I tracked him down. I thought maybe learning about him would help you figure out what kind of father you want to be. But then again, what do I know?

I love you, Ryden. Always and forever.
Love, Meg.

The next page has a sealed envelope taped to it with Hope's name on the front. And the page after that has an address, email address, and phone number for Michael Taylor. How could she possibly have…?

You know what? I can't think about that right now.

I close the book and sit back on the couch, trying to process everything I've read.

"Mom," I say. I don't really raise my voice, but I know she can hear me.

She comes out of her room.

"You didn't read it?" I ask.

"No."

"Well, I think maybe you should." I hold it out to her.

She looks at me, unsure, but takes it and opens to the first page.

I stare out the living room window while she reads. Our

neighbor across the street is putting freshly carved jack-o'-lanterns on her front stoop. I wonder if they're going to bake the seeds. Mom and I used to do that when I was little and still into Halloween.

"She found Michael," Mom whispers. Her face is white with shock.

"Apparently. How do you think she did it? How did she even know his *name*? Did she talk to you about it?"

Mom shakes her head. "She must have gotten a copy of your birth certificate somewhere. Can you find that stuff out on the Internet?"

"I have no idea. I've never tried."

"Me neither."

"Maybe she hired someone?" I say. "To track him down? Maybe she used her parents' money?"

"Maybe."

There's a long pause.

"Well," Mom says, "what are you going to do?"

I let out an exhausted, painful sigh. "I have absolutely no idea."

Chapter 33

I don't go to school or work for a week.

I make Mom and me sandwiches for lunch and help her with her projects. Mostly I just glue stuff, since it's pretty hard to screw that up.

Hope starts eating solidish foods—cheese and avocado seem to be her favorites—and she picks up the chunks with her fingers and feeds herself. I have no idea when or how or where she learned to do that. It's like she woke up one day this week and just *knew*. She seems pretty damn proud of herself for it too. All smiles and squealing and bouncing around in her seat.

She's got another tooth coming in, but Joni's Washington Square Park soundtrack is helping.

I spend as much time at the lake as possible, since in a matter of days, it will be too cold. Hope comes with me, bundled up under lots of layers.

I call and text Joni several times a day, but she never answers or calls back. I'd thought…hoped…that once a little time went by, she wouldn't be so mad. After all, she said not to drag her into my problems *until* I make peace with the way my life is now. Okay, so maybe I'm still working on that. But it wasn't a "never." It was just a "not now." I think, anyway.

I've been thinking a lot about Michael too. I'd kind of given up on finding him—you can only be mocked by Google so much before you start to feel defeated. And yet, I know how to contact him. He lives in New Jersey. I could call him or email him or go meet him. I could do a much more refined Google search and find out if he's an ex-convict on parole or what he does for a living or if he's got other kids. I could show up on his doorstep and finally feel whatever you feel when you look in the eyes of the guy who helped give you life. I think I'm going to.

Declan comes over for dinner Friday night, a week after the Purple Notebook Day. He brings us stuff: a rattle in the shape of a tyrannosaurus rex head ("Your mom told me she likes freaky things," he explains.) and a steering wheel cover with a black-and-white soccer ball pattern on it for me ("I own an auto supply store, so if you ever need anything…").

He looks at me, waiting for my reaction.

I stare at the steering wheel thing in my hand. It's kind of a weird gift to give someone, isn't it? Like, here's a random item for your car that no one could possibly ever need.

"I don't play soccer anymore." As soon as it comes out of my mouth, I feel bad. Apparently I can't go a single day without being a douche to someone who's trying to be nice to me.

Declan's face falls. "Oh. I didn't know that," he says. "Well, you can come by any time and exchange it for something else if you want."

I shake my head and force myself to put a little effort into the conversation. It's not like I have a ton of people on my side right now. And if my mom's biker boyfriend is offering to be my friend, well, I'm not in a position to turn it down. "Nah, this is cool. Thanks." I hold out a hand, and he shakes it.

"No problem, man."

My mom, who's been standing a few feet away, watching the whole exchange, lets out an audible breath, and says, "Why don't we go into the kitchen? Dinner will be ready in a few."

Declan looks at her and smiles, his eyes taking on that so-in-love look that Mom's been sporting lately, and it hits me like a soccer-ball-patterned steering wheel cover to the face—this guy is going to be around for a long time.

He hands her a bag, and she takes out a bottle of wine and a bakery box that looks like it contains some sort of pie or cake.

"Thanks, babe," she says and rises up on her tippy toes to give him a quick kiss.

"Did you ride your motorcycle over here?" I ask Declan as we head to the kitchen.

He raises his eyebrows. "What makes you think I have a motorcycle?"

I nod at his outfit as I put Hope in her swing. "I dunno, the leather jacket, the boots, the beard. I have a friend who reads books about bikers, and you look exactly like the guy from the cover."

Declan laughs. "Okay, you caught me. I had a bike for a long time. But I got rid of it when I had my daughter. Figured

I shouldn't take so many risks, since I want to be around to see her grow up."

That gets my attention. "You have a daughter?"

He nods. "She's three. She lives with her mother in Portsmouth half the time."

I glance at Mom. She's smiling to herself as she fills the water glasses.

All throughout dinner, Mom and Declan laugh and talk and brush their hands against each other's and smile dopily across the table. Declan asks me a lot of questions—and he doesn't stick to the safe subjects, like school and work.

"I can't imagine what it's like being a single dad at your age, Ryden," he says as Hope starts fussing. I get up to make her a bottle. "It's hard enough for me, and I only have my daughter every other week. And I'm thirty-seven. How has it been for you?" He's looking at me like he really wants to know the answer.

"It sucks," I say completely, one hundred percent honestly, and everyone laughs. "But I'm figuring it out. Trying to, anyway. Mom's been amazing."

He looks at her but responds to me. "She is amazing, isn't she?"

"Oh, stop," Mom says, brushing her bangs back from her face. "I'm only doing what anyone else would do in my situation."

"No, you're not," Declan and I say at the same time, and everyone laughs again.

I set Hope in my lap, and she latches onto her bottle right away.

Mom beams, like she can't believe how well the evening is

going. Honestly, neither can I. Is this what it's like to have two parents? Not that Declan is my father or that I would ever want him to pretend to be. But the whole "two adults, two kids, sitting around the dinner table, laughing and sharing stories, everyone getting along swimmingly" scenario. It's so incredibly foreign.

Declan starts clearing the table as Mom sets out the pie he brought. Even in these simple, basic actions, you can see how happy they are.

He knows everything, and he still loves her. I don't know much about his story, apart from the fact that he has a daughter, but I bet he's told her all about his shit too, whatever it is, and she still loves him. It's so much easier when there're no secrets. When you're with the right person, at least.

Which makes me think of Joni again.

I pull my phone out of my pocket and dial her number. It goes straight to voice mail.

I wish she were here with us. I wish she would look at me again the way Declan looks at my mom.

I miss her. And it's not about the sex, and it's not about pretending my life is different than it is. That didn't really work anyway. It's about *her*.

It's her stupid jokes and weird, made-up games and her bag full of candy and her wacky outfits and how she meets people wherever she goes. It's the way she's always blowing her hair out of her eyes instead of pushing it back with her hand or securing it with a clip. It's how she skips instead of runs, and how she's so badass in so many ways, with the tattoos and whatnot, but also into ridiculously girly things like romance novels and unicorns.

I miss her magic room. I miss *her magic*, period.

For the first time, I see it: my and Joni's relationship has absolutely *nothing* to do with Meg. Joni isn't a means of escape. She's her own destination—someone to go *to*, not to use as a means to get *away*.

And I completely blew it.

"Mom," I say, my voice coming out in more of a whisper than I thought it would.

She's pulled her chair close to Declan's, and she's feeding him spoonfuls of pie and ice cream. "Yeah, bud?"

"I need to go out for a little while."

Her forehead wrinkles. "Everything okay?"

"Yeah, I just…need to do something."

"Do you want us to watch Hope?" she asks.

"Nah, I'll take her with me." Mom looks surprised but doesn't comment. "You two look like you need some alone time anyway." I give her a raised eyebrow.

Mom and Declan laugh. Huh, funny how they didn't disagree.

"I'll text you when I'm on my way home. Don't want to walk in on anything unsavory…"

"Oh, shut up, Ry," Mom says, still laughing. "Have fun."

"Uh, yeah, you too, I guess."

I grab Hope and all her stuff and practically run to the Sable, my plan taking shape with every step forward. Every step closer to Joni.

Chapter 34

Elijah's in the garage, as always, working on a painting I haven't seen before. It's a series of faces that look like they're melting. Normally I would ask him what that's about, but I don't have time for that right now.

"Hey, Elijah," I say. "Is Joni home?"

He's clearly surprised to see me. His eyes zero in on Hope, who's in her car seat, sound asleep from the ride. "She's really pissed at you, dude," he says, still staring at the baby.

"I know. Just tell me, is she here?"

He nods. "She's in her room. She hasn't really left there all week, except to go to school. I don't even think she's been going to work. Probably trying to avoid your lying ass."

I'm already on my way toward the front door. "Thanks," I call back.

I ring the bell, and a middle-aged woman comes to the door. Joni's stepmother. Her skin is the same shade as Elijah's, but her hair, which is cropped close to her scalp, isn't quite as light. She's wearing a sweatshirt with a picture of a golden retriever puppy on it. "Can I help you?" she asks.

"I'm here to see Joni. Um, please. My name is Ryden Brooks."

"Oh, yes. Ryden Brooks. We know *allll* about you." She doesn't look very happy with me.

"I've tried calling, but she won't answer her phone. I really need to talk to her. Explain everything. Apologize," I say.

She stares me down a while longer, arms crossed, considering. A few times, her eyes flicker toward Hope.

"Please," I say again. "Just give me a chance."

Finally she drops her arms to her sides. "Wait here." She closes the door in my face.

I stand there for a few minutes, but she doesn't come back. So I sit on the porch steps, facing the front lawn. It's a huge expanse of green. The flowers that lined the walkway the first time I was here are mostly dead now. Stupid fall.

About fifteen minutes later, Joni's stepmom returns. "She doesn't want to see you."

I shake my head. "I'm not leaving until she at least tells me that herself." I'll sit here as long as I have to. Really, where else do I have to be?

She sighs and disappears again.

A few minutes later, I hear Joni's voice. "What do you want?"

I stand up and turn to face her. She's on the other side of the screen, wearing the simplest outfit I've ever seen her in: baggy jeans and a gray hoodie. She's not wearing her nose ring. She gasps when she sees Hope sleeping in her car seat by my feet. Her eyes get a little watery.

"What are you doing, Ryden?"

I reach into Hope's diaper bag and pull out a baggie with

a silver twist tie around the top. "I brought you candy," I say, holding it up. It's filled with Smarties and rock candy and sour gummy worms and tiny boxes of Nerds and all kinds of other stuff. "I stopped at the candy store on the way over. I figure it's my turn to bring you a peace offering."

She covers her face with her hands and shakes her head. "You can't bribe me with candy and expect everything to go back to the way it was."

"I'm not—I mean, I would never think that. I just know you like candy, so I wanted to bring you some. You bring—brought—me stuff when I wasn't in a good mood, and it always helped." I take a deep breath. "Actually, it wasn't the food that made it better. It was you. *You* make everything better, Joni."

She moves her hands away from her face and looks up slowly.

I take that as a signal to keep talking. "I've missed you so much this week, you have no idea. I know I have no right to show up here and ask you to listen to me like this, but I...I don't know. I want us to start over. I want you to know every-thing about me, and I want to know everything about you. Even the shitty parts. I can't change the past or pretend it didn't happen, like you said, but I'm hoping there's a way to move forward from it. And I really want you to be there for that."

I break off, gasping a little. The words rushed out, and I kind of forgot to breathe. Joni watches me, silent.

When I get my air back, I say, "So, first step toward you knowing everything about me: this is Hope." I hold Hope's car seat so it's close to our eye level, lift one of her sleeping baby hands, and wave it at Joni. "Her name is Hope Rosa Brooks, and her mother's name was Megan Elizabeth Reynolds. She's seven and a half months old, she loves weird-looking monster toys with googly eyes and big teeth, and I'm pretty sure I'm her least favorite person in the world. But we're working on it." I hold Joni's gaze. "She also loves your Washington Square Park soundtrack."

"Ryden…"

"Yeah?" I can't stop the hope that surges through me. I'm putting everything out there—it has to work. It just has to.

"I…"

"Yeah?"

"I can't do this. It's too little too late."

"Joni, please. I—" I stop myself as my brain skips ahead of my mouth and I realize what I was about to say. I was about to tell her I loved her. Where did that come from? I can't be in *love* with her. It's only been seven months since Meg died. Seven and a half. Whatever. It's too soon. *Way* too soon. Instead, I say, "I miss you."

She shakes her head at me sadly. "Bye, Ryden." She starts to close the door.

"No! Wait!" I spring into action, pulling open the screen door and sticking my foot in the doorjamb so she can't close the interior door on me. She stops, sighs, and waits.

She wants honesty? Well, then that's what she's gonna get.

"Please don't walk away from me. I feel like if you do, I'll never get you back, and I'm really not okay with that."

She doesn't move. Her eyes narrow, but they're somehow less sad than they were a minute ago. She's giving me the chance to say whatever I need to say or do whatever I need to do to change her mind once and for all.

Time to pull out the big guns.

I look her straight in the eye and blurt out, "I got my scar when I was eleven years old." Joni opens her mouth, then closes it, listening. "I was on my way home from my friend's house a few streets over, and I noticed this Frisbee stuck in the branches of a tree right near the house of this family who had, like, nine or ten kids. The ones in my school were really popular. I got this idea in my head that I would climb the tree and get the Frisbee and knock on their door and say, 'Behold! I have come to return your Frisbee!' And they'd all be grateful and think I was so brave, and word would spread around the neighborhood and on the school bus that I was their hero."

I keep rambling. "So I climbed the tree. Turned out the Frisbee was a lot higher than it seemed from below, but I got it out and tossed it to the ground. Except then I couldn't get down. I couldn't get a good perspective on the branches or footholds to lower myself down, and I was too scared to jump. So I ended up sitting in that tree, stuck, for hours."

Joni giggles. *Yes.* It's working.

I smile. "It gets worse. So after a while of sitting there, having no idea how I was going to get down, I had to pee. Knowing I had nowhere to go made me have to pee even more. So I peed from the tree."

"No!" Joni covers her mouth with her hand.

"Yes. But I couldn't figure out how to do it from my sitting position without getting pee all over me, so I stood up on the branch. And as I was zipping myself back up, I lost my balance and fell. I whacked my face on a few branches on the way down." I point to my eyebrow. "Needed four stitches."

Joni shakes her head, amazed. "You're lucky you didn't lose your eye."

"Tell me about it." I run my thumb over my scar. "I've never told anyone the real story before. Not Meg, not even my mom. I told her I was playing hockey in the street with the kids in the neighborhood and someone accidentally knocked me in the face with a hockey stick. You and I are officially the only people in the world who know the truth."

Joni fiddles with the spring on the screen door hinge for a minute, chewing on her bottom lip.

I wait.

She steps outside. "Come on. Let's go for a walk." She starts across the lawn. "And bring the candy."

Chapter 35

J oni leads the way to a little park. It's not much more than a small playground, a couple of benches, and a few trees, but the sky is just about dark, and we're the only ones here. It's a good spot.

She sits on a bench near a small cluster of old maple trees. Even in the muted streetlight, you can tell the leaves have turned shades of deep red and orange. A few are still green though, like they're clinging to the summer. Some just went straight to brown. Dead.

I take a seat next to Joni and put Hope's car seat on my other side, but she's starting to wake up, so I lift her out and hold her against my chest.

The crying starts immediately. "Sorry," I tell Joni without looking at her, getting out Hope's diaper-changing stuff and making quick work of her dirty diaper. I give her a pacifier and put on the Washington Square Park noises, rocking her in my arms and shushing her.

A few minutes later, she's quieted down.

I can't really avoid Joni any longer, so I look at her. She's watching me.

"What?"

"You're really good at that," she says.

"At what?"

"The baby stuff." She nods toward Hope.

"You're joking, right? I'm total crap at this."

Joni's eyebrows scrunch together. "No, you're not. You're a natural. You know, the first time I ever saw you, you were saving that kid from falling off the shelf at the store. Remember?"

I nod.

"At first, you let him try to reach the bag on his own, which I thought was really cool of you. Not everyone would do that. A lot of people would just yell at him to get down. It was how I knew I liked you. And then when he fell, you sprang into action without missing a beat, like helping that kid was second nature."

We fall into silence again, and I think about what she said.

Have I gotten better at the dad thing recently? I'm still not "really good" or a "natural," but I think she might be right—maybe I'm better than I was. Joni's soundtrack has been a life-saver, and I've had more time this past week to focus on the baby. Looking at her and not seeing Meg mirrored back at me helps. And, I don't know, ever since reading Meg's final confession, I think I've let the bad fade away.

The silence goes on way too long. Joni's waiting for me to say something. So I share the first thing that comes to mind. "Copse." Random, I know.

She glances around the park. "Cops? Where? What?"

"No, not cops. Copse. With an *e* at the end. As in, 'We're sitting near a copse of trees.' I've always liked that word."

She laughs a little. "You and your words. What did you get on the Reading SAT?"

"I didn't take it. I was signed up for the October test last year, but then the shit hit the fan and I didn't go. I'm supposed to take it this November, but I'll probably bail again since I'm not going to college now anyway."

"You're really smart, Ryden. You don't need soccer to go to college."

I shrug. "I'll probably go to community college next year. Can't really live in a dorm with a baby." I look down at Hope and run a hand over her head. "I think my mom's been trying to tell me that for months, actually."

"I'd like to meet your mom," Joni says.

"You will, I promise. Just not tonight because I'm pretty sure she's having sex with her boyfriend right about now."

"Um, gross?"

"Tell me about it."

More silence. Joni opens the bag of candy, thinks a minute, then opens a box of the Nerds. She holds the bag out to me, and I pick out a Swedish Fish.

"I thought for sure you were gonna go for a gummy worm," I say.

"Can't. Gelatin. Not vegetarian." She pours Nerds into her mouth.

"Oh. Shit. Sorry."

"No worries. You just have to eat 'em." She smiles. It's not a huge smile, but at least it's real.

"Okay." It feels good to be talking with her again, even if it's about candy. "So, um, thanks for hearing me out today."

"You're welcome. Thanks for being a pain in the ass and making me listen to you."

"You're welcome."

"Can I ask you something?"

"Anything," I say and mean it.

"I want to hear more about Meg." The name sounds impossibly strange coming from Joni's lips. "You told me about how she got pregnant and died, but I'd really like to know more about her as a person. Why you loved her in the first place."

I blink. "Are you sure?"

She bites into an Airhead. "Yup."

I talk for a long time, and she listens closely, sometimes asking questions, sometimes not.

The last thing I say, as Joni pops the final piece of candy in her mouth, is, "I didn't go to her funeral."

Joni looks surprised by that. "Why not?"

I take a deep breath, and it shudders on the way out.

"Because I was really fucked up. She died and I became a father all in the same day. Nothing made any sense."

Joni moves her hand toward me like she's about to put it on my thigh for encouragement. But then halfway there, she pulls her hand back—slowly, like she's trying to make the motion seem meaningless—and places it back in her lap.

Guess we aren't going back to normal as quickly as I'd hoped.

"She was trying to hold on, to stay pregnant for as long as possible so the baby had a better chance of being healthy," I continue. "In one of her journals, it said that the doctor wanted her to have an early C-section, to get the baby out and give Meg's body a chance to bounce back, but she wouldn't do it." I shake my head, thinking how different things could have been if she had. "She would have had to have a C-section anyway, 'cause she was too weak to push the baby out the natural way, but she was waiting as long as she could. And then, when she was a little more than eight months pregnant, her body failed."

"What do you mean, failed?"

I clear my throat and check my emotions. "It was a Sunday afternoon, and I was at her house, sitting with her as she watched some movie. I don't even remember what it was. She looked like she had fallen asleep. Her eyes were closed and her mouth was hanging open. But her chest wasn't rising and falling as it should have been—the space between her breaths was way too long and uneven. I called her parents into the room and grabbed my phone and called 911. We kept talking to her, trying to get her to hold on while we waited for the EMTs to arrive, but her eyes wouldn't open. They wouldn't let me in the ambulance."

I pause a minute. I will not cry. I will *not* cry.

"Anyway, I drove to the hospital. But they wouldn't let me back to see her or tell me how she was doing. And then, after I have no idea how long, I was being led to the NICU by a nurse, and she was pointing at Hope through the window. She was so small—a few weeks early—and hooked up to oxygen machines, but the nurse said she was going to be fine. I asked her about Meg, and her face got sad and all she said was, 'Congratulations. You're a daddy,' and she walked away."

"She didn't tell you what happened to Meg?" Joni sounds outraged.

I shake my head. "I went back to the waiting room and waited for a long time. They wouldn't tell me anything because I wasn't a blood relative. And Meg's parents seemed to have forgotten about me. Or they didn't care. The hospital people just kept talking about how the baby was doing—because I *was* Hope's blood relative. I was *the* relative. I had more say over what happened to Hope than anyone. But I didn't care. All I wanted to know was when I could see Meg and if she was going to be all right."

I look at Joni and am surprised to see that she's crying. Not sobbing or anything, but thin tears are trickling down her cheeks. "So what happened?" she asks.

"My mom got there, demanded to speak to someone who knew what was going on, and found out what had happened: Meg had died midsurgery, before Hope was even out. She didn't live long enough to be a mother, not for one second." I pause to steady my voice and my breathing. "And that was it. Hope came home with me after she got the all clear, and I never saw Meg or her parents again. When the funeral happened, I was too out of it to know, frantically trying to figure out how to take care of a newborn." I shoot Joni a sideways glance. "Let's just say it wasn't a great time for me."

"You never got to say good-bye," she whispers.

"Nope."

She wipes her face with the sleeve of her hoodie. "You know what I think?"

"What?"

"I think you need that chance. To say good-bye. She got to leave you the journals as her good-bye, but you don't have anything like that. You need closure."

I smile a little. "That sounds amazing, really, but I don't know how it's possible, except for waiting it out."

She shakes her head. "No. We need to have a funeral for her."

I stare at her. "How are we supposed to do that? She's been dead for months, and she's not buried anywhere. She was cremated."

Joni shrugs. "We can have a memorial service, where every-one says something and you all say good-bye together. Alan can come, and Meg's sister, and your mom, and whoever else you want. Maybe we can light some candles."

I nod slowly, thinking. "Are you sure you're okay with that?"

"Of course."

My mind starts to turn with the possibilities. "Mabel told me her parents keep her ashes in their living room. She would hate that. Maybe…" *No, it's too crazy. We couldn't.*

But then again, just because it's crazy doesn't mean it's wrong.

"Maybe," I say again, "we could take them, or get Mabel to

take them, and we could scatter her ashes at the lake, like Meg would have wanted."

Joni's eyes go wide. "You want to steal her ashes from her parents," she repeats.

"Yeah. Too much?"

"Probably," she says.

"Yeah."

She shrugs. "But it's worth a shot."

"Really?"

"Sure, why not."

My phone beeps in my pocket. It's a text from my mom asking if I'm all right. Guess they're done having sex. I text back that I'm fine and I'll be home soon.

"I have to go," I say. "Can we talk more about this tomorrow?"

She nods. "You going to be at work?"

"No, my mom told them I'm not coming back until Monday."

"Wait—you haven't been at work all week either?"

I shake my head.

"And I thought I was being all crafty to avoid you." She laughs. After a second, so do I. It feels pretty freaking phenomenal to laugh with her again.

I put Hope in her car seat and we start back toward Joni's house. I want to hold her hand, but I don't dare reach for it. It's up to her to make the first move.

"Hey, Ryden?" she asks quietly as we walk.

"Yeah?"

"One more thing. I want you to know I'm okay with you

having a baby," she says. "It doesn't change the way I feel about you."

Feel, as in present tense. Phew.

"Thanks. You have no idea how good it is to hear that," I say. "But…"

Shit. But what?

I stop and wait for her to finish her sentence. She stops too.

"A couple of things. One—you cannot lie to me, about *anything*, ever again. It's really not okay."

I nod. "I know. I won't. I promise."

"And two…I can't be her mother," she says.

"Joni, I would never expect you to—"

"No, listen," she says, cutting me off. Her voice is gentle, but I can tell she's about to say something serious. Again. "Even if the three of us are together a lot, you have to do the feeding and diaper-changing and stuff. It can't be my responsibility. And I can't babysit either. I can't fall into that routine. Because I feel like it would be really hard to get out of the habit, and I may not know what I'm doing after high school, but I know I need a *lot* more time before I even think about becoming a parent. Does that make sense?"

I nod. "Total sense."

"You can't rely on me like you relied on Alan. When I'm around, it's because you want to be with me, not because you need help with Hope. Okay?"

"Okay. Yes, got it."

She exhales. "Good. Now let's go steal some ashes."

Chapter 36

I 'll do it," Mabel says without hesitation.

I pull the phone from my ear and stare at it. Has *everyone* in the world gone nuts? You'd think this sort of thing would require a fair amount of coercion. Apparently not. "You will?"

"It's what Meg would have wanted. Plus, I doubt my parents will even notice—they're off in la-la land pretty much twenty-four seven these days."

"That was a lot easier than I thought it'd be."

"When does this whole thing go down?" Mabel asks.

"I was thinking next weekend? Sunday?"

"Sounds good. Did you tell Alan about it yet?"

"Not yet. I figured I'd ask you about the ashes first."

"Admit it: you're scared to call him," she says.

Oh Jesus. "What do you know about it?"

"He told me what happened—we talk, you know. Though if I didn't hear it from him, I would have heard about it from *someone*. You didn't exactly choose the most private place for your mental breakdown."

"It wasn't a mental—" Oh, hell. "Are people at school talking about it?"

"Um, *yeah*. I mean, everyone knows you're dealing with a lot so no one's, like, making fun of you or anything. You could probably drive a bus full of nuns into the lake and still be Mr. Popularity. But the Shoshanna/Dave gossip is delicious. Of *course* people are talking about it."

I sigh. "So you think Alan's gonna forgive me long enough to come to the memorial? We can't really do it without him."

"Guess you won't know until you try."

"Yeah."

There's a brief silence. "He told me about Joni."

I chew on the inside of my bottom lip. "He did?"

"Yeah."

"So, um, what do you think?"

"It's not any of my business…"

"But?"

She laughs. "But…it's good she's there for you. Helping you at the party and all that."

"She was the one who came up with the idea for the memorial," I tell her.

"She sounds like a good person."

"She is. Well, see ya, Mabel."

"See ya, Ryden."

I end the call and dial Alan's number before I talk myself out of it.

"Hello?"

"Hey, Alan, it's Ryden."

"I know."

"Right. '99 Problems.'"

"Nah. You're 'I Used to Love H.E.R.' by Common now."

Wonderful. "Well, I wanted to say I'm really sorry about pretty much everything, and thank you for everything you've done for me and Hope. I really do appreciate it, even if it doesn't seem like it."

There's silence on the other end of the line.

"And, um, we're going to have a memorial for Meg. Next Sunday at the hidden spot at the lake your family took her to when you were kids."

"I haven't been there in years," Alan says. "How do you know about that place?"

"She took me there. It sorta became our place."

"Oh." A pause. "I didn't know that."

"Anyway, Mabel's going to steal Meg's ashes from her house, and we're going to say a few words and scatter them there. You want to come?"

"Hold up—Mabel's going to *steal her ashes*? Are you fucking crazy? Is *she* fucking crazy?"

Finally, a logical response to this insane plan. "Uh, I guess?"

I can almost see Alan shaking his head in the silence that follows. But then he says, "You bet your ass I'll be there."

• • •

All week, I've been counting down the days to the memorial.

I've had so much schoolwork to catch up on from the week

I missed—though Mrs. Schonhorn said if I study hard for her test next week and get at least an eighty-five, she'll let the homework I missed slide. Love that woman.

Plus, I've had to deal with all the gossipy bullshit at school. Half the guys think I'm a hero for hooking up with Shoshanna, and the other half think I broke the bro code by trying to sleep with Dave's girlfriend. Half the girls think I'm a total asshole who was using Shoshanna, while the other half throw themselves at me now that I'm "ready to start dating again." They're all a bunch of fuckheads.

I see Shoshanna every day in AP English, but she barely looks at me. I don't blame her. I haven't seen Dave much now that I'm off the team and spending lunch in the library to catch up on work. I hear they broke up though.

Joni hasn't been able to come over all week because we've both been really busy with work and homework. But I've seen her at work almost every day, and we're almost back to normal—joking, laughing, talking. No touching. Not yet.

Anyway, it's probably weird that I've been looking forward to the memorial—something else for my future therapist to analyze—but it's really kept me going. It will be nice to have all the people who are important to me in one place to remember Meg. 'Cause that happens, like, never. Or maybe I'm just looking forward to introducing Joni to my mother.

Sunday morning arrives, and I put on my favorite jeans and a button-down shirt. I wash my hair too. Now that Hope isn't crying quite so much, I have a little more time to work with in the shower. I'm never going to take little things, like having time to use conditioner, for granted ever again.

Joni borrows Elijah's car and meets me at my house.

I'm sitting on the stoop when she rolls up. She looks amazing. Bright red dress that's tight around the top and then flares out at her waist and black cowboy boots. Her nose ring is a black stone. I stand as she walks over and have to stop myself from pulling her into my arms and kissing the top of her head.

"Hey," she says, smiling.

"You look really beautiful."

She looks down at her dress. "You sure? I wasn't sure if the red would be appropriate or not. I have another dress in the car in case—"

"It's perfect."

Joni rocks back on her heels, her hands on her hips. "Thanks. You look nice too." She reaches up tentatively and brushes a thumb across my eyebrow scar, the corner of her mouth quirking up. Then her face becomes serious. "Are you sure you want me to come today?"

"Of course I do. Why?"

"I don't know, because I didn't know Meg? It's only going to be people who knew her and loved her. I don't know if they'd appreciate me being there."

I take both her hands and look her in the eye. "I really want you to be there. Besides, everyone already knows you're coming."

She gives me a nervous smile. "Okay."

"Come on." I nod toward the house.

She follows me inside, and we find my mother in the living room, dancing around to Sia's "Chandelier" with Hope in her arms. Mom stops when she sees us and holds a hand out to Joni. "You must be Joni. I'm Deanna."

Joni shakes her hand. "Great song," she says.

Mom laughs. "Oh yeah, we're going to get along just fine."

• • •

Mom, Joni, Hope, and I meet Alan and Mabel at the turnoff to the one-lane road that leads to the dirt road, and they follow us in their car as we drive farther and farther into the woods until we reach the point where we have to go on foot. The beach at this time of year—bare and chilly, the water uninviting—reminds me of the last time I was here with Meg. We huddled together under a blanket, watching the water as if we weren't on a deadline. I can't believe that was nearly a whole year ago.

Mom squeezes my hand. "This is really beautiful, bud," she whispers.

I nod. Now that we're here, the anticipation has disappeared, leaving only nerves and a slightly sick-to-my-stomach feeling in its place.

I get the candles out of my bag, and Mom helps me put them in the sand and make it look all pretty. Then Mabel removes a shoe box from the shopping bag she brought with her. Inside the box is a gallon-size Ziploc bag. And inside the bag are the ashes. Mabel holds it out to me, like she's actually expecting me to take it, like it's nothing. "I left the box where it was on the windowsill," she explains. "My parents will never look inside."

"What do you mean?" Mom asks. "Your parents don't know you took them? Oh, I don't know how I feel about—"

"It's okay," Mabel says. She sounds really sure of herself. "I left some behind. For them to scatter themselves, if—when—they ever decide to."

She's still waiting for me to take the bag, but I can't move. That's *Meg* in there. All that's left of her are millions of tiny gray flakes, one indistinguishable from the next, like the stuff that comes out of our vacuum when we empty the canister.

My gut lurches, and I force my feet to move. I barely make it to the edge of the woods before I throw up. I stay there, heaving, until there's nothing left to come out. I feel a hand on my back. "It's okay, Ryden," Mom says quietly. "We don't have to do this if you're having second thoughts."

I right myself and wipe my mouth with the tissue she's holding out to me. "No. Let's do it." Everyone is waiting over on the beach, looking solemn. The bag of ashes is sitting on the sand now. Mabel is holding Hope.

I clear my throat and walk slowly back. "Sorry, guys."

"Don't apologize," Alan says, staring at the bag of ashes. "I feel like doing the same thing."

"Okay, well…" I say. "I guess we should start. Who, uh… who would like to say something?"

One by one, we talk about Meg. The good stuff: the stuff

we loved about her, the stuff we'll miss most about her. There are lots of tears.

Mabel goes first. She talks about birthdays and Christmases and family vacations and how she feels like she doesn't have a family anymore now that Meg's gone. Mom says how she didn't know Meg long but she's so honored to have been part of her life. And she thanks her for her amazing granddaughter. Alan talks as if Meg's there with us and tells her the entire plot of the most recent Korean import he saw. It's what he *doesn't* say that's the most clear though—he misses talking to his best friend about random everyday stuff. Joni doesn't say anything but places her hand on my arm to let me know she's there, and that's all I need.

When it's my turn to talk, I pull the pink note-book—*Ryden*—out of my bag. Here's what I figure: anything I say in my own words won't do Meg justice, won't even begin to articulate what she meant to me, what we went through together. Alan, Mabel, and Joni haven't read the pink note-book yet. What better way to say good-bye than to read her last words aloud?

I take Hope out of Mabel's arms and hitch her on my hip while I hold the notebook in my other hand and begin to read.

I take a deep breath. "Dear Ryden…"

• • •

The only thing left to do is let her ashes go. The six of us stare at the bag for a ridiculously long time, each waiting for someone else to make the first move. The candles have mostly flickered out, and it's getting cold. Hope is fussing in my arms. She's probably hungry. I smooth a hand over her hair. Time to get this show on the road.

They're just ashes. It's nothing to be afraid of. I pick up the bag and wordlessly walk to the waterline. I close my eyes, rest my head against Hope's, breathing in the combination of her baby smell and the fresh lake air, and then look up at the sky. "We'll miss you forever," I whisper and open the bag, holding it out to the wind.

In less than a minute, all the ashes are gone, carried away on the breeze, on their way to becoming part of the sand or soil or a bird's nest or the waves, working their way into the earth until they're nothing but a memory

Chapter 37

Joni finally kisses me a couple of weeks later, at work one Thursday night. She does it right in the middle of the freezer section, as we're stocking boxes of rice-crust pizza. I reach back for her to pass me another handful of pizza boxes, but she grabs my wrist instead. I turn, and her lips collide with mine. I don't waste a single second. I kick the freezer door shut and pull her to me. Her kiss is even better than I remembered. She walks me back until I'm pressed against the cold door, but the heat between the two of us is enough to keep me warm.

How the hell did I get so lucky? I don't deserve her. But if she wants to be with me—and right now it seems she does—I'm sure as hell not going to say no.

When we part, the world zooms back into focus. I look around quickly. No managers or coworkers in sight. Excellent.

"Let me drive you home tonight?" I murmur against Joni's ear. "There's something I want to talk to you about."

"Will there be more kissing?" she asks, grinning.

"I'll have to think about it," I say with a wink.

• • •

"What are you doing Thanksgiving weekend?" I ask Joni as we drive toward Clinton.

"The usual dinner stuff on Thursday. I already put my Tofurky order in at work. Why?"

"Well, you know how Meg found my father's address and stuff?" We haven't really talked about the pink journal since I read from it at the memorial, but I know she hasn't forgotten.

"Yeah."

"I was thinking about taking a trip down to New Jersey. To…I don't know…see."

She looks at me. "Really?"

"Yeah. Why, bad idea?"

"No, I think it's great, if that's what you want to do."

"So will you go with me? We could leave the Friday after Thanksgiving and be back by Sunday."

She places her hand on top of mine, resting on the gearshift. "Absolutely."

• • •

"Are you going to call him first?" Mom asks as she helps me load my and Hope's bags into the car. She's been completely supportive of my decision to go meet Michael, but I can tell there's a part of her that's worried. Whether it's worry that I'll find some spark I've been missing in my relationship with her, or that Michael won't be as receptive to me as I hope he will, or that even if he is, I won't get the answers I'm looking for, I can't tell.

"I don't think so. I'd rather say whatever I need to say in one shot, instead of splitting it up between phone conversations and stuff."

She closes the trunk. "What is it that you're going to say?"

"I haven't really gotten that far yet."

She pulls me into a hug and holds me tighter than usual. "Good luck, Ryden. Call me if you need anything. Drive safely. I love you."

"I love you too, Mom."

"And I love you, little monster," she says, nuzzling her nose against Hope's. "Have fun, you guys."

I swing by Joni's, load her and her bag into the car, and hit the highway. I hand her my phone. "You're in charge of the GPS," I tell her. "I already input the address into the system, but let me know when there are turns coming up. It's almost a six-hour drive, so we'll have to stop for diaper-change breaks. And you can have control of the radio if you want. I don't really care what we listen to. No hip-hop though."

She flips to the same pop/rock station my mom always listens to and starts singing along with a Katy Perry song. Okay, maybe I shouldn't have relinquished control of the radio quite so easily.

A while later, when we lose the station, instead of searching for another, Joni turns it off.

"What are you going to say when you meet him?" she asks.

That's the Question of the Day. "I don't know." I'd hoped all the driving would help me come up with something. So far, it hasn't.

"Okay," she says. "Why do you want to meet him?"

The answer hits my lips automatically. "I feel like I won't ever truly know how to be a dad until I meet mine."

"But you're—"

"I know what you're going to say. Don't."

"What?"

"You're going to say that I'm already a good dad and he won't be able to tell me anything I don't already know."

"Yep, that's pretty much exactly what I was going to say."

We drive in silence for a long time after that.

Well, sort of silence.

Because there's been this quiet hum in my head ever since I laid eyes on Michael's contact info, and the closer I get to him, the louder it's becoming. The hum grows into a full-on chorus, a chorus of people I know. And all the things they've told me— all the advice I refused to listen to—are suddenly resounding in my brain in multipart harmony:

Joni insisting I'm already doing an okay job at being a dad. I mean, the last few weeks *have* been better. Hope doesn't seem to hate me lately. Could it have been *my* anger and guilt she was sensing and reacting to this whole time? Maybe I've been doing better, so she has too?

And that thing Alan said. How I was obsessing so much over finding the journals, finding Michael, finding the *mystical secret to fatherhood*, that I was completely missing the point. That my quest to become a good dad was actually making me a bad one.

And my mom, the way she looked at me like I'd lost my

mind when I told her I thought Michael, someone who *knew* he had a kid on the way and *left anyway*, could help me figure out how to be a parent while my own mother couldn't.

I pull over onto the side of the highway, flip on my hazards, bring my head to the steering wheel, and squeeze my eyes tight, trying to think.

"Hey, Joni?"

"Yo."

"Can you Google something for me?"

"Sure. What?"

"Michael Taylor, Edison, New Jersey. Do an image search."

I can feel Joni's questioning stare burning a hole into the side of my face, but I don't open my eyes.

A few minutes later, she says, "Got it."

I lift my head and take the phone from her. There he is: a good-looking, late-thirtyish guy with olive skin, brown eyes, slicked-back black hair, and glasses. He looks familiar in the most unfamiliar way possible. I've never seen him before in my life, but I've seen pieces of him every day in the mirror. My nose is his nose, my smile is his smile.

The photo is of a youth soccer team. The kids look like they're about ten or so. Michael is wearing a pullover jacket that says *Coach. He's the coach of a fucking kids' soccer team.* Which means I probably got my athletic ability from him. And which means one of those kids is probably my half-brother.

I stare at the photo, clicking the pieces together. Michael is a dad. He's wearing a ring in the picture, so he's probably a husband too. He's a stand-up guy who coaches his kids' sports teams. He's clean-cut, well put together.

He is, according to the look of this picture, a good person. He doesn't quite resemble the long-haired, piano-playing, marathon-running guy from my imagination, but he's not a drug addict or in prison or in some sort of creepy religious cult either. And he's not dead.

Which means he *could* have looked me up, could have put in the effort to get to know me. He just didn't want to.

I click off the screen and turn around. Hope's snug in her car seat, a little baby who has no idea what's going on. She looks at me.

Suddenly the chorus reaches the climax of the damn operatic masterpiece, and they sing as loud as they can, right in my face.

Hope's eyes are no longer blue. I don't know when they changed, but they're a bright, stunning green. They're not dark like Meg's, like I thought they'd be. They're like mine.

Even though life has been really fucking hard lately and it's going to be really fucking hard for the foreseeable future, and even though I'd go back and do it all differently if it meant Meg would still be alive and I'd get the chance to play soccer at UCLA…I love this baby. She's more than just Meg's legacy. She's my daughter too.

I'm her dad. I don't need a face-to-face with my non-father to tell me how to begin. I'm already in it, even if the game started before I was warmed up and in position.

One of these days, the "Da-da-da" is going to turn into her first word. So I should work on being ready for it.

Because I'm all she has. It's not her fault she was born into all this bullshit. I'm starting to get that it's the ways I'm *different* from Michael that are important. (Why the *hell* did it take me driving halfway to New Jersey to see it?) All I need to know is how *not* to be the guy he was when Mom was pregnant. And I've already done that.

I shift back in my seat. Joni waits patiently, looking out the passenger-side window, trying to give me as much privacy as possible in this cramped car.

An idea strikes me. An idea so awesome it might actually be the best idea I've ever had.

Wordlessly, I hand her the phone and pull onto the road again. She flips the radio back on.

When we approach the George Washington Bridge, Joni says, "Okay, you're going to merge onto the lower level of the bridge, and after you cross over to New Jersey, you're going to take I-95 South."

"What happens if I don't get on the bridge?" I ask.

"Uh...you'll head into Manhattan."

I nod. "Got it."

The bridge exit approaches, and I drive right past it.

"That was it, Ryden. That was our exit," Joni says, pointing behind her. "What are you doing?"

I shoot her a smile, the first since this long car trip started. "I'm taking you to Washington Square Park."

Her face jolts in confusion. "But what about your father?"

"I think I know everything I need to know about him."

Several beats of silence go by as the traffic grows more congested and the buildings to our left grow taller. And then, all at once, Joni claps her hands, bouncing up and down in her seat. "Holy crap! I can't *wait* to show you Washington Square Park! You're going to love it. Hope's going to love it too. It's magical."

I laugh, thinking of Joni's magic room, of a weekend in New York, and of all the possibilities of an unmapped future.

I look straight ahead at the city coming into view and tell her the absolute, one hundred percent truth.

"I can't wait."

Acknowledgments

This book took a long time to write, which means there were so many amazing people who helped me in various ways along the journey. Please bear with me while I throw some props their way.

To my husband, Paul Bausch, thank you, as always, for being awesome and supportive and excited. And thank you for being interested in cancer research and women's rights (and all kinds of other good stuff) and sending me the article that sparked Ryden and Meg's story.

Thank you to my mother, Susan Miller, to whom this book is dedicated, for being the inspiration for the wonderful parents in this book. And huge thanks as well to the rest of my family: Jim Verdi, Robert and Alyssa Verdi, my nephew Jacob, and John Miller.

Kate McKean, thank you for being such a smart, insistent, cheerleader agent. Ryden never would have gotten to where he is without you.

To my editor Annette Pollert-Morgan, I'm so thrilled/honored/lucky that you "got" this story. Your faith and support throughout this journey, and the fact that you fell in love with Ryden at first sight, has meant everything.

To the incredible Sourcebooks Fire team—Kate Prosswimmer, Katy Lynch, Elizabeth Boyer, Jillian Bergsma, Sabrina Baskey, Heather Moore, Alex Yeadon, Todd Stocke, Dominique Raccah, and my cover designer, Jeanine Henderson—THANK YOU for all you do.

Sarah Ketchersid, thank you for discussing this book so long ago over beers and saying, "What if she's already dead at the start of the book?"

Big, big shout-out to everyone at the New School, the Lucky 13s, the Binders Full of YA Writers, and all the awesome book bloggers.

Here comes the long list! Thank you to all the people I can always count on to come to my parties and buy my books and give me notes and just be all around cool and supportive: Alison Cherry, Bridget Burke, Carolyn Demisch, Caron Levis, Casey Cipriani, Colleen Mathis, Connie Kiselak, Cristin Whitley, Cynthia Farina, Dahlia Adler, David Levithan, Debra Tackney, Dhonielle Clayton, Frank Scallon, Kevin Joinville, Laurie Boyle-Crompton, Lindsay Ribar, Mary G. Thompson, Michael Armstrong, Mindy Raf, Nicole Lisa, Renia Shukis, Riddhi Parekh, Roseanne Almanzar, Sarah Doudna, Sona Charaipotra, Steven Shaw, Victoria Marano.

Four people in particular read this book more than anyone else and offered such insanely amazing advice, I don't know what I'd do without them. Alyson Gerber, you are my hard work and perseverance guru. Caela Carter, your positivity and talent are truly inspiring. Corey Ann Haydu, each thing you do impresses me more than the last. And Amy Ewing, you're not just a crazy-talented writer and amazing friend, you are my rock. Thank you all for being you.

Finally, I'd be remiss if I concluded without mentioning my author idol, Ned Vizzini. Your work has been such a huge inspiration for me, and as far as I'm concerned, you will forever be the master of writing about tough subjects in an honest, unafraid, sometimes serious, sometimes not way. Thank you. We miss you.

The Summer I Wasn't Me
Jessica Verdi

Lexi has a secret.

She never meant for her mom to find out. And now she's afraid that what's left of her family is going to fall apart for good.

Lexi knows she can fix everything. She can change. She can learn to like boys. New Horizons summer camp has promised to transform her life, and there's nothing she wants more than to start over. But sometimes love has its own path…

Praise for *The Summer I Wasn't Me*:

"A powerful indictment of reparative therapy—a sweet love story—and an unforgettable main character!"

—Nancy Garden, author of *Annie on My Mind*

"Verdi has offered an uncomfortable, but realistic, journey into conversion (or reparative) therapy programs. This title is recommended as a quality piece of fiction in a teen collection, and especially as part of an LGBTQ collection."

—*VOYA*

My Life After Now
Jessica Verdi

What now?

Lucy just had the worst week ever. And suddenly, it's all too much—she wants out. Out of her house, out of her head, out of her life. She wants to be a whole new Lucy. So she does something the old Lucy would never dream of.

And now her life will never be the same. Now, how will she be able to have a boyfriend? What will she tell her friends? How will she face her family? Now, every moment is a precious gift. She never thought being positive could be so negative. But now, everything's different...because now she's living with HIV.

Praise for *My Life After Now*:

"Debut author Verdi paints Lucy's devastation and her tangled emotions with honestly and compassion...telling Lucy's story with realism and hope."

—*Publishers Weekly*

"Verdi forces her readers to face Lucy's dilemma with unflinching honestly and unfaltering compassion. A gem of a novel."

—*RT Book Reviews*, 4½ Stars, Top Pick of the Month

About the Author

Jessica Verdi lives in Brooklyn, New York, and received her MFA in Creative Writing from The New School. She seeks out good stories and finds inspiration from the people she meets and her travels around the world. Jessica is also the author of *My Life After Now* and *The Summer I Wasn't Me*. Visit her at jessicaverdi.com and follow her on Twitter @jessverdi.